D1558764

THE GOOD DIE TWICE

A Chase Dagger Mystery

THE GOOD DIE TWICE

A Chase Dagger Mystery

Lee Driver

Full Moon Publishing

Published by
Full Moon Publishing
P.O. Box 408
Schererville, IN 46375

Library of Congress Catalog Number 99-62925
ISBN 0-9666021-1-0

10 9 8 7 6 5 4 3 2 1

Published November 1999
Printed in the United States of America

ACKNOWLEDGEMENTS

Since my talents fall short in the categories of police procedural, editing, graphics, parrot behavior, and many other subjects too numerous to mention, I have had to rely on experts in these fields. My profound thanks to:

George J. Behnle, Jr., retired chief investigator for the Cook County medical examiner, for his tireless guidance and vast knowledge.

My editor, Chris Roerden, who can take a paragraph of hodgepodge and make meaning out of it so effortlessly.

William Sherlock of the Illinois State Police Forensic Science Center in Chicago for sharing tidbits of his endless areas of expertise.

Parrot psychologist Liz Wilson, whose extensive list of credentials includes certified veterinary technician, writer, lecturer, teacher, and writer for *Parrots Magazine*. She was kind enough to lend her keen eye to detail to ensure that Einstein was a true macaw in every sense of the word.

The members of Mystery Writers of America, Sisters in Crime, and the DorothyL Internet List for their advice, inspiration, and support.

Last but not least, my special thanks to:

Kay, Sally, and Tina, my pre-publication critiquers, who love reading mysteries almost as much as I love writing them.

My husband, Bill, family members, and friends for their continued support.

The Good Die Twice

1

Nocturnal wildlife played a deadly game of hide-and-seek a hundred feet below the gray hawk. Silently the hawk glided, silhouetted against the full moon, wings flat and graceful. It circled slowly, its underwing coverts trapping the rising air currents. Nature had no reason to fear the hawk, not at night. The hawk was a diurnal predator, it preyed only by day. But even in daylight, the animal kingdom didn't have to fear this particular gray hawk. The only animals in danger both day and night were two-legged.

The hawk folded its forty-inch wing span and perched on top of a pole. The warm, westerly breeze off Lake Michigan rippled through its feathers. In the distance, a train rumbled, its horn blasts echoing through the woods.

The hawk possesses the greatest eyesight in the animal world. Its eyesight not only outdistances a human's, but its visual acuity is also eight times more powerful.

The hawk can distinguish the various sounds prevalent during the day and those more common at night. It can distinguish between mating calls, distress and cries of pain. And it knows animal sounds from human.

Angry voices made the hawk jerk its head around. Swooping down for a closer look, it searched in the direction of the sounds, near buildings with windows facing the lake.

The buildings were tucked on the north side of a bluff where thick woods created a cozy backdrop. Clusters of townhouses faced the lake, each having its own deck with stairs leading down to the beach.

The hawk settled on a deck railing and cocked its head. The voices were coming from the end unit. Three figures could be seen beyond the French doors. Light filtered through the slices of vertical blinds revealing stark white end chairs and a sofa.

Two men were struggling with a woman. A muffled pop shuddered through the hawk. The odors were strong ... gunpowder and blood. A deadly combination. The woman crumpled to the floor. Her long, blonde hair flowed gracefully around her head. A stain seeped through her white dress and between her breasts. The woman lay motionless, blue eyes open in shock, lips parted slightly. The stain grew, spreading onto the white rug.

A bright speck danced toward the fireplace. The hawk followed the object with curiosity. With unusual human-like intellect, it studied its surroundings as if looking for landmarks. By the time it returned its gaze to the French doors, the blinds were drawn tight.

With quick wing beats the hawk took flight, made a pass over the townhouses, and flew off. It climbed higher, over treetops, across a ravine toward a huge building with spiraling towers. It searched the balconies for a white scarf tied to a door handle, located it, and disappeared through the open balcony door.

2

"Dagger, wake up."

"Hmmmm?" The interruption sounded distant, part of his dream. Dagger lifted his head from the pillow and glared at the clock radio. "It's only four o'clock. Go back to your room, Sara."

Sara hit the wall switch, which turned on both bedside lamps. Shielding his eyes from the light, Dagger groaned. Through his splayed fingers he watched Sara pick through his pile of clothes on the floor. She was clad in black from neck to toes, colors she had been taught to wear on stakeouts.

"Hurry," Sara ordered, flinging his black shirt and slacks at him. "A woman has been murdered." She dropped the bombshell and retreated to her side of their hotel suite.

Dagger dragged his body to the edge of the bed and blinked the sleep from his eyes. He struggled with the pant legs as Sara breezed through the doorway again.

"What's taking you so long?" She had her dark waist-length hair pulled around to the side and was braiding it. Pinpoints of blue-green were encased in almond-shaped eyes. "Hurry, hurry."

"If she's dead," Dagger mumbled through the black shirt he pulled over his head, "I doubt she's going anywhere."

"Are you sure this is the place?" Dagger parked his dark blue van at the end of the block and killed the lights.

"I think so."

"Think?" Dagger raked his fingers through his shoulder-length hair.

"There's only one way to find out."

The dark woods provided an excellent cover as they approached the back of the townhouses. A layer of mist snaked out from the woods and creatures chattered in the branches. The July air was humid, dewy, and blades of grass felt saturated and slippery under their shoes.

Dagger held a flashlight in one hand but it was turned off. He stopped and listened. Birds were just starting to awaken and were filling the air with their incessant chirping.

Sara stopped and listened, too. She was able to filter out all the wildlife noises. Shaking her head, she proceeded up the asphalt drive to the side of the townhouse with Dagger close behind. Glancing at nearby trees, then at the lake ahead, she announced, "This is the one." She turned her attention to the deck and started to climb over the railing.

Dagger grabbed her arm. "Wait. How can you be so sure?" He looked down the lakefront at the row of town-houses. "It could be any one of them."

"It's an end unit."

As silent and agile as a cat, Sara climbed over the railing and stayed close to the building as she listened for sounds beyond the French doors. "I don't hear anything."

The sky toward the east was turning a dark blue as daybreak was fast approaching. Sometimes, if you blinked, you could miss it entirely. Dagger crossed the patio and turned the flashlight on. Other than the patio doors, there weren't any other entrances on this side of the townhouse.

"Come on," he whispered. They retraced their steps to the back of the townhouse. Dagger shined the flashlight on the back door to check for evidence of a break-in. There wasn't any. While Sara held the flashlight, Dagger maneuvered a lock pick and the tumblers gave with a click. With gloved hands, he carefully turned the doorknob and they entered through what looked like a utility room.

Piping was exposed where they assumed a washer and dryer would be installed. Moving cautiously, they listened for any noise on the other side of the door. Sara shined the flashlight on the tiled floor looking for the usual evidence of a crime—drops of blood, suspicious footprints—but there weren't any.

Slowly, Dagger opened the door that led to the kitchen. The interior was damp, musty. Sara flashed a beam of light on a wall switch just as Dagger flipped on the lights.

Sara quickly moved to the living room. Large globe lights extended from the ceiling fans. The white upholstered furniture and thick area rug were unstained. Puzzled, she said, "I don't understand. I saw her. I saw the blood."

Dagger leaned against the island counter separating the living room from the kitchen. He gathered his collar-length hair into a rubber band and tried analyzing the situation.

Sara was not one to let her imagination run wild. Yet, there wasn't a body. There wasn't even a hint of a crime. He opened the vertical blinds and unlocked the French doors. After sliding back the screen, he stepped out onto the wooden deck. He motioned to Sara.

Reluctantly, Sara followed and walked out to the railing closest to the adjoining unit. Getting her bearings, she looked out at the lake, the navy blue sky now a lighter hue with hints of pink and yellow near the horizon. She faced the townhouse again and stared at the French doors.

Dagger studied the intensity in her face as she started to chew on one of her knuckles. It was a nervous habit she had started after her grandmother, Ada Kills Bull, passed away. He had thought she would slowly give up the habit, but if anything, it had only gotten worse.

"I don't understand," Sara said again. Frustrated, she went back inside and crouched down. She felt the carpeting. It was dry. She wiped her fingers across the solid oak floor. "It isn't even dusty."

Dagger slid the screen shut. "The place has been closed up. It wouldn't get dusty."

"It's almost TOO clean." Sara got down on all fours.

She was tenacious, Dagger had to say that much for her. She looked up at him with those dazzling eyes pleading for him to help confirm her sanity.

"If you want, Sara, I could have the police come over and coat the place with luminol. If there is any residue of blood ..."

Sara shook her head. "I can't do that, Dagger. The police will want to know where I was when I saw the murder and why I didn't do anything, and wonder how I escaped the killers."

"I'm sorry, Sara. You're right."

Her eyes searched every crevice as if unseen magnifying lenses were attached to her irises. A slight smile crept across her face as she crawled toward the fireplace. Reaching under the fake logs, she retrieved a sparkling object.

"I saw something fall off of the woman as she fell to the floor," Sara explained.

"It's an earring, a black topaz or something. Sucker's at least fifty carats." He held it up to the light. "Sure is a strange color." He folded the earring inside his hankie and slipped it in his pocket. "Now all we need is the body."

3

In the lobby of the Dunes Resort a bell captain and waitress were setting a long table for the continental breakfast. The colorful mosaic-tiled floor was dotted with thick Persian area rugs.

Dagger tugged at the collar of his shirt. His stubble was itchy and the lobby was a bit too warm. He wanted a hot shower, some breakfast, and a fast ride home. This was not how his one-day surveillance was supposed to end. A client by the name of Hardaway had hired Dagger Investigations to follow Mrs. Hardaway and find out to whom she was giving away corporate secrets. Dagger had followed her to the Dunes Resort where she was spending the night with her husband's business partner. Getting glossy eight-by-tens for pissed off husbands were not cases Dagger Investigations usually handled. But the amount of money Stu Hardaway was paying was enough incentive for Dagger to drag out his audio equipment.

The Dunes Resort was an eighty-year-old hotel getaway near Michigan City, Indiana. During its lifetime it had gone through numerous renovations. The new owners had invested a huge sum of money in the latest updates including the building of the townhouses on the lakefront.

The desk clerk returned. "Which unit did you say?" The red-haired woman rested the bifocals on the tip of her nose. She studied the pamphlet unfolded on the counter. Her lapel pin said MARIA.

"This one." Sara pointed to the corner unit in the photo.

Dagger explained, "We saw it last night but it was occupied and we didn't want to disturb them. If they are checking out today, we would like to take a look inside."

Maria bent her head to peer over her glasses at them. "That's impossible. Those units won't be available for rent until August. No one could have been in there last night."

"But they look finished," Sara protested.

"The last items to be installed are the washers and dryers, and that won't be for another week." Maria folded up the brochure and handed it to them. "Take this with you if you'd like. It's easy to get turned around here, there's so much property." She handed Dagger a business card. "This is our Guest Services Department. I can have them call you when they have additional information if you'd like."

Dagger wrote his name and phone number on the back of the card and handed it to her. "I'm in Cedar Point, Indiana. Just on the Indiana/Illinois border, about an hour from here. They can reach me at this number."

4

"Did you miss us?" Sara slid open the grated door to the bird aviary. The forty-by-thirty-foot room housed a large climbing tree that reached to within a few feet of the cathedral ceiling. Large skylights provided natural sunlight and fluorescent bulbs set on timers dimmed the lights gradually in the evening.

Feeding stations were strategically placed. One side of the room held a large birdbath with a showerhead operated by a chain. The tiled floor around the shower drained to a grating in the corner. Astro-turf under the tree made the room look more like a park than an oversized birdcage.

On a branch high in the tree a colorful scarlet macaw eyed Sara suspiciously as she approached. It buried its head under one wing and refused to budge.

"Look what I have for you." Sara held out a handful of dandelions in one hand and sunflower seeds in the other. "Einstein, don't be like that. We were only gone two days."

"Don't baby him, Sara." Dagger waited for the color printer to finish spitting out pictures. "Come take a look at these."

Dagger's makeshift office was cordoned off in the corner of the living room by a forty-inch-high paneled wall. It was just outside the aviary so Einstein could see a familiar face and not feel anxious. It had taken Einstein almost a month to settle down in his new surroundings after being cooped up in a small apartment above a bar.

Sara no sooner left the aviary, when the macaw spread its scarlet red, blue and gold wings, flew down and landed on a wooden perch by the doorway to his room.

"AWWWKK, BABY ME, BABY ME," Einstein blurted.

Sara smiled at Einstein who bobbed his head up and down.

"AWWWKK, BABY ME." Einstein stabbed at the grating with his powerful beak.

"What do you think?" Dagger placed the composite pictures on the desk. Using the computer and Sara's recollection of the features of the two men, Dagger had the computer draw composites of the alleged killers.

Sara studied the images. "His face is too full and this one had more of a receding hairline."

Dagger returned to the computer and made the alterations to the composites. "You know, we are spending a lot of time on a murder we can't prove. We couldn't find one sign of violence in any of the townhouses." He shifted his gaze to the couch where the late edition of the morning paper was strewn. "You haven't found any mention of anything in the paper either."

"You don't believe me?"

Dagger ran his hands through his hair and leaned back

in his chair. He had worked enough cases to know a dead-end when he saw one. But it was difficult to stare into Sara's innocent face and tell her his first inclination was that she imagined it all. Instead he pointed to the monitor and asked, "How's this?"

"Yes, that's better."

Dagger sent the pictures to print.

A heavy knock rattled the kitchen screen door. "Hey, anybody home? Have I got the right place?"

Dagger yelled, "Come on in, Simon."

Simon made his way through the kitchen and into the living room. What might have once been a muscular chest had given way to gravity. A thick middle rested comfortably over Simon's belt. His cherub face and twinkling eyes made him appear to be constantly smiling. Perspiration was already forming at the hairline of his short-cropped Afro. With the temperatures nearing eighty-five degrees, Simon wore his regulation uniform shorts. It was difficult to imagine that those spindly legs and bony knees could support such a massive torso.

"MR. POSTMAN. PLEASE, MR. POSTMAN. AWWWKK." Einstein fanned out his feathers and did a little dance on his perch.

Simon's laugh was deep, which brought the word *jolly* immediately to mind. "Hello to you, too, Einstein."

"Coffee, Simon?" Sara offered.

The visitor nodded and cocked his head slightly as Sara left the room, a vision of shapely legs in a pair of low-riding denim shorts. He set his mailbag on the quarry tile floor and looked around the expansive living room with its high ceiling, skylights, and polished steel-beam staircase. At the top of the staircase was a catwalk that dissected the width of the living room.

Sara hadn't owned much furniture, so Dagger had contributed his black leather sofa, love seat, and entertainment center. She did have a television set and VCR, but only after her grandmother had discovered educational tapes that her granddaughter could use. The earth-toned area rugs and Sara's bed were the only items she had kept after her grandmother died.

Simon did a slow three-hundred-and-sixty-degree turn as he surveyed the converted dealer showroom. "This sure beats that apartment and office of yours."

"You've got that right." Dagger stood up and stretched his tall, lean body. His features were chiseled with dark eyes set deep and a continuous five o'clock shadow. He had muscular arms and workman's hands, which were callused and rough. Dagger had already started work on the Florida room he was adding to Sara's house.

"Is that an electrified gate you got out front?"

"Should be. But it's just a monitored gate that we can open remotely. Too many people think this property is a nature walk open to the public."

Simon sauntered over to the doorway to Einstein's room. "What a set-up. Ya like your new home, Einstein?" Einstein bobbed his head up and down and shrieked. "I guess you do. You've got a swing, climbing ropes." He looked at the tall tree on one side of the room. "It looks like a goddamn rain forest in here."

"That's the idea. We wanted Einstein to feel at home."

"Humidity must play havoc with your computer."

"Sometimes. But when it gets too warm, we just close Einstein off in his room and turn on the air."

Simon gazed through the large plate glass windows at the property which extended as far as he could see. "Three hundred acres of reservation land out there, huh?"

"With a stream, a lot of natural preserve, open prairie, and a few bluffs overlooking a fishing stream."

"Damn." Simon did another slow survey of the living areas, the wall of bookcases, and the aviary. "So this was going to be an auto dealership."

"Pretty fortunate for Sara's grandparents. They didn't have to build a house. Once it was revealed the land shouldn't have been sold to the dealer, the building was left as is." Dagger nodded toward the aviary. "That was supposed to be the service area. It already had the plumbing for washing cars."

"I like those government boys. Always on top of things," Simon chuckled. "But why such a long driveway?"

Dagger leaned against the paneled wall, legs crossed at the ankles. "The dealership had planned to position the new and used car lots closer to the road to entice shoppers. So they set the building back a couple hundred feet." Dagger asked, "Did you have any trouble getting your route changed?"

"Nope. Seniority has its upside. Besides, you shouldn't be trottin' off to your post office box every day. And it's a good thing I'm your mailman, too. Who else would understand all this *Soldier of Fortune, Mercenary Today, Spy Network* magazines you get?"

"Nowadays, everyone with Y2K-phobia subscribes to these magazines."

"Yeah, but that mercenary school in Kentucky you attended still has you on their mailing list. What are they teaching now? How to look like that Saddam Whozzits in fifteen days?"

Einstein flew to the catwalk railing. "SQUAWK, GUGE, GONJI, KILL STRIKE, UZI, MI-FORTY SEVEN ..."

"Hey." Dagger pointed a finger at Einstein. "Put a clamp on it."

Einstein turned and ruffled his feathers at Dagger.

"See," Simon motioned toward the macaw. "Even the bird remembers the weapons and all those deadly self-defense courses you took."

Dagger handed some of the mail back to Simon saying, "Do me a favor and mark these *Return to Sender*. I'm more into Tai Chi these days."

Simon rubbed a hand through his graying Afro and took the mail from Dagger. He let his gaze drift toward the kitchen. "How's the little lady? Is she getting used to her grandmother's passing?"

Dagger followed his gaze. "Some days I find her out back by the grave talking to her grandmother. She was all the family Sara had left. But I think Einstein really fills a large part of that void." Dagger dug through stacks of papers and notes on his desk, shoved them aside, and made room for today's mail.

"I see you're still neat and orderly." A piece of mail slipped to the floor. Simon quickly retrieved it and threw it back on the stack. "How are the living arrangements working out?"

"Place is big enough that we're able to stay out of each other's way." Dagger jabbed an index finger under the flap of an envelope and tore open a bill from the phone company. "And the rent I pay for Einstein and me gives Sara an income."

A twinkle crept into Simon's eyes. "Seems to me it would be kinda hard to keep your mind on business with that gorgeous creature living under the same roof."

Dagger gave his broad shoulders a shrug. "Never mix business with pleasure. Besides, Sara's more like a little sister to me." Dagger couldn't help but smile at Sara's transformation in just six short months. She had been so shy and withdrawn when he had met her. He had looked over and there she was, standing in the doorway of his office over a local bar, looking like some native of a South Pacific island with her almond-shaped eyes, olive complexion, and waist-length hair.

Back then, Sara had been instrumental in helping Dagger solve a case. They complemented each other well. She had unusual talents that could benefit his firm, and he needed an office and a place to live that didn't frown on a rowdy macaw. And Sara knew more about macaws than even the man in charge of the Aviary House at Brookfield Zoo.

Simon's bushy eyebrows slowly crept up his broad forehead. "Brother and sister? Right. You gonna tell me those twenty steps up to that sweet thing's bedroom doesn't give you that itch during some lonely nights? You gonna tell me living and working in this close proximity doesn't make things a little too tempting?"

Dagger gave a hopeless shake of his head. "The only thing I'm tempted to do is turn her over my knee. It has been a struggle getting her used to being around people after being secluded here with her grandmother."

"She used to do the shopping for her grandmother, didn't she?"

"Sure, early in the morning before the stores were crowded. I made the mistake of taking her to the mall once, after her grandmother died. I thought it would be good to expose her to as much of the outside world as possible, as soon as possible. Talk about an anxiety attack." Dagger leaned closer. "I ended up calling her a baby. Then those big, blue-green eyes started to fill with tears and ..."

Simon smiled broadly. "Oh yeah, let me guess. Those women get that bottom lip a-quivering and you feel like an absolute jackass."

"Right. And then the tears hang on the bottom lashes, just hanging, never falling. And the lashes are moving up and down from the weight." Dagger shook his head of thick hair and laughed. "How on earth do women do that?"

"You've got no patience, Chase Dagger. Women need patience." Simon winced as Einstein let out a diatribe of screeches as he flew from the catwalk to the aviary.

Dagger motioned Simon toward the couch while sliding shut first the grated door and then the clear Plexiglas door on the aviary. The Plexiglas door provided excellent sound-proofing. Dagger carried some papers in his hand and took a seat next to Simon. He tossed a quick glance over his shoulder toward the doorway, leaned in and whispered, "Well, those days that I used to look at Sara sideways and reduce her to tears are gone. Now that I taught her how to shoot, she has a backbone. Now that she has learned some self-defense, she challenges me on everything from taking care of Einstein to doing my job. She even had me throw out all my coated fry pans because, little did I know, the coating emits toxic fumes that could kill birds. Between Einstein and Sara, I don't know which one is going to drive me crazy first."

"Crazy." Simon huffed. "You're loving every minute of it. You want her to be that shy, timid girl again because then you won't be attracted to her." He leaned in and whispered, "Unless you haven't noticed, but I'm sure you have, she ain't no girl. She's a full grown woman." He eye-balled his friend suspiciously. "Is she doing your laundry?"

Dagger shook his head.

"Are you buying her monthly personals?"

"No."

Simon clamped a thick hand on Dagger's shoulder. "Then you're safe for now."

"Take a look at these pictures, Simon. Ever see these guys before?"

"Uh huh. Changing the subject already." Simon studied the pictures of the two men. "They don't look ugly enough to be inmates. Are they relatives?"

"Not quite. Just some suspicious characters who piqued Sara's interest." He placed the pictures on the coffee table. "Have your cop friends told you about any missing persons? A woman around thirty, maybe? Or any homicides from last night?"

"Just gang shit, but no young woman."

"Anything else new around town?"

"Just that hoity-toity cocktail party Friday night for the rich fat cats."

Dagger arched one eyebrow.

"Here you go, Simon." Sara placed a tray containing cups of coffee and a plate of cookies on the coffee table.

"Why thank you, little lady." Simon helped himself to refreshments. Sara curled up on the love seat and waited for Simon's reaction. "Ummm. Chocolate chip. My favorite."

Sara pressed her fist to her mouth and absentmindedly started to chew on a knuckle. To her it was a way to keep her hands from shaking. But her knuckles were looking raw, the skin cracking. Dagger reached over and pulled her hand away so she clenched it tightly in her lap.

Simon handed one last piece of mail to Dagger. "I saved the best for last. I'm sure this is your invite to that hoity-toity affair. It's being given by Robert Tyler, the rich dude who owns thousands of hotels around the globe."

"And I should know this Tyler guy?"

"He's a very, very close friend of Leyton Monroe, the newspaper tycoon." A narrow smile curled up one corner of Simon's mouth. "I'm surprised Monroe's daughter hasn't called to personally invite you."

Sara averted her attention to the photos on the coffee table. She remembered Sheila Monroe. At the time Sara met Dagger, he was engaged to Sheila. It had been only a couple of days before the wedding. But Dagger never made it to the wedding.

Dagger poured himself a cup of coffee and took the invite from Simon. "Spending time at a social event with Sheila and her father is not my idea of an enjoyable evening."

Simon pointed a thick finger at the bottom of the invitation where it read *Number of Guests* and whispered, "You don't have to go alone."

5

Cedar Point was one of the largest suburbs in northwest Indiana. Some called it a mini-Chicago with its close, thirty-minute proximity to downtown Chicago. Unfortunately, the Chicago skyline was a little more picturesque than Cedar Point's. Just east of Cedar Point one could see the belching smokestacks from the Gary steel mills spewing a haze that settled across the entire lakeshore on calm days.

With its population around 125,000, Cedar Point was slightly smaller than South Bend, Indiana. It had seen its income derivation change from industry to technology in just twenty-five short years. Its Center for Performing Arts had produced plays comparable in talent and scope to Broadway, bringing in audiences from Chicago and Indianapolis, which was three hours to the south.

Ten miles of Lake Michigan beaches were kept pristine by city workers, volunteers, and owners of the beachfront properties. The Cedar Point Yacht Club accepted boats only over thirty feet in length. For several years avid fishermen challenged the elitist rule in court only to be turned down by judges who owned no less than thirty-five-foot Bayliners.

The Tyler mansion claimed a five-block area just one mile from the yacht club. With a widow's walk on each end, the estate appeared like a fortress resting on top of a hill, its circular drive lined with limousines and vanity cars.

From the front seat of Dagger's car, Sara stared apprehensively at the forty-room mansion and the bubbling fountain in the middle of the circular drive. The setting sun cast long shadows across the immaculate landscape. She tugged nervously on the spaghetti straps of her black dress.

"You okay?" Dagger gave her hand a squeeze as he brought the Ford Torino to a stop. A hubcap clattered to the brick drive and rolled to the valet's feet. The engine belched and sputtered, refusing to quit, until at last, with one final shudder, it stopped.

The valet looked too old to be parking cars. Dagger guessed him to be part of security. Old man Tyler probably didn't want any of the luxury cars of the attendees stolen. The valet's thick eyebrows hovered over his beady eyes surveying the cancerous rust spots dotting the aged black Ford Torino.

Dagger dropped his car keys into the valet's hand. "Treat my baby good." Dagger patted his arm. "It's priceless."

"Yeah, I bet." But the valet's attention was quickly drawn to Sara as she stepped out of the car, the slit of her dress exposing a shapely leg, her long hair shiny and framing her face. The last of the sun's rays caught the blue-green of her eyes.

Dagger wrapped a protective arm around her waist. "You'll do just fine, Sara."

"I think I need more practice walking in these heels."
Her black ankle-wrap heels were a little more than two
inches high. She stepped gingerly up the stairs to the main
entrance.

"Think of it as walking on your tiptoes."

"I don't know which is worse, the heels or the panty
hose. Women actually wear these things all day long?"

Dagger laughed. Everything about Sara was so refresh-
ingly uncomplicated. She had never worn nylons or heels
before today. Even the dab of eye shadow and mascara she
was wearing had been applied and removed three times until
she had gotten the hang of it.

Sara had always led a simple life with her grandmother,
raising their own vegetables, eating fish out of the stream, and
wearing clothes hand-sewn by Ada Kills Bull. Sara didn't
know how to drive, had been home-schooled, yet seemed to
know a little about a lot and was a quick learner.

They made a striking couple, Sara with her long, dark
hair which the sun had streaked a variety of colors, and
Dagger in his tuxedo with his thick hair pulled back in a
pony tail, a diamond stud earring in his left ear, his features
angular, eyes mysterious.

They entered the foyer. Sara gaped at the crystal chan-
delier hanging over their heads. Loud voices and laughter
spilled out from the ballroom and classical music played
softly in the background. Dagger felt as if they were part of
a herd of cattle being directed through one central doorway.

As they drew nearer, Dagger understood why. Everyone
was being steered through a metal detector. A tuxedo-clad
security guard had a wire snaking up under his jacket,

around his neck, and into his ear.

Just as Dagger expected, as he and Sara walked through the doorway, the metal detector rang out. The husky security guard motioned Sara through and asked Dagger to check his pockets.

"I'm sure you're looking for this." Dagger pulled a Smith & Wesson Shorty .45 from his belt holster.

Another security guard appeared out of nowhere. He had large, flat features, and a mouth in permanent frown mode. His name badge said MEYERS. Meyers checked that the safety was on and then examined the pistol.

"You've got a goddamn Trijicon night sight on this baby. What were you going to do? Go hunting in Mr. Tyler's back-yard tonight?"

Dagger pulled out a business card. "I have a license."

Meyers reluctantly took the card and snickered. "You can get your toy back when you leave." He motioned Dagger through the doorway.

"Did you know they were going to check?" Sara whispered.

"Of course. That's why I gave you my Bersa .380 to carry in your purse."

"You should have seen Prince Charles' face when I asked him point blank how long he had been having an affair." Sheila Monroe threw back her head and gave a throaty laugh. A large emerald pendant surrounded by dia-monds draped her slender neck. Her white, glittery, off-the-shoulder dress fit her slender body like a second skin.

Sheila's audience consisted of three female college friends, two co-workers at *The Daily Herald*, and three male hopeful suitors.

"He's available now, Sugar. You should interview him again." Laurette's Georgia accent was heavy and sometimes exaggerated. Her hazel eyes flashed as she fluffed the bangs of her short red hair. Laurette was Sheila's closest friend and had been slated to be her maid of honor.

Molly's deep dimples pinched at her cheeks. She was the first to see Dagger at the bar. Her squeaky voice sounded more like a little girl's. "Uh, oh. Look who's here, Sheila. I guess we can bring our bridesmaid dresses out of storage."

Sheila's shoulder-length platinum hair swung freely as she turned in the direction of the bar. She brushed one side of her hair behind her ear with her fingers, revealing an engagement ring she had yet to remove. Her heart skipped into her throat. Dagger always did look good in a tuxedo. But then again, he looked good in anything he wore. She had even gotten used to Dagger's penchant for wearing black.

She especially loved how his eyes seemed to always rest in shadow, making him appear sensually dangerous. Being a reporter, she was adept at pulling information from people, men especially. But Dagger was like a closed book, answering in cryptic sentences, sometimes answering only with a smoldering gaze that would send a shiver of excitement through her body. She could forgive him anything, even for canceling their wedding two days before the gala affair. She watched him accept two drinks from the bartender.

"Well, well. Who is that gorgeous creature with Dagger?" Sal Wormley lifted his wire-frame glasses. Coarse red hair stood straight up, as though searching for sunlight. The freckles dotting his white skin were the same color as his hair.

"Put a sock in it, Worm. She isn't WITH Dagger. She works FOR him," Sheila clarified.

"She works FOR him?" Laurette drawled, "or UNDER him?" This got a laugh from everyone.

"You two haven't even been dating again, have you?" Molly squeaked.

"We've kept in touch. Just needed some time apart, that's all. My god, Dagger's thirty years old. Of course he's going to get cold feet getting married for the first time." Sheila checked her engagement ring, rubbed her thumb across the top as if to shine it.

"Did you ever see so much jewelry in your life?" Dagger asked over the rim of his martini glass. Sara didn't have to respond. Her eyes looked like a deer's in headlights, part fear, part excitement.

The room was filled with the Cedar Point elite in politics, business, philanthropy, art, you name it. Women were coifed, curled, painted, squeezed into dresses, toes pinched inside sequined shoes. Men were stuffed into tuxedos they hadn't had on since New Year's Eve. Some owned as many tuxedos as business suits. But the men were scarce and Dagger figured out why.

A reading room near the bar was emitting billows of

smoke. Although smoking was not permitted in the house, the emergence of the latest trend in cigar smoking prompted Robert Tyler to convert his reading room into a cigar room.

"I guess that's where most of the men disappeared to." Dagger's gaze roamed the ballroom, feeling eyes on him. He located the source. "I think we've been spotted. Let's get this over with."

Sara felt the room closing in. So many people, so many stares. The impulse to flee was compelling. She grabbed Dagger's arm and whispered, "I want to go home, Dagger. NOW."

Dagger lifted her glass to her lips. "Take a deep breath and a long sip."

"I don't want anything to drink." Her eyes darted around the room, and she clamped her bottom lip between her teeth.

"Look at me, Sara." His gaze was penetrating, almost threatening—if she hadn't known him better—but his touch was gentle as he brushed her hair away from her face. "I'm not going to let anything happen, okay? We're going to drink their liquor and eat their two-hundred-dollar-a-plate meal. If you want to swipe a few crystal goblets, I have more than enough room in my pockets." A nervous smile tugged at Sara's lips. "Don't fail me now, Sara. I can't face Sheila and her cronies on my own."

After a couple sips of champagne, Sara released her grip on Dagger's arm and they made their way across the room.

Sheila smiled seductively, her eyes running the length of Dagger's frame as he approached. After wrapping an arm around his waist and planting a kiss on his cheek, Sheila proceeded to place herself between Dagger and Sara.

Dagger didn't reciprocate the hug.

"You're looking good, Sheila."

"Of course." Sheila tried clasping Dagger's hand but he moved his martini to his left hand. "You remember Molly, Laurette, Jim, Worm, Kelly." Sheila continued the introductions, completely ignoring Sara. When the men turned their attention to Sara, Sheila was forced to introduce her. "Oh, and this is Dagger's ... just what is it you do, Dear? Receptionist? Secretary?" Eyelashes too long to be real fluttered.

Sara held her hand out to the men. "Sara Morningsky."

The men lurched forward. The women watched for Sheila's reaction.

Pumping her hand a little too strongly, Worm stammered, "Sal Wormley, cub reporter at *The Daily Herald*."

"So, Sugar," Laurette asked Dagger, "I hear you've moved."

"My former landlord didn't care too much for Einstein."

"Einstein?" remarked a pudgy young man who was sweating profusely. His Napoleon haircut was plastered to his damp forehead.

"Dagger's mangy bird," Sheila explained.

"Actually, he's a beautiful scarlet macaw and he's quite intelligent," Sara offered.

"Einstein is in love with Sara." Dagger stole a glance toward Sara, which was difficult to do since Sheila was blocking his view.

"I bet." Worm's glasses started to fog up.

The young men watched Sara, studying her full lips and turquoise eyes. The women looked in unison again to Sheila for her reaction. Their gaze shifted constantly as if the women were spectators at a tennis match.

Sheila asked Dagger, "Have you seen Daddy yet, Honey?"

Honey? An uneasy feeling crept up his spine. Dagger's gaze drifted to Sheila's left hand where she flashed her engagement ring. Sheila sprinkled endearing terms a little too freely for his liking. Obviously, he thought, he must be the only one who understood what unengaged meant. "I'm sure I'm the last person he wants to talk to." Dagger intercepted a waiter and exchanged his empty glass for a fresh martini.

Laurette pressed on. "Are you in a big ole' house or a tiny little apartment, Dagger?"

"Actually, it's a converted car showroom."

"How tacky," Sheila muttered.

Dagger continued, "I'm adding on to it, though. I like working with my hands."

Molly's baby voice chimed in, "That's what Sheila tells us."

The women smiled coyly. Dagger could feel Sheila's breast pressing against him, her tight grasp around his waist almost stifling.

Sara took a sip of champagne and caught a glimpse of Sheila's engagement ring. All the apprehension Sara had felt in the car, arriving at a house full of people she didn't know, letting Dagger coax her out of her secure house in hopes of getting her used to being around other people—none of it had prepared her for this. She wanted to curl up and die, run for the safety and security of

THE GOOD DIE TWICE   39

familiar surroundings.

Worm turned to Sara and asked, "So, where do you live?"

In all sincerity, with the innocence of her naive eighteen years, the young woman replied simply, "With Dagger."

6

The silence hung like a dark cloud. Even women standing nearby, friends of Sheila's mother, had eavesdropped on their conversation. Sheila could feel her face turning red.

Molly forced a smile and as she turned to leave said, "I guess that means my bridesmaid's dress stays in storage."

"It's actually Sara's house," Dagger clarified.

Sara's face flushed. "Of course, we have separate living quarters," she stammered. But the damage had been done. She felt the room closing in, the large chandeliers hanging dangerously close, the stares too numerous.

A five-piece band struck up a song in the corner of the room. Sheila pulled on Dagger's sleeve. "Dance with me," she ordered.

"I think I'll go find the ladies room." Sara left quickly, trying desperately not to trip in the heels. One of the security guards directed her up the staircase.

"When were you planning on telling me that you and your little friend were shacking up? And to announce it in front of my friends. How clever of the little ..."

"Just stop it." Dagger pulled her arms away from his neck, grabbed her by the forearm, and pulled her away from the dance floor. "Come on." He found a study down the hall from the ballroom. It was ornate with thick wainscoting and dark wood. Once he closed the door, Sheila tried to kiss him but he held her back.

"I don't know how many different ways I have to say that we're through, Sheila. I'm sorry but we just are not going to make it."

She folded her arms in front of her, eyes flashing. Years of sunbathing and tanning booths had encouraged tiny lines around her eyes. Her face was thin with lips to match, and the constant sucking on cigarettes had caused tiny creases to form above her top lip. "You aren't one to just jump into bed with someone, Dagger. My god, I ought to know. It took me, what? Six, eight dates? You meet her three days before our wedding and all of a sudden the wedding is off? Was she that great of a fuck?"

Dagger pointed a finger barely an inch from her face. "Watch it." His dark eyes seemed to withdraw, the pupils enlarge. He felt the more he tried to pull away, the more she thought he wanted her. The more disdain he displayed, the more it seemed to encourage her. He didn't know how many times he could deny that he slept with Sara. Sheila wasn't going to believe him.

"STOP IT." Dagger moved away from the door, away from Sheila. "This isn't about Sara. How many times do I have to tell you? It's about you. Listen to yourself. Is it that hard for you to accept the fact that we are wrong for each other?"

"Yes," Sheila whispered. "I love you, Dagger. I don't want anyone else."

Dagger emitted an exasperated sigh and moved over to the window, hands jammed in his pants pockets. Globe lights lit up the brick walkway below leading from the patio. Guests stood in clusters sipping their drinks. All he had ever wanted when he met Sheila was to have an in with the Cedar Point elite, build up his business with some higher-paying customers. All he had was a little too much scotch one night, and next thing he knew Sheila was picking out an engagement ring.

"Whining doesn't fit you, Sheila. The only thing I ever was to you was a slap in the face to your father. You've told me yourself you used to bring home boyfriends in leather jackets riding Harleys just to give your father gray hair."

Sheila trailed her fingers along the dark mahogany desktop, all the while moving closer to Dagger. "So, you didn't sleep with Sara?"

"No, but even if I did, it isn't any of your business, Sheila."

Her eyes flashed. "Even if you did ...?"

"See, you're reading into it again." Dagger looked down at her left hand. "Give me back the ring. I don't appreciate your giving people the impression the wedding is just on hold."

Sheila looked at the ring, the marquis cut with tiny baguettes. She clasped her hand to her chest. "No, I won't. I'm going to give you as long as you want to reconsider. Besides, what else am I going to do with a Bill

Blass wedding gown?"

Dagger shrugged. It's cubic zirconia anyway."

She clenched her fist, moved her hand behind her back in a childish gesture. "No, it isn't."

Dagger shook his head. "You had the damn thing appraised. Why should I be surprised?" He checked his watch and wondered what Sara was up to. Was she lost somewhere in this forty-plus room mausoleum? Or did she run to the car and is now hiding in the backseat?

"Dagger!"

He jerked his gaze to her and suddenly realized she had been talking to him.

"I don't have time for this." He walked out leaving Sheila standing in the middle of the room spouting something very unladylike.

Sara had never seen a washroom this large. If it was supposed to be a bathroom, why were there two couches, a makeup table, and a television set?

She checked her reflection in the mirror, ran a hand through her hair. What little curl she had coaxed out of it earlier had disappeared, giving way to the weight. She pulled her hair behind one ear the way Sheila wore hers. But it eased its way out. She ran a hand across her throat. The necklace Sheila wore looked real. Sara didn't own any jewelry. It was too cumbersome.

Examining her features in the mirror, she felt her arms and legs could use some trimming, her eyes were too far apart and too odd-shaped, her lips too full. Turning, she checked the back of her dress, which clung to her rear end, another part of her body she felt was too muscular. She gave a resigned sigh and sat down on one of the couches. It felt good just getting off her feet. What would feel better would be to get out of the shoes. She fumbled with the straps, pulled off the shoes, and wiggled her toes. Relief, splendid relief. Dangling the heels in one hand, she left the washroom.

Returning to the ballroom didn't tempt her. Facing Sheila and her friends after what Sara had just blurted out would be too embarrassing. Instead, she walked past the stairway and down the hall, which was carpeted in a thick, rich Oriental design. She paused at the railing and stared down at the clusters of people.

Some of the women looked like the models Sara had seen in the catalogs Dagger brought home for her to look through. He had wanted her to add more clothes to her near-ly empty closet, but she had not yet been up to shopping in crowds. Instead, she thumbed through the colorful pictures of women with flawless skin and expensive clothes.

Sheila and her friends were like the models. Their hair was perfect, glossy as if coated with some plastic film. Those with low-cut dresses seemed to have something push-ing their cleavage up to their throats. And their lips were pouty as if they had been stung by a swarm of bees. Sara had read that some women have plastic surgery to increase their bust size, their butts, even their lips.

Sighing, Sara turned away from the railing and wan-dered farther down the hall. Family pictures hung on a wall covered in a velvet-textured wallpaper, picking up the peach and navy hues of the carpeting.

She had heard that Robert Tyler had two sons, but Sara had yet to meet any of the Tylers. The family photos appeared several years old—two boys in hockey uniforms, the same boys in baseball uniforms, school prom tuxes, and college caps and gowns. Next was a picture of a man, very distinguished-looking with thick, graying hair and dressed in expensive-looking clothes. He was standing next to a woman with brown hair and a streak of gray at her temple. Sara guessed her to be proud of that one streak. The older son exhibited an identical streak. Probably ran in her family. The couple and the boys were standing outside a resort hotel, somewhere warm, palm trees in the background.

Photos that seemed more recent showed one of the boys several years older with a baby and a wife. The other son was photographed standing near huts, looking tan and shirt-less. Another picture showed the same adventurous son, rather attractive, in a pose resembling the male models in a catalog.

Another portrait in an expensive, ornate frame showed the father again but this time with more gray hair, a trimmer build, and a different woman. She had blonde hair swept up and surrounded by cream-colored flowers, which matched her lace gown. She had bright blue eyes and clung to the man. He wore a tuxedo with a spray of baby's breath in his lapel. It looked like a wedding picture.

Next to the wedding picture hung another picture of the young woman, a close-up of her flawless skin and long blonde hair. Sara studied the picture more closely and then realized where she had seen the woman before.

7

Sara and Dagger leaned against the opposite wall and stared at the portrait. Dagger shook his head. "This is unreal." He had already asked Sara twice if she was sure it was the same woman.

Sara said, "It doesn't make sense, though. Why would Mr. Tyler hold a party if his wife is dead or missing?"

"Maybe he doesn't know it. Maybe she's supposed to be out of town."

"Or maybe he killed her and told everyone she was out of town."

"DAGGER!" The booming voice came from the top of the stairway. A barrel-chested man with thick white hair that fit like a helmet walked toward the two. He gave an approving glance down Sara's form, a disapproving glance at the heels dangling from her hand. He pulled back his shoulders and tilted his head back, giving Sara the same arrogant stare down his pointed nose that Dagger had received on more than one occasion. With an arch of a bushy brow he turned his gaze to the young man. Dagger felt as if Dad had just caught his son and date necking in a darkened living room.

But the glint in his eyes told Dagger, *good taste.*

"Mr. Monroe." Dagger wanted to flatten him right on his pompous ass.

Leyton Monroe pointed to a study down the hall, saying, "If I could have a minute of your time."

Sara watched the men leave and understood why Dagger didn't like Sheila's father. And it seemed to her that Monroe wasn't too fond of Dagger, either. She returned her gaze to the portraits on the wall, studying details of the woman's face, the woman who was obviously Robert Tyler's second wife, the woman she had seen lying on a blood-soaked white carpet in a townhouse at the Dunes Resort a little more than forty hours earlier.

"Handsome fella, isn't he?" The voice was silken, a tone slightly higher than a radio announcer.

Sara turned to see the man in the photo, the mountain climber, model, all-around sports enthusiast. He was even better looking in person, with sun-bleached hair and soft brown eyes. Any woman would kill for his flawless complexion. Although he stood just under six feet tall, athletics helped him to fill out his tuxedo rather nicely. And as if on a personal crusade against formal attire, he left his tie off and his shirt collar open.

The man held his hand out and clasped Sara's with a firm grip. He smiled, revealing dazzling white teeth a little too even to be god-given. "I'm Nicholas Tyler. But you can call me Nick."

Sara found Nick a little reluctant to give her back her

hand. "Sara Morningsky."

Lifting his glass in a toast, Nick glanced at the shoes dangling from Sara's fingers, then at her feet. "Sore?"

Sara smiled, color rising to her cheeks. "I'm not used to wearing heels."

"You are about as fresh as a breath of springtime." He turned his hand and brought the top of her's to his mouth, pressing his lips just a little too long and touching her skin lightly with his tongue.

Sara pulled her hand back and smiled, saying, "And you're just plain fresh."

"You're quick." Nick turned and looked at the portraits. "Great-looking family, don't you think?"

"Who is everyone?"

"Eric is my brother. He's the married one." Nick pointed at the picture of a dark-haired version of himself. "That's Eric Jr. He's three. Cute kid. Takes after Uncle Nicholas." Nick flashed another toothy grin. "And the brunette who now has dyed red hair, which my brother hates, is the gold-digging Edie Winthrop, my wonderful sister-in-law."

"You sound like the brother scorned. Did Edie pick Eric over you?"

Nick shook his head, wisps of blonde hair falling across his forehead. "She's not my type. Besides, she's several years older than me." He flashed Sara his boyish grin again. "I don't like old ladies. She's like a horse that's been ridden hard." He casually draped an arm around Sara's shoulder.

"This is your mother?" Sara pointed at the photo with the two sons at the resort.

Nick's boyish grin faded. "Theresa Tyler. She was the

prima donna of socialites. She could throw a party together in two hours, wrote the etiquette books. And she still had time for us kids."

"You talk in the past tense."

"My mother died about nine years ago. Ovarian cancer. They diagnosed it in the summer and she died right before Christmas."

Sara watched his eyes. A sadness washed over him for the first time. But he quickly recovered. He flagged down a passing waiter and retrieved two glasses of champagne, setting his empty glass on the tray. He handed a drink to Sara. She took a polite sip. She had never seen so much liquor flowing. Everywhere she turned there were waiters, even outside the restroom. She found herself curious about how much of a head start Nick had gotten. There was a slight slur to his words and a glaze to his eyes.

She pointed to the most recent wedding portrait and asked, "So this is your stepmother? She doesn't look much older than you."

"Oh, yes. That is my step-mom. My mother's body wasn't even cold and my father had to find someone to fill her side of the bed." His words were laced with sarcasm. He took another sip of champagne.

"She's beautiful. Almost looks like a model."

"She was. A thousand dollars an hour is what she earned. That face graced the cover of many a fashion magazine. I'm surprised you hadn't heard of the great Rachel. She used only her first name. Her full name was Rachel Liddie, rhymes with tittie." Nick grinned again and gave Sara's shoulder a squeeze, stroking her skin with his fingers.

Sara stared at his roaming fingers. "Could you practice your drumbeat elsewhere?"

Nick removed his arm from her shoulder. "Sorry about that." He turned his attention to the individual portrait of Rachel. "If you ask me, she could have done a lot better than my old man. But, hell, when you're after money, you shoot for the moon. Right?"

Sara looked over her shoulder toward the stairway, down to the ballroom. "Where is your stepmother? It would be nice to meet the host and hostess."

"It's really quite pitiful." Nick stifled a drunken laugh. "Stepmumzey is dead."

8

"The secret is to never use a lighter, always a wooden match." Leyton Monroe blew out the match and held his cigar out. "And never puff on it to get it going."

"It helps to smoke only cigars that cost fifty dollars or more," Dagger added dryly.

Leyton filled out the entire width of the wing-backed chair. A basket of silk flowers sat inside a nearby fireplace. The room had a feminine touch to it in its pastel colors and antique roll-top desk. Dagger had declined the offer of a cigar.

"You know that damn wedding was going to cost me a hundred thousand dollars." Leyton finally took a slow puff on his cigar, closing his eyes and savoring the taste. When he opened his eyes, he looked at Dagger and smiled. "Good thing I put a clause in the contract that I could cancel up to twenty-four hours beforehand. I knew that wedding wasn't going to take place."

Dagger settled back in his chair and crossed his right ankle over his left knee. He felt a little too old to be lectured to, especially by the likes of Leyton Monroe, who had made his money by crafty legal maneuvers.

"Well then, I guess we both got what we wanted," Dagger said.

"My daughter deserves better than you—a private dick who lasted six months in the marines, two years in college, and was kicked out of the police academy. Your father was a two-bit hustler who lived at the race track and died crossing a street, too greedy with his winnings to see a semi big as life barreling down on him."

Dagger's eyes challenged him. "You two are a lot alike. You just do your hustling behind people's backs. They never see you or your high-priced lawyers coming."

If he was ruffled, Leyton didn't show it. It didn't surprise Dagger that Leyton had checked him out. Dagger would have been surprised if he hadn't.

"See, I know my daughter pretty well. You'll never make the kind of money that would keep Sheila in tennis bracelets and Gucci pumps." Leyton paused to take a sip of his brandy. "She likes to push my buttons, always has. Had her navel pierced when she was sixteen. Went to her high school prom with a Hell's Angels wannabe. Dropped out of college her first year because she didn't like the weather in New York. She wanted to go to college in Hawaii. My daughter is not marriage material."

"Finally, we agree on something." Dagger shifted in his seat and played with the earring in his left ear.

Leyton took another long drag and blew the smoke out slowly toward the ceiling light. His cheeks reddened as though exhaling was too strenuous. "Sheila does not want to be strapped down by kids or a stove. She'd be hiring nannies and having meals catered. Now, what I like about you is you also aren't marriage material. The only reason she wants you is because she knows I don't approve. So if she holds a torch for you, she'll never have the chance to meet Mr. Right, who just might lure her to that little cottage with the picket fence."

Dagger was finally getting the picture. "So as long as she's pining for me, she'll always be right where you want her."

"Now you're getting it." The broad smile brought his plump cheeks close to kissing his eyeballs. "She'll stay at the newspaper and take over when I retire, keep it in the family. She's my only child, so who else do I have to follow in my footsteps?" Leyton's eyes twinkled. They were like two college roommates joined by a masterful plan, co-conspirators.

Fat chance, Dagger thought.

Leyton reached into his pocket and pulled out a piece of paper. "You should find this quite adequate. If anything, you should be able to replace that shit-can you call a car."

Dagger's blood pressure hit boiling point as he stared at the check made out to him for two hundred thousand dollars. He glared at Leyton as he slowly folded it in half.

"Not enough?" Leyton's eyes mocked him.

What Leyton didn't know was that money didn't matter to Dagger. Leyton thought money mattered to everyone, that everyone had a price.

"Exactly what am I supposed to do for this money?"

Leyton gave a nod of his head as if perturbed he had to spell it out. "Do what you do best … keep stringing her along."

9

"You seem shocked, Sara." Nick took a long swallow of champagne and emptied his glass.

"It's just that she was so young. For your father to have lost two wives is such a pity. When did she die?"

"About five years ago."

Sara tried to hide her surprise. Five years ago. Then who was it that was murdered? "How did she die?"

Nick set their glasses on a narrow table under a trophy case and leaned against the wall. He seemed to have to think hard for an answer and she wondered if the champagne was the culprit. "Rachel went out sailing one night. Got a little too tipsy and ..." Nick motioned with his hands as if diving.

"Was she alone?"

"No. It was a sixty-footer with a two-man crew. They ran out of wind and out of gas. Drifted for hours."

"Did anyone see her fall overboard?"

Nick raised his eyebrows. "My, you are full of questions."

"Sorry. I'm just naturally curious, I guess. Someone that young and your father that rich, people might think he

54

would be a suspect."

"It would be the other way around, really. If it was my father who fell overboard and my step-mom who got his money, then it might draw suspicion to my step-mom."

"I take it they found her body."

Nick shook his head. "Never did."

"What do you want, Sheila? You usually cozy up to me only when you want something." Worm maneuvered Sheila around the dance floor to a brass band tune.

"You've always wanted a big assignment. Now you've got one. I want you to find out everything you can about Sara Morningsky."

Worm laughed. "Why thank you, boss lady. That should win me a Pulitzer."

Sheila pressed her body closer to Worm, letting her lips touch his ear. "Just think, you can ask her out on a few dates, get her talking, a little dinner, a few drinks, loose lips sink ships."

Worm pulled away from Sheila, digested what she said, then smiled.

"Is he asleep?" Sara asked as she sat down on the black leather sofa.

Dagger turned away from the aviary, making sure the padlock was secured. It hadn't taken long for Einstein to figure out how to slide open the grated door to the aviary. Having a fondness for chewing, he would leave gnaw marks on furniture when they weren't around to police him.

"Yes, he's asleep." He eyed her yellow jogging suit. "You didn't waste any time getting out of those panty hose."

"They were sheer torture."

Dagger stripped out of his tuxedo jacket and sat down. He pulled the check from his pocket and handed it to Sara.

"That would be tempting to a lot of people," she said. "He probably thinks that rusty Ford is all you drive. He hasn't seen the van or the other cars in the garage?"

"No, and neither has Sheila. I save them for surveillance purposes." He took the check back and tossed it on the table in disgust. Leaning against the cushions, Dagger stretched his legs across the coffee table, hands clasped across his chest. There was many a night he fell asleep in this position. "The absolute gall of that man. To think he could buy someone."

"And you want him to think he has?"

Dagger nodded. "Until I figure out exactly what I can do with the check that would do him the most harm."

Sara wanted to ask him if that meant he would continue to date Sheila. Instead, she hugged her knees to her chest and changed the subject.

"Nick invited me to his birthday party tomorrow."

"See, tonight wasn't so bad after all, was it?"

"No. Once I focused my attention on the mystery of Rachel's disappearance, I forgot all about my nervousness."

"Oh yes. Rachel."

"It was her, Dagger. I'm sure of it."

"Okay," Dagger conceded. "We'll go together. Sheila invited me and I told her I would meet her there. This could be good. We should be able to find out more about Rachel."

Sara picked up a pad of paper and jotted down notes. "We should check to see if Robert Tyler had Rachel sign a pre-nuptial agreement and what effect her death had on anyone's inheritance."

"Good idea." Dagger stripped out of his shirt and walked to his bedroom to change clothes.

Sara tried not to stare at Dagger's firm, tanned torso. His arms were muscular, his stomach flat. She didn't understand the strange feelings that came over her whenever she saw him.

Dagger returned wearing loose-fitting cotton drawstring pants and pullover shirt. He pulled the rubber band from his hair and rubbed his scalp with his fingers. There was a slight curl to his hair resembling a relaxed permanent.

He sat down next to Sara and plopped his legs back on the oak coffee table. "Add another note to check the police report on Rachel's death. Maybe some of the crew members are still around."

"Then we need to find out where everyone was that night."

"You can pick Nick's brain on that one," Dagger said. "Sheila might have some information, too. The Tylers were like a second family to her. I think their fathers went to high school and college together."

"Do you think Sheila dated any of them?"

Dagger shrugged. "Never asked. Guess it's possible."

Dagger removed the lid from a painted box. He lifted out the earring they had found at the townhouse. Dagger rolled the piece of jewelry around between two fingers and watched how the light reflected off the small diamonds circling the larger stone. "This is very well made. I think I should bait them by mentioning I have a new client who found it at the Dunes Resort."

"Yes, we took care of the problem. When can we meet?" The hotel suite was spacious with bulky furniture in conservative brown and gray tones. The man with the phone pressed to his ear looked like a furniture mover or nightclub bouncer. His biceps were the size of a normal man's thigh. Dark, curly hair hugged his large head and his eyes turned down at the corners. He had a deceiving choir-boy look to his face. "Why so late?" He asked. He turned to the two men seated on the couch as he hung up the phone. "We'll get the rest of our money tomorrow night."

"I don't like it, Luke. We should have been paid in full the minute we iced the lady." Mince dragged one leg over an armrest of the couch, the laces of his untied tennis shoes dangling. His balding head made him appear older and his pudge face was marred with enough bumps and craters to resemble a misshapen bag of flour.

Sections of the newspaper were scattered around the couch and coffee table. The men looked as out of place in a four-star hotel suite as a homeless man at Buckingham Palace.

"Nobody pays in full. You get half before and the balance after the job. That's what we agreed to." Luke gathered up the papers and stacked them on the table. "You guys are absolute slobs."

"We should up the ante," Joey added, pacing as he chugged a can of beer. His eyes seemed too close together, his nose too pointed and slim, like the rest of his body. He wiped the back of his hand across his mouth.

"We're lucky we're being paid anything. You two fucked up. You weren't supposed to kill her."

"Hey." Mince pulled his feet off the table. "Nobody gave us a Plan B. She was trying to escape. How many times do I have to say it?"

Joey argued, "You weren't there, Luke. I know we were supposed to keep her alive. But what did you want? A woman on the loose or a dead woman?"

"At least you got rid of the body." Luke crumpled his beer can with one hand.

Mince and Joey exchanged glances.

10

Sara was up early Saturday morning making blueberry scones. After placing the pan in the oven, she went looking for Dagger.

She cautiously peered into Dagger's bedroom, a room she still didn't feel comfortable entering. It was the only other part of the house she considered his private domain. After all, he was paying rent and deserved some privacy.

Sunlight sprayed in through the blinds. A variety of floral aromas seeped into the room through the opened windows. In the distance, the wildflowers transformed the backyard into a botanical garden.

Dagger carried his taste in black and gray into his décor. A king-sized bed and wall unit in a black lacquer finish occupied one side of the room with a matching dresser and entertainment center. The room was almost as large as the aviary but without the high ceiling. Dagger had his own bathroom and walk-in closet.

A geometric-patterned bedspread in black and gray hues accented the gray wall-to-wall carpeting. Dagger had transformed the opposite side of the room into a mini-gym with a treadmill, exercise bike, weight machine, and mirrored walls. One section of the mirrored wall was ajar. It was a hidden door to Dagger's secret room, accessible only by a code.

Dagger called out, "In here, Sara." Dagger had created this windowless room to house a variety of toys. A long-range semi-automatic rifle hung on a wall next to handguns, night scopes, night-vision goggles, wiretapping equipment, bulletproof vests, a Ruger police carbine, and numerous other items purchased, traded, confiscated, and retrieved by honest and sometimes not-so-honest techniques. Bright high-intensity lights no larger than inverted cone cups hung from the ceiling.

"Do you know a Sergeant Jerry Martinez?"

Dagger thumbed through boxes of printer paper as he mumbled, "Yes. Padre Martinez is bringing us a copy of the original missing person report on Rachel Tyler. Is he here?"

"Yes. He's coming up the drive."

"Did I hear the phone ring?"

"Sal Wormley called."

Dagger looked up from the supply drawer. "Let me guess. He wants to take you to lunch or dinner."

Sara chewed on her bottom lip. "Not a good idea?"

"Not HIS idea. Sounds like Sheila has him on a fact-finding expedition." Dagger shoved a filing drawer shut with one knee.

Sara stepped closer. "What is that?"

"Remember that check from Leyton Monroe?" He held up several sheets of blank paper and the check. "Pretty good match, don't you think?"

He had a devilish twinkle in his eye that had taken Sara very little time to recognize. He thoroughly enjoyed his work and especially liked those times he could be creative. And right now his creative juices were on overload.

The paper was identical in color to Leyton Monroe's check. It was light blue with tiny threads running through it like the threads found in currency paper.

Sara stood close enough to smell his aftershave, subtle, woodsy. He didn't shave daily. It seemed useless because no sooner did he shave then his face looked as if it had been dusted with tiny grains of black dirt. When she leaned forward, her hair drifted over her shoulder, cascading down to her waist. She flipped it back over her shoulder but it stubbornly refused to obey.

Beneath Dagger's open-collared shirt she could see the black leather cord necklace that had once belonged to her grandmother. A sterling silver charm in the shape of a wolf's head hung from the cord. Its eyes were made of turquoise stones. He had found it strange that Ada Kills Bull had placed the necklace and a note to him in her jewelry box. It was as though Ada knew she was going to die.

Dagger held the sample paper in one hand, the check in the other. "What do you think? We do a little clip art to duplicate the border and typestyle and scan in his signature. *Voila*. We have signed checks from Leyton Monroe."

Sara smiled slowly. "And what do you plan to do with blank checks, forged, I might add?" She fingered the cuffed edge of her denim shorts and stood with one foot snaked around her ankle as if in a bizarre yoga position.

"I'm not sure yet, but think of the possibilities."

The front door knocker banged three times. In the background they heard Einstein shriek, "COMPANY, SQUAARK. COME IN."

They exited the secret room and Dagger closed the mirrored wall.

Sergeant Martinez wasted no time shedding his frayed sportcoat revealing his shoulder holster. He was shorter than Dagger and stocky, with a forehead made larger by his receding gray hairline. A fresh scar on his left cheek was starting to heal.

Dagger said, "I hope the other guy looks worse."

Padre stroked his scar. "Let's just say he won't be resisting arrest again."

Dagger introduced Sara to Padre just as a blur of color flew past them.

Einstein clamped his claws onto the perch by Dagger's desk. The macaw had been trained to only use the catwalk railing or the perches. Other than the ones in the aviary, there was one bolted to the back of the sofa and one attached to the paneled wall by Dagger's desk. "AWK, UP AGAINST THE WALL AND SPREAD 'UM. AWWWKK."

They all laughed. Padre said, "You still around, Einstein?"

Einstein dipped his head up and down in response, training one yellow-ringed black eye on him.

Dagger handed Einstein a Brazil nut and ran his hand down the macaw's back whispering, "Be a good boy and go to your room." Einstein flew off with his treat in his beak. Dagger closed both doors to the aviary, minimizing the noise level.

Padre explained to Sara, "Dagger and I met during a bank robbery, so to speak. The perps were going to keep everyone as hostages. Dagger created some kinda bomb using a piece of fuse, some metal nuts or bolts, and a cigarette. Just big enough to divert attention but small enough so it didn't blow us all to hell. I ain't never seen nothing like it."

"Guess I watched a little too much TV as a kid." Dagger motioned Padre over to the couch.

Sara sat down on the love seat and gathered her legs under her. "Why does Dagger call you Padre?"

Dagger explained, "Jerry attended two years of seminary school until he realized he wanted to hold a gun instead of a bible."

Nudging the case folder on Rachel, Padre said, "That's your file. I made you a copy but you have no idea how you got it." Padre gave Dagger a knowing wink. It wasn't unusual for information to conveniently fall into Padre's lap. Leaning forward, elbows on his knees, he asked, "Why the interest? She's been dead for what, five years now?"

"Five years next week," Dagger replied. "But," he paused, choosing their cover carefully, "I have a client who saw her a couple days ago."

Padre scoffed. "You're kidding. Where?"

"At the Dunes Resort in Michigan City. Unfortunately, this time she was dead, murdered, we think."

"Were you the investigating officer?" Sara asked.

"No. Cal Dobrowski was. He's retired now." Padre thought for a moment, ran his fingertip gingerly across his scar. "But if your client saw her, why didn't he, or she, call the police?"

Dagger flashed a quick glance at Sara. Then retrieved the two composite pictures from his desk. "Let's just say it's complicated."

"You haven't changed. You're doing what you do best," Padre countered, "being evasive."

Dagger laid the pictures on the table and sat down. "Do you recognize either of these two?"

Padre examined the pictures carefully. "I suppose having a crime unit check for fingerprints didn't occur to you."

"The place was clean."

Padre laid the pictures back down. "So, you were there."

Dagger stacked the pictures in a neat pile and shoved them in a file folder. If it had been any other cop, Dagger would have been dragged into the precinct by now. He handed Padre the folder. "You can take the pictures with you. I have another set."

Padre gazed curiously at Sara whose gaze darted from Dagger to the pictures.

Sara stood. "Would you like something to drink?"

"Something cold." Padre watched her leave and then turned to Dagger.

Dagger opened the box and showed Padre the earring. "This is the only thing I was able to locate. The victim was wearing it."

Padre examined the earring. "Why did you wait two days to call me?"

"Jezzus, Padre. What's with the third degree?" Dagger clasped his hands behind his head and leaned back, staring up at the hazy sky beyond the skylights.

Sara returned and handed Padre a glass of lemonade. Dagger shifted his eyes from her to the kitchen, signaling her to disappear.

"Just trying to get something to go on."

Once Sara left, Dagger straightened up and said, "My client happened to be at the Tyler house last night and saw a picture of Rachel. I have to tell you it's difficult for me to believe the story since I saw no sign of a struggle when I searched that townhouse. But my client is a very credible witness."

"Have you checked with the Michigan City police?"

"I thought it would be rather awkward for me since they'd probably drag my ass in for questioning. However," Dagger grinned, "you are in a better position to pick their collective brains."

"Sounds like a plan. And I'll fax them these pictures." He placed the earring on the table.

"Just make sure the press doesn't get wind of this. Don't mention the earring to the Michigan City cops, and, god forbid, don't mention my name. Sara and I are attending another party at the Tylers tonight. We'll slip in a few delicate questions, maybe drop a few not-too-delicate time bombs."

Padre held the cold glass to his forehead. "Damn, you keep it warm in here." He pushed wisps of wet hair off his forehead and thumbed through the case file again. "According to this report, Harbor Rentals provides boats and crew members for charter cruises. Tyler hired two men to pilot his boat the night of Rachel's disappearance. At the last minute, Tyler was called away on business so Rachel

THE GOOD DIE TWICE 67

went by herself. The reports detail where everyone was that night and the testimonies from Pete Foster and Grant Oakley, the crew members. And there's also an extensive background check on Rachel."

Dagger jotted notes in the margins of his copy. "So, where and why would a young woman hide out for five years?"

Sara returned carrying freshly washed vegetables in a bowl. She slid open the two doors and entered the aviary. She filled one of the food bowls and stood in the doorway watching the macaw.

"What about Robert Tyler? Was he a suspect?" Dagger asked

Padre replied, "No. He was madly in love with his wife, according to all these notes. Some of her modeling friends agreed that Rachel was treated like a queen by Robert Tyler."

"But did she love him?" Dagger asked.

"Supposedly."

Padre closed the file folder. "If it were a kidnapping, and believe me a kidnapper could have gotten a lot of money out of old man Tyler, there was never a ransom note."

Einstein flew back into the living room and perched near Dagger's desk. "AWK, DUNES RESORT, DUNES RESORT." Einstein fanned his colorful wings as if circulating the room air.

Dagger rose from the couch, his brows forming a straight line. "Wait a minute. Einstein might have something there." He sat down at his computer and accessed America On-Line.

"What are you doing?" Padre walked over to the desk and leaned his arms on the ledge, weight shifted. He jammed a fist just under his scar.

Sara cradled Einstein, kissed the top of his head. "Be good."

Dagger said, "I'm checking all the holdings of Tyler International."

"AWWWKK, DUNES RESORT, AWK." Einstein craned his neck to see the monitor.

Padre returned to the couch. "So, Sara, how long have you been working for Dagger Investigations?" He watched her fold herself gracefully onto the floor in front of the coffee table, her long hair touching the floor.

"Just a few months." Sara studied her hands nervously.

"GOTCHA!" Dagger leaped from the chair. "Einstein, you are a genius."

"What did you find?" Padre asked.

Dagger showed Padre the printout. "Tyler International owns the Dunes Resort. It was acquired three years before Rachel died, the first time."

"Interesting." Padre studied the printout, then glanced at Einstein. "How did your bird know that?"

"I vaguely remember talking to Simon some time last year about good stocks to get into. Tyler International was one of them. I must have listed some of the resorts Tyler owns and Einstein associated the name Tyler with the Dunes Resort." Dagger puffed up like a proud father.

Sara squirted lotion in the palm of her hands and worked the cream into the ragged skin on her knuckles. She said, "Who better to have access to a new construction site than one of the Tylers?"

Dagger studied the list of suspects he had made. "The question is: Which Tyler?"

11

Padre left after they agreed to keep in touch to compare notes. Padre would take a few days off and drive out to Michigan City to have a look around the Dunes Resort.

"How do they look?" Dagger held up the samples of the forged checks. "All I have to do is keep my eyes and ears open tonight and I should come up with the appropriate recipients of Leyton Monroe's generosity."

Sara's eyes widened. "You're going to give Mr. Monroe's money away?"

He crooked his finger and tapped it under her chin. "Nah, just helping him spend it." The intercom from the front gate rang out. "That's probably Hardaway." Dagger left his project on the worktable and exited the secret room. He lifted the cover to the fake thermostat on the wall and punched a button to close the mirrored door.

Stu Hardaway looked like a short version of Danny Thomas, with a honker of a nose and hairy knuckles. A chunk of cigar jutted out from between his plump lips.

"I'm sorry, Mr. Hardaway, but we don't allow smoking," Sara said gently.

Stu Hardaway stared indignantly at Sara, as if he were just refused seating at the Le Janiere Restaurant at the Ritz Carlton Hotel.

"I won't be here long enough for you to even get a whiff of it, Honey," Stu barked.

Sara stepped out onto the stoop and held the screen door open. "I smelled it the moment you got out of your car. If you don't mind."

Stu jerked his head at Dagger, waiting for him to get his hired help in line.

Dagger said, "Don't worry. Your smelly turd will be safe outside."

"AWK, STINKY, STINKY." Einstein added his two cents while hanging upside down by the grated door.

Stu slapped his suitcase on Dagger's desk. Three large-stoned rings were squeezed over his sausage fingers. One had a large "S" in diamonds surrounded by black onyx stones. A thick gold chain link necklace around his compressed neck held a large pendant in the shape of a dollar sign.

"Crissake," Stu muttered. "You've got some smelly bird in here with filthy bird shit all over and you're worried about my cigar? Now I've heard everything."

Sara waited until Stu tossed the cigar out the opened door, then she crossed the room to the aviary. "Einstein doesn't stink and he's trained."

Stu laughed showing gold caps in two of his molars. "A bird that shits in a litter box." He shook his head, causing wisps of thin hair to break free from whatever spray had held them in one place.

"Not a litter box but at least in a specific area," Dagger clarified.

Stu cast a gaze toward Einstein, saying, "Hope you don't go outside during hunting season, you oversized crow."

Einstein climbed on the perch by his door, lifted his wings, and fanned out his tail. He made several hacking motions toward Stu.

"Let's finish this up, Stu, before I sic my guard parrot on you." Dagger popped the tape into the machine and pressed the PLAY button.

Stu stood vigil over the tape player, gleefully smiling as he heard his wife and her paramour trade company secrets of acquisitions and bidding contracts, all the conversations Dagger had taped during his trip to the Dunes Resort.

"Your ass is fried now, you whore."

Dagger pressed the STOP/EJECT button. "You do realize that you might not be able to use this tape in a courtroom."

Stu handed Dagger an envelope of cash. "I don't think it will make it to a courtroom. Just as long as I get that bloodsucking wife out of my life and be able to keep my hardearned money, I'll be perfectly happy."

Sara stood at the kitchen door watching Stu Hardaway drive away in his Lexus. Dagger counted out the hundred-dollar bills on his desk.

"Why do people get married if they don't even like each other?" Sara slid open the door to Einstein's room on her way to Dagger's desk. She eyed the stacks of money.

Dagger scooped up the money and banded the stacks. "Sometimes people don't show their true selves until after they are married."

"I think the lucky one is Mrs. Hardaway. Stu Hardaway is a self-righteous, sexist pig."

Dagger smiled. "Don't hold back, Sara."

"I don't think I could stand living ten minutes under the same roof with him. Especially those cigars." She shivered at the mention of the foul-smelling tobacco.

He handed her the bundles of cash. "Want to do the honors and put these in the safe?"

"How much did we milk him for?" Sara asked as she retreated to the vault.

"Thirty thousand." Dagger smiled. Six months before she would never have asked such a question. He had created a monster. And Simon was right—he wouldn't have it any other way.

12

"PARTY TIME, PARTY TIME," Einstein shrieked as he flew from the tree to the birdbath. He pulled on a chain, spraying himself with a shower of water. Turning around several times, he flapped his wings and chattered incessantly.

"We won't be long, Einstein. I promise." Sara filled two of Einstein's food dishes with fresh vegetables. She hung a braided rope filled with Brazil nuts from one of the tree limbs and placed several interlocking toys on the floor. "That should keep you busy while we're gone."

Dagger peered into the aviary and whistled, admiring the aqua-colored, chiffon-tiered dress Sara wore. The color matched her eyes. "Absolutely gorgeous."

Einstein let out a shrill whistle. "GORGEOUS, AWWWKK." He flew to the tree and shook the water from his feathers. Sara laughed and ran from the room, scolding Einstein for spraying her dress.

Dagger slid the grated door shut and turned the key in the padlock. "Behave yourself while we're gone."

"HELLO, HELLO, AWK. DAGGER INVESTIGA-

TIONS. YOU LOSE IT, WE'LL FIND IT. AWK."

"Sorry, buddy. You won't be able to answer the phone from in there." Dagger shook the door to make sure the lock held. He slipped a black sportcoat on over his black dress pants and black shirt. He wasn't sure he liked the idea of Nick having his sights set on Sara. He felt like her protector. Sara's grandmother had been Sara's confidante, her sounding board, teacher. Since Ada's death, Dagger was the only person Sara trusted.

Dagger gave Sara a puzzled look.

Sara asked, "What?"

"I just wondered ... have you ever dated?"

Sara dropped her gaze, fumbled with her purse. "I think I left my comb upstairs."

As he watched her climb the stairs, Dagger whispered, "Oh my god."

"Just remember," Dagger warned Sara as they entered the main dining room. "If he tries anything, you kick the shit out of him."

"Dagger, please!" Sara felt her face flush.

"And don't forget why we're here."

The main dining room was in a different wing from the ballroom where they had mingled Friday night. The table, covered with a festive cloth, was set for nine people, a bit more intimate than the previous star-studded event. The table could easily seat twice as many, but tonight the staff had provided additional space between each seating. Sara was sure there must be something in an etiquette book that dictated how to host a party for fewer than eighteen people.

Fragrant, colorful floral arrangements graced the table. Sara had no idea why each place setting needed so much silverware. Friday night there had been a buffet and her napkin had contained only the customary knife and fork. This was entirely different. She had half-expected a barbecue with hamburgers and hot dogs, not china in a rose pattern that matched the wallpaper, or polished silver and crystal wineglasses.

Today there were no security people, no valet, no metal detectors. And another thing Sara readily noticed—it wasn't a formal dress gathering.

"Dagger, Darling." Sheila drifted over from the opened French doors that overlooked the gardens. Her halter top was cropped just above her navel, exposing tanned shoulders and midriff. Sheila gave Sara's dress a casual glance, then turned toward Nick who was standing by the bar. "Nicholas, I didn't know you were taking Sara to the prom tonight."

"Sheila, shut up." Dagger's stare was icy, but Sheila ignored him.

Sara never thought to ask Nick what the dress code was. Her fingers played with one of the chiffon tiers and she focused her attention on a woman with auburn hair. She wore white pants and a short-sleeved white top with gold studs forming the image of a building. Sara guessed the building to be a replica of one of the Tyler resorts, probably from one of Tyler's hotel gift shops.

Nick appeared with a beer for Dagger and a glass of wine for Sara. "Pay no attention to her, Sara. Sheila once wore a swimsuit to a pool party. She didn't read the fine print that said to bring your own cue stick."

Everyone laughed except Sheila. Sara distanced herself from Dagger's former fiancee and walked out onto the balcony. Flat white buildings could be seen in the distance. She remembered Nick telling her they had their own greenhouses and a mile away from the mansion was a stable. The Tyler estate was like something Sara had seen in vacation brochures. It could be a resort on its own. And there was a lot of land here to ... bury someone? The thought struck her suddenly, but it was comical and Sara found herself laughing at the thought of Rachel Tyler climbing out of her grave to declare herself alive, almost.

The balcony seemed a quiet sanctuary if it weren't for Sheila's loud voice. Sara moved away from the doors and toward the far end of the balcony where a myriad of potted plants huddled. She admired the flowering hibiscus trees. They were in full bloom and she inhaled their aroma. Another plant with red flowers and stems clothed with woolly hairs of a reddish/purplish color was unique but she was disappointed that the flowers didn't have a scent.

"Thank god Sheila has you to pick on."

Sara turned to see the auburn-haired woman, her hair short and forming a fluff of curls around her face. Her lips were covered with flaming red lipstick.

Sara asked, "Why is that?"

"Because then the bitch can leave me alone." She laughed and held out her hand to Sara. "Edie Tyler. And you must be the young lady who is driving Sheila right up the wall."

"I don't mean to." Sara noticed Edie's two-inch nails

had gold studs embedded in the bright red polish. It was hard for Sara to believe that Edie could button her clothes or even get into those horrid panty hose with nails that long.

Edie laughed again. "Innocence and modesty. Quite a rarity around these halls."

Sara noticed a look in Edie's eyes that seemed amused at Sara's discomfort even if her words chastised Sheila's behavior. Sara self-consciously ran her hands down the front of her dress, as if keeping the chiffon layers from swaying would make her dress appear more informal.

"The table seems set for a formal dinner."

"The Tylers don't know the meaning of informal. Although Sheila looks casually dressed in that swatch of fabric she calls a top and those low-riding flared pants, the outfit cost over five hundred dollars. And those straw-colored matching sandals set her back, oh, I'd say about one hundred dollars."

Numerous gold bangled bracelets clanged on Edie's wrist as she raised her wine glass to her lips. Sara didn't know how she did it, but Edie didn't leave a lipstick smudge on the glass. Her green eyes were an unusual color, a vibrant kelly green.

"You have nice eyes." Sara felt a compliment might do wonders to win her a supporter.

The gold bangles clanged again as Edie fluffed a hand through her hair. "Green today, blue tomorrow. I have a drawer full of every color in the rainbow."

Sara glanced at Edie's nails. "It must be hard to put them in."

Edie shrugged. "That's what maids are for."

Sara caught the look again, subtle but transparent enough for even Sara to read it. Arrogance. There was probably a feminine way of being arrogant without flashing it the way Stu Hardaway did.

They stared out toward a river in the distance. It came right up to the Tyler property where several boats were moored. Amazing what money could buy, Sara thought. Tyler had his own river and access to the lake without ever having to trailer his boat to the marina.

"It must be tough being the only woman in the house," Sara said. "I mean, since Rachel Tyler passed away." Edie arched a picture-perfect eyebrow but said nothing. Sara plodded on. "I saw the family portraits yesterday when I was upstairs. Nick explained who everyone was. She is ... was ... beautiful." Sara forced a smile. "I bet she drove Sheila crazy, too."

Edie finally smiled. "Probably for the first time in her life Sheila was intimidated. With Robert and Leyton being so close, Sheila considered herself the adopted daughter of Robert Tyler, the anointed little sister to Eric and big sister to Nicholas. Then Rachel comes on the scene, twenty-eight years Robert's junior, a couple of years older than Sheila. She had the attention of every man who laid eyes on her. A thousand-dollar-an-hour model. She had it all." Edie took a long sip of wine and studied Sara curiously. "Now, ask yourself. Why would a young woman who had more than enough admirers and could have her pick of any man, pick an old fart like Robert Tyler?"

Sara shrugged. "Maybe she loved him."

Edie jerked her head back and laughed aloud, a very

unfeminine, raucous laugh that pierced the humid air. She placed a hand heavy with numerous rings on Sara's shoulder and squeezed. "Sweetheart, you are so naive." She was still laughing as the dinner bell rang and they seated themselves around the table.

Robert Tyler sat at the head of the table looking very much like a king. A paisley ascot hugged his neck, tucked dapperly under a starched white shirt. Gold cuff links shaped like anchors peeked out from under his navy sportcoat. His hair was thick, a pleasant blend of gray and brown accented by strands of silver. His nails were manicured, hands smooth and unscarred.

Sara liked his voice. It was smooth and gentle. She could understand why a woman like Rachel would be attracted to him.

"Nicholas, who is your beautiful friend ... this week?" Robert laughed at his own joke, and—as is typical of a lord of the kingdom—the subjects followed suit. Robert's gray eyes twinkled.

Nick rested his arm across the back of Sara's chair, the sleeve of his white poet's shirt softly touching her hair. "This is Sara, Dad. Sara Morningsky."

"You have beautiful features, Dear." The woman seated to Robert's left was Leyton Monroe's wife, Anna. A nest of platinum curls rested on top of her head. "What nationality are you, Sara?"

Sara blinked quickly and glanced across the table at Dagger. "I'm pretty much a mixture, really." The less said the better, Dagger always told her.

Several waiters set platters of food on the table. Robert

stabbed a filet mignon and passed the platter to Sara. "Let me guess," he said. "I bet you have some Arapaho, Shoshoni, maybe even Apachi. The nose isn't right for Blackfoot." He stared at Sara, his gaze taking in the shape of her eyes, her cheekbones. "If I were a betting man, I'd say you had some mythical Anasazi genes in you."

"But blue-green eyes, Dear?" Anna chirped again. "That certainly can't be from your Native American heritage."

"Actually, there was a Navaho princess back in the eighteen hundreds who was known as Blue Eyes. Although," Sara admitted, "I have never traced my family tree."

"Well, maybe you should, Dear."

Sara stared at the pool of blood surrounding the filets. Her stomach did a flop. She swallowed hard and passed the platter to Nicholas. She passed the next platter of venison and added more salad to her plate.

"Please," Leyton bellowed, "let's not talk about Native Americans. I have enough problems fighting your people for fishing rights in Wisconsin."

Sara felt the hair at the nape of her neck rise. She saw Anna place her hand on Leyton's plump arm but one scowl from him had her removing it immediately. His eyes, surrounded by folds of skin, appeared cold and unfriendly.

"We get limited on the number of fish we can catch," Leyton continued, "but YOUR people have no limits. They even hunt with bow and arrow." He reached across the table and stabbed a filet off the platter before Nick had a chance to pass the platter to Edie. He dropped it on his plate splattering red juice on his shirt. Anna promptly dipped her linen

napkin in her water glass and tried to dab the blood off
Leyton's shirt. "I don't know who's draining the government coffers more—you people or the blacks. My tax dollars at work," he muttered. "We should have wiped all
Indians off the face of the earth."

"LEYTON," Anna yelled, her scorn falling on deaf ears.

Sara scooped mashed potatoes onto her plate and in
a quiet voice countered, "I believe YOUR people already
tried that." She heard a chuckle from Robert and Nick.
And out of the corner of her eye, she saw Dagger smiling approvingly.

Leyton raised his hand to one of the waiters and ordered
a scotch and water.

"Leyton, put a sock in it," Edie blurted. "This is Nick's
birthday. If anyone is allowed to make a fool of himself, it
should be Nicholas."

"Here, here." Robert raised his wine glass. "To
Nicholas. May he someday stop trying to find himself and
settle in at Tyler International."

13

"Your little secretary eats like a bird. I take it she's a vegetarian since she turned green when she saw the filets." Sheila leaned against the bar between Dagger and Eric. Nick was opening gifts at the far end of the dining room table. Edie and Anna sat nearby sampling the desserts. Sara sat across from Nick drinking a cup of tea.

The staff had cleared the table and reset it with fresh linen. The credenza near the French doors had been set up with desserts, coffee, and hot water. The opposite side of the room looked like a library with a wall of bookshelves and a number of upholstered chairs surrounding an octagon-shaped coffee table.

Dagger sighed heavily. "She has a name, Sheila. And, no, she's not a vegetarian. She eats chicken and fish. It's red meat she doesn't like."

"There are a lot of people who don't like red meat." Eric set his empty beer bottle on the bar. Eric had two of his mother's patented traits—a one-inch white streak of hair at his temple and eyes which were a little too small and close together. Although he was taller, Eric wasn't as muscular as his father and brother. He turned to Sheila. "Have you and Dagger set another wedding date yet?"

"You'll have to ask Dagger." Sheila ran her hand down the lapel of Dagger's jacket.

Dagger set his beer bottle on the bar and excused himself. He located Robert by the credenza pouring a cup of coffee. Dagger did the same. Edie and Anna howled with laughter at something Nick said. Just a small family gathering, the way Robert Tyler insisted.

Dagger studied the pictures on the wall. More family portraits and another close-up portrait of Rachel. Pulling out a computer composite picture of Rachel, the detective said, "She was beautiful."

"Yes, she was," Robert replied.

"I saw Rachel's picture upstairs in the hallway yesterday."

Robert took a sip of coffee and eyed Dagger curiously, then looked at the printout. "Yes?"

"It's a pretty good likeness, don't you think?"

Robert studied the printout. "Where did you get it?"

"I have a new client who told me she saw this woman Thursday night at the Dunes Resort."

Robert's hand trembled and he set the cup and saucer down quickly, spilling coffee on the credenza. "Rachel ... ALIVE?"

Talking dulled to a low hum, then ceased. Eric and Sheila joined the group at the table.

Stepping from the balcony, Leyton demanded, "What do you mean Rachel is alive?"

Robert swiped a hand through his hair and staggered to

the table where he slowly lowered himself into a chair.

Dagger took a seat next to him. "I was hoping to discuss this privately with you."

"I should have known you would be the one bringing these tall tales." Leyton pulled back his shoulders and fixed a twisted smile on Dagger.

"What on earth are you talking about?" Anna flitted over as fast as her short legs could carry her. She plopped down into the chair next to Robert and patted his arm sympathetically.

"Can we go to your study and discuss this?" Dagger actually had no problem discussing it publicly. Sara's job was to watch everyone's reaction.

"A little late for that," Leyton blurted, walking off in a huff to fix another drink. But he returned quickly.

"She can't be alive. After all this time." Robert gladly accepted the drink Leyton brought him.

"I didn't say she was alive. I said I had a client who saw someone who looked like her." Dagger placed the printout on the table. "My client says she witnessed the woman's murder."

Leyton paced the marble floor as if it were his own relative he were hearing about. "Preposterous!"

"I, I don't understand," Robert stammered.

"It can't be Rachel," Anna said. "If she were alive, she would have contacted Robert. Where would she have been all this time?"

"Who is this client?" Edie demanded. "We have a right to know."

Eric chimed in. "The police have a right to know."

"Preposterous!" Leyton mumbled again. "Don't listen to him, Robert. Dagger has a habit of working the most outrageous cases, the weirder, the better."

Sheila slid close to Dagger, saying, "Honey, is this witness reliable?"

Dagger half turned and leveled an icy stare. Sheila backed off and found refuge next to her father.

"The witness is reliable in spite of the fact that we never found a body. The only proof I have that the victim might have been your wife is an earring I found at the murder scene."

14

"Your boss certainly knows how to bring a quick close to a party." Nick led Sara into a room in the East Wing.

"I'm sorry if it ruined your birthday." Sara stopped when she saw the king-sized bed. Nick had led her to his bedroom. Strange-looking artifacts hung from the walls alongside colorful maps. The room wasn't as large as Sara's bedroom. She was surprised. And his taste in decor leaned toward safari with animal print draperies and bedspread. It was vintage Nick, seeing how much traveling he had done in his young life.

"No problem. Old folks are kinda boring anyway." He unbuttoned his shirt and threw it over the horn of a rhino jutting out from the wall behind the door. "Don't worry," Nick said tossing a nod toward the rhino. "It was a road kill." A crater-sized dimple formed in Nick's cheek as he smiled and winked. He made no move to put on another shirt.

Alarms rang in Sara's head. She looked back at the closed door, feeling imprisoned without escape. Her eyes darted nervously around the room. "Would it surprise you any if Rachel had been alive all this time?"

Nick appeared to space out, staring at nothing in particular, his thoughts occupied. Just as quickly, he jerked his head up, smiled, and moved slowly toward her, lifting her hair and moving it behind her shoulder. "I find it highly unlikely," Nick finally replied. "She loved playing queen of the castle, and I don't think she would have wasted one minute settling back into her role." His gaze moved down to Sara's chest, his smile broadened.

Sara looked down to see her nipples hard and protruding. No wonder Dagger always lectured her to wear underwear. The air conditioning had been pumping full force, even downstairs in the dining room. Now she wondered if her lack of underwear had been apparent in front of the Tylers and Leytons. She felt the color rush to her cheeks. She turned away, walked toward the patio doors. But Nick settled a tight grip around her waist.

She wasn't sure what Nick had on his mind but his hold on her was anything but friendly. Sara panicked. Her elbow found the spot just below his rib cage. While he was temporarily stunned, she hiked up her dress, turned, and high kicked him in the chest before throwing him over her shoulder.

Nick landed with a thud, his head thumping against the leg of a rattan throne chair. He lay still for several seconds, staring up at the ceiling, as if mentally checking that all his bones were intact. Then he broke out in a high-pitched giggle.

"Goddamn." Nick giggled again, propping himself up on one elbow. "Hey, I didn't know you liked it rough."

Sara fled, opening the door and tearing down the hallway. She could hear Nick yelling after her, "Hey, I was only kidding."

Sara turned down another hall and found refuge in a vestibule. Overhead track lighting shone down on a painting of three nude women taking a bath. Voices echoed down the hall, growing louder, approaching but then turning away. Sara peered around the corner and saw the two men from the Dunes Resort, the men who had killed Rachel Tyler. They were with another man who was built like a refrigerator, rock hard. She could almost feel the floor shake as they walked.

She pulled back against the wall, then just before the door near the end of the hall closed, she glanced at it again. And from the direction she had fled, she heard Nick calling out her name.

"Sara, I'm sorry. Please, let me make it up to you."

His voice was getting closer. With her shoulders pressed against the wall, she held her breath, hoping Nick wasn't looking for her down this hall. Dagger's words came back to her. "Have you ever been on a date?" Maybe she shouldn't have remained silent. Maybe she should have told him the only thing she knew about romance was what she had seen in the movie theatres.

It was her grandmother who had insisted Sara go to the movies. She thought it would be good for her. Sometimes she would sit through three movies. She didn't know any of the actors and hadn't read any movie reviews. Once, she found herself in a movie with the words flashing across the bottom of the screen. What the actors were doing on screen was shocking but she would have been more embarrassed to run out of the show. So she stayed and listened to the people panting in the audience. She had been too embarrassed to tell her grandmother. But her grandmother must have suspected because soon after she had a woman-to-woman talk with her about the birds and the bees.

Sara would watch people on dates at the show, at the beach, or walking in the park. The only thing that seemed to have prepared her for this was Dagger's self-defense lessons. She didn't think romance was supposed to necessitate self-defense.

She heard Nick call her name again, but his voice was fading. He was moving away. Sara made her way to the end of the hall. Leaning against a door, she heard voices. The door to the adjacent room was open. It was a bedroom, immense, with a fireplace, dressing table, and a lounge chair that looked like something out of a Cleopatra movie. Two carpeted stairs led up to a four-poster bed covered in a floral bedspread. Floral pillows had been generously tossed against the headboard.

Sara closed the bedroom door and stared at a huge portrait of Rachel hanging over the fireplace. Moving closer, Sara could see why men were enamored with the woman. Her beauty was flawless.

The sun was setting in the distance, casting a strange orange glow to the landscape. Hoping the balconies connected the rooms, Sara stepped outside only to discover the balcony to the adjacent room was more than forty feet away. She tried to listen for voices but too many conflicting noises were coming from the animals and birds in the nearby trees.

Sara had no choice but to kick off her shoes. Now she understood the downside to wearing nylons.

The change was quick. Sara rarely had to think long about it. Just a slight focus and the dress fell away, discarded, as much a nuisance as the nylons. The gray hawk took flight, landing on the railing of the adjacent balcony, its sturdy talons clinging tightly. Its feathers ruffled in the mild breeze and the setting sun wrapped the hawk in warmth. Its eyesight and hearing were keen, just as they had been the night Rachel was murdered.

Sara Morningsky was a shape-shifter. Once thought only to be the subject of tall tales told by the elders about men who would shift into wolves and prey upon livestock or unsuspecting men, Sara knew firsthand that a shape-shifter was anything but a myth. Nor was it a curse. Sara's grandmother had always called it a gift. Sara could shift into a gray hawk or gray wolf. And even in her human form she possessed the keen senses of the hawk and wolf.

Cautiously, the hawk turned its head and peered into the room. One of the men, the shorter one with the cratered face, had fired the gun that killed Rachel. He was seated in a barrel chair by the patio door. The other two men stood in the shadows. But the draperies blocked the hawk's view of the person seated behind the desk. Whoever was seated there just set a lit cigar in an ashtray. The hawk lifted off, spread its forty-inch wingspan and flew to a tree branch where it might have a better angle of sight.

* * *

"Use your head, Sheila. I thought you wanted to be known as a hard-hitting reporter, not some dame who rode her Dad's coattails up the ladder."

"I do." Sheila struggled to keep up with Dagger's long strides as they climbed the winding staircase. "Where are you going?"

"I'm looking for Nick."

"You mean you're looking for Sara." Sheila stopped in front of Nick's opened bedroom door. "Well, the bed's made so I guess her virtue is still intact." Sheila pulled Dagger into the bedroom and shut the door.

"Sheila, keep your head on the case, not sex."

"What case?"

Dagger unwrapped her arms from around his neck, her lips leaving a trail down his neck as if marking her territory. He held her at arm's length. "Rachel Tyler was alive prior to four o'clock Thursday morning. She has been missing for five years. Where has she been and who killed her? I would think you would be chomping at the bit on this one."

Sheila rolled her eyes and turned away. Sitting down on the bed, she said, "Give me something more to go on than a missing body that suddenly shows up now and is missing again." She pulled off her shoes and watched coyly as Dagger sat down next to her. Turning, she forced Dagger down on the bed and straddled him. His protesting seemed mute. She was on him like a raging nymph, forcing her tongue into his mouth and his hands over his head.

Dagger? Dagger heard Sara's voice but it sounded as if

it were in his head.

He broke free from Sheila saying, "Sara," like a man calling out a lover's name in his sleep. He forced himself up, sending Sheila tumbling off the bed.

Sara, why is it I can hear you in my head? Dagger asked in thought only. The voice was more distinct than just someone listening to his conscience. It was as clear as if she were standing next to him.

Dagger? Come quick. I'm outside Robert Tyler's bedroom at the end of a maze of halls. It's past an alcove.

Sheila crawled up off the floor and blew a strand of platinum hair from her forehead. "Sara? You're calling another woman's name while you're kissing me?"

"Not now, Sheila." Dagger tore out of the bedroom and down the hall. *Sara, what do you mean you're outside of Tyler's bedroom?*

I saw the killers, Dagger. They are in the room next to Mr. Tyler's bedroom but I can't see who they are talking to.

Why is it I can hear you in my head?

I didn't know if we could communicate this way. Grandmother and I were able to whenever I shifted. I guess now you and I can.

So we can talk to each other in our heads? It dawned on Dagger what Sara had said. He opened the door to Robert Tyler's bedroom and found Sara's shoes by the ficus tree and her nylons and dress out on the balcony. He looked out and saw the gray hawk in the tree fifty feet away. Leaving the dress on the balcony, Dagger picked up Sara's nylons and shoved them in the pocket of his sportcoat.

I don't see them anymore.

Sara, get back here, now.

The gray hawk flew back to the balcony. The shift happened so quickly Dagger couldn't distinguish at what point the hawk became Sara. He had even turned away as if she might be totally nude before putting her dress back on, but the hawk had somehow drifted into the dress and came up as Sara, fully clothed.

Stepping back into the room, Sara picked up her shoes and looked around for her nylons.

Dagger grabbed her by the shoulders, pressing gently. "Sara, don't ever do that in strange surroundings again. It is still daylight outside. Someone might have seen you." Dagger looked around the bedroom. "For all we know, he might have surveillance cameras in the room. Did you check first?" Sara shook her head no. Her eyes, large and bright, filled quickly and her bottom lip started quivering. He tried not to focus on her lips. "What if someone had come into the room besides me? Sara, you have to think first. Do you understand?"

Sara nodded, turning her bottom eyelashes into tiny springboards catapulting the teardrops up. They seemed to be suspended for the longest time before plummeting onto her high cheeks.

Dagger's defenses broke down. He gathered her in his arms and held her tight. He whispered, "Don't ever do that again, Sara. Please."

"I won't. I'm sorry, Dagger."

"Well, well. Isn't this a Kodak moment." Sheila stood in the doorway, one fist jammed onto her hip. "You leave me in bed to come play with your receptionist. How so like you,

you poor excuse for a ..."

Dagger broke the embrace. "I left you two minutes ago, Sheila. I doubt even I could have accomplished much in that little time."

"Oh really?" Sheila walked over and pulled something protruding from Dagger's pocket. "Looks like you got a pretty good start." She held up Sara's pantyhose.

Sara swiped them from Sheila's fingers and retreated to the master bathroom.

"Don't pretend to be jealous." Dagger walked out of the room and entered the adjacent room, not bothering to knock first. It was empty. "Did you see anyone come out of this room?"

"What? No."

Dagger checked the oversized mahogany desk. Other than a calendar and notepad, it was tidy, a little too neat. He looked at the high-backed chairs, the barrel chair by the balcony. There wasn't a scrap of paper, a burned out cigar, a jacket, a hint of who might have been there. He opened another door on the opposite side of the room. It opened to another hallway.

"Just great. Just fucking great."

"What? Dagger, what is it?" Sheila demanded.

"Nothing." He rushed past her but then stopped. Lifting up her left hand, he eyed the engagement ring she still wore. "You can take this off now." He pulled the check out of his pocket and ripped it in half. "And tell your father I really don't need the money."

"What is this?" She held the two halves of the check together, saw the check made out to Dagger and signed by her father.

"Your father tried to pay me to string you along, assuming, quite correctly, that I am too much of an ass to go through with the wedding. This keeps you tied up, out of the dating market, and more likely to stay single and follow in Daddy's footsteps at *The Daily Herald*." He could tell by the look on her face that she didn't believe him. "Just ask him."

15

At six the next morning, Sara and Dagger found themselves at Skizzy's Pawn Shop. A *Closed* sign was pressed against the door glass. Dagger rapped loudly.

"Are you sure he's in?"

"He's always in. Skizzy lives here." After another minute of pounding, the shade lifted. A set of beady eyes peered out. Chains and bolts were unfastened and the door was pulled open a scant two inches.

"Are you alone?" Skizzy stretched a bony neck out the door. His features looked alien, with bulging eyes and a nose too small for his face. His eyes jerked from side to side. "Come on in, quick, quick." He slammed the door shut behind them and refastened all the chains and bolts. Tufts of short, gray hair stuck out around his head, and what was gathered in a long pony tail was attempting to wrestle its way free from the rubber band.

Dagger held out a large bag and a cup of coffee. "We come bearing gifts."

"Store-bought with preservatives meant to render us like zombies?"

Sara took a step back from Skizzy. Dagger wrapped a reassuring arm around her shoulder. "No, Sara made the coffee. The vegetables are from our garden and the bread Sara made with all natural ingredients."

Skizzy peered into the bag. "Thank you. Smells good." Skizzy stood a little taller than Sara. He wore a stained tee shirt over a ragged pair of green camouflage pants, and battered tennis shoes. His conversation then turned private, carried out in a whisper as if a conversation with himself. "Can't have labels in your garbage. Then they'll know what you eat, what stores you shop at. They can track your comings and goings." He noticed Sara for the first time. "This the subject?"

"Yes. Sara Morningsky, Skizzy Borden."

"No relation to Lizzy." Skizzy didn't even laugh at his own joke. He just motioned for them to follow him past the glass cases of jewelry, through a curtained doorway, and into a small sitting room with a bed, television set, and a wall of books. Skizzy pressed a button under one of the shelves and the bookcase opened, revealing a steep staircase.

He led them down to a paneled basement. Bright fluorescent bulbs illuminated the room. It felt damp in this makeshift bunker. Shelving units held gallons of distilled water and canned goods, minus their labels. The cans were marked with a felt pen.

"Skizzy?" Sara whispered to Dagger. "What is that short for?"

Her voice echoed off the walls and settled on Skizzy's ears. "Paranoid schizophrenic," Skizzy said. "But I don't understand why." He pointed a black box with blinking green lights at the walls and did a slow, three-hundred-and-sixty-degree turn.

"What's he doing," Sara asked.

"Checking to see if aliens came in during the night and bugged the place." Dagger's smile toward Skizzy was genuine, affectionate. Skizzy hadn't been right since he'd returned from 'Nam. He had supplied Dagger with a lot of equipment, all homemade. Sometimes Dagger thought Skizzy acted crazy so people would leave him alone.

Sara chuckled. "You are kidding."

Skizzy turned a beady eye at her, continued to check the green light on his meter. "Never know how far away they are. They could be jamming my signal now."

"Who?" Sara asked with wide-eyed innocence.

Skizzy's eyebrow jerked up, his neck twitched. "You know who." He focused on his meter again. "They can monitor our phone calls from blocks away or from a helicopter. But I'm one step ahead, yes sir." He seemed to be talking to himself again, asking questions and even providing the answers. Finally, he said, "I guess it's okay."

Pulling out a drawer, he set several cards and blank documents on the desk. "So you told me you need a Social Security card, driver's license, gun registration, and a birth certificate."

"Yes." Dagger instructed Sara to stand in front of a white screen.

"Are you sure this is going to work?" Sara clamped her bottom lip between her teeth.

"Don't do that, Sara. It doesn't look good on a driver's

license."

Sara straightened the eyelet collar on her floral sundress. Dagger brushed her hair away from her eyes.

"My fake I.D.s always work." Skizzy checked the film in the camera.

"Skizzy is the best." Dagger stepped back behind Skizzy and motioned with his fingers for Sara to smile.

"I don't know why we have to go through all this." Sara checked the buttons on her dress and clasped her hands in front of her.

"Trust me. I know Sheila is going to have Sal Wormley turn every stone in the states to find information on you, and when there isn't any, she's going to get suspicious."

Skizzy snapped several shots. "Dagger knows what he's talking about. He knows how the deceitful mind thinks. I, on the other hand, know a conspiracy when I see one. Take these new driver's licenses, for instance, with these holograms. It's just like the metallic strip in the hundred-dollar bills. It's a way for the government to track us. They know where we are at all times and how much money we are leaving and entering the country with."

Sara's brows knitted. "Why do they want to do that?"

Skizzy looked at Dagger as if to ask what planet he found her on. "That's how they control us, girl. Big brother is watching. We have to stay one step ahead."

Dagger leaned against an X-Files poster on the wall which read, *We Are Not Alone*. "Skizzy believes the government has for years covered up the truth that aliens are living among us. Soon, we will all be duplicated, just like in the movie, *Invasion of the Body Snatchers*." A wide grin spread across Dagger's face.

Skizzy snapped another picture. "Keep laughing. But I'll be the only survivor. You'll see." He turned his computer on. "Now give me that dainty little hand of yours, Sara. I need your prints." As Sara's fingerprints appeared on the monitor, Skizzy continued, "Y'all don't know it, but every baby born since nineteen hundred and ninety-seven has had a computer chip implanted in its neck." He gave a serious wink and nod to Sara. "It's another way for them to keep track of us. And everyone who goes in for surgery, the government's having the doctors put a chip in their necks, too. Can't trust the government."

Sara watched in amazement as her picture appeared on the monitor next to her fingerprints. Then the two merged. "Is this legal?"

Skizzy and Dagger laughed. Sara's face flushed. Skizzy asked Sara, "You've been working with Dagger how long?" The printer spit out the driver's license and ran it through a plastic coating machine. "How can someone not have a birth certificate?" He waved a liver-spotted hand through the air, saying, "Forget it, none of my business."

"No problem, Skizzy," Dagger said. "Sara was delivered by her grandmother on a reservation. She never had a birth certificate."

"I'll date your driver's license back a couple years, your gun registration current as well as your Social Security card. And I have some yellowed paper I can print your birth certificate on."

Sara said, "I don't understand. All anyone has to do is check the Social Security and Department of Motor Vehicle computers and they'll know I'm not in there."

Skizzy smiled broadly, revealing a mouth crammed with teeth fighting each other for room. "That's the beauty of it. All the computers will show your I.D.s have always been in there."

"Skizzy's a bit of a hacker and worth every penny." Dagger pulled out his wallet and laid five hundred dollars on the table.

A bell rang overhead. Skizzy walked over to a television monitor showing the front entrance. Someone was peering through the window. "Damn drunks. Can't read." Skizzy looked at the stack of bills. "You brought all twenties, right?"

"Yes." Dagger turned to Sara saying, "Can't have any of those detectable fifty and hundred-dollar bills." He handed Skizzy the two composite pictures. "See if you can find these two in your computer. I'm looking for a third guy, too, so pictures of their known associates would help." He also handed him several phone numbers. "I would like a listing of all calls to and from these numbers for the past five years." The numbers were for all the phones at the Tyler mansion.

"Five years?" Skizzy moaned.

"Yes, but you can narrow it down to only those that are repeated with unusual frequency." Dagger repositioned the thick watch on his wrist and checked the time.

"I suppose you want this yesterday?"

Dagger's dark eyes smiled. "Of course."

16

"I can't believe this looks so real." Sara held up her birth certificate. She and Dagger stood on opposite sides of their oval-shaped, granite and chrome kitchen counter. Halogen lights hung from a wide beam suspended from the ceiling. The room looked like an industrial kitchen designed for a chef school. Clean lines, a lot of light, an abundance of cabinets, and plenty of room. A wall of windows overlooked the flower garden. The walls matched the granite countertops. Herbs and flowers hung upside down from a rod in the greenhouse just off the kitchen. A vase filled with yellow roses sat in the middle of a chrome and granite kitchen table.

Dagger downed half a glass of fresh-squeezed orange juice. In the background they could hear Einstein screeching, "GOOD MORNING. RISE AND SHINE. AWWWKK."

"You should put the birth certificate in the safe and always carry the driver's license, Social Security card, and gun registration," Dagger instructed. "What time are you meeting Sal Wormley for lunch?"

THE GOOD DIE TWICE

"One o'clock."

Dagger saw the name on the card that accompanied the roses. "You didn't say much about your evening with Nick. Are these roses an apology for something?"

Sara shrugged. "I should probably be the one sending him roses. He got a little pushy and I had to push back."

"Good girl. I knew you could take care of yourself."

Sara noticed the thick file folder and notes on the Rachel Tyler case. "Have you found out anything new?"

"Interesting rags-to-riches story. Rachel Lidowski was the only child of a steelworker and housewife. She changed her name to Rachel Liddie at the age of sixteen when she entered a local modeling contest. The rest is history. Her face graced the covers of *Seventeen, Cosmopolitan, McCall's,* all the fashion magazines, as well as the New York and Paris runways." Dagger leaned over, elbows on the counter, studying the flawless face. It was a face no one would forget. Unique, one of a kind. "All that attention and she was still able to keep her head on straight."

Sara picked up one of the photographs. "Why did she give it all up so young?"

"Very few models remain marketable after the age of twenty-four, twenty-five. There's always another fresh sixteen-year-old face to replace them." Dagger studied some of the notes, took a sip of his juice. "She's almost a little too good to be true. No scandalous headlines, no partying til all hours on the drug scene. She came from a pretty strict background. The all-American girl, mom and apple pie."

"You don't trust the report?"

Dagger shrugged. "There's always a flaw, even in a masterpiece." He smiled a crooked smile, his dark eyes twinkled. "After all, look at us."

The buzzer at the front gate rang. "COMPANY, COMPANY, AWK."

As they walked past the aviary to the surveillance monitor for the front gate, Einstein had his claws clamped to one of the bars on his door, his beak protruding between the bars. "AWWWKK, COMPANY."

"We know, Einstein. Calm down," Sara whispered. She stroked Einstein's head.

Dagger checked the monitor. "You won't believe this. It's Robert Tyler."

Robert refused cream and sugar, preferring his coffee black. They sat around the coffee table in the living room. Wearing a short-sleeved peach shirt with Cedar Point CC on the pocket, Robert looked ready for a game of golf. He sat stirring his coffee for two minutes making idle conversation, never drinking.

"That is really a beautiful bird you have there."

Einstein eyed their visitor through the bars. He flew over to the birdbath and pulled the chain, spraying himself with water.

"You've put a lot of work into his aviary," Robert added.

"I've had Einstein for five years. I would never give him up."

"Leyton tells me that's the major disagreement between you and Sheila." Robert finally took a sip of his coffee, glancing briefly at Sara through the steam wafting up from his cup. "Sheila says this is Sara's house."

"Yes," Dagger replied. "I rent office and living space for me and Einstein."

Sara walked over to the computer and busied herself going through the list of businesses Tyler International owned. As far as anyone knew, Sara was just a secretary, which was fine with her and Dagger. People tended to disregard her, speak more freely, open up. Robert kept glancing over at her. She looked down at the blue leggings and oversized floral shirt she had changed into after visiting Skizzy and wondered if she was underdressed.

Dagger's gaze shifted from Sara to Robert. Leaning forward, he watched as Robert's hand started to tremble, the same tremble he had displayed the day before when Dagger showed him the computer drawing of Rachel.

"I think I killed her," Robert whispered.

Dagger cocked his head, his ponytail flipping across his shoulder. "Come again?"

"Rachel." Robert blinked several times, stared down at his manicured nails. "I received a call around midnight last Wednesday, Thursday, whatever day. It was a female voice, sounded frantic. I didn't recognize it at first. And when I did, I said, 'Rachel? Is that you?' Then there was a dial tone." His gray eyes appeared to glaze over. Robert Tyler looked old, suddenly aged in twenty-four hours and feeling a need to unburden his soul.

"What did you do?" Dagger asked.

"I walked the floors wondering if I had dreamt the damn thing. Maybe it just sounded like her. Maybe I had a few too many nightcaps."

"Do you have Caller I.D. on your phone?"

"I didn't even think to use it. I didn't tell anyone about the call for fear they would think I was in need of a shrink."

Dagger leaned over and lifted up the lid on the heart-shaped box on the table. He handed Robert the earring.

"Does this look familiar?"

"My god, yes. It was Rachel's. I gave her money on her trip to Australia to buy herself something special."

Dagger placed the earring back into the box. "So you feel if you had taken the call seriously, you might have saved her life?"

Robert rested his elbows on his knees and steepled his hands under his chin. "Something like that. I put that phone call completely out of my mind because it was so out-landish. If Rachel were alive, why did she wait til now to contact me? I need you to find out where she has been all this time. Once we find that out, I think we'll find out who she was running from and who finished the job they started five years ago." He pulled a check from his pocket and handed it to Dagger. "This should be sufficient for a retain-er. Let me know if you need more."

17

Nick plied himself with coffee as he shook the cobwebs from his head.

Lily stood vigil, her face masked with motherly concern. "Anything else, Master Nicholas?"

"Did my brother come home for lunch?"

"I'm here." Eric turned to Lily. "That will be all." Once she left, Eric poured himself a cup of coffee and sat next to Nick at the dining room table. The picture of Rachel stared down at them.

"She was supposed to be dead," Nick whispered.

"I guess we need some answers, don't we?"

"God, I should have drunk more last night so I wouldn't have to deal with this." Nick pressed his hands to his head.

"Seems to me, little brother, that's how you have been drowning it out for the past five years."

Nick pulled his hands away and glared at Eric. "And why shouldn't I?" His hands started to shake. "I'm responsible. I killed her."

Eric clamped a hand on his brother's shoulder. "You should be celebrating, Nick. You didn't kill her. She was alive all this time."

"But how could that be?" Nick massaged his temples vigorously. "If only I could remember." He reached for his glass of lemonade but Eric intercepted.

Eric brought the glass up to his nose. "Dammit, Nick!" He carry the glass to the balcony and flung the contents over the railing outside. "How can you remember anything if you live your life in a haze?"

Nick leaned back and closed his eyes to the bright sunlight. When he opened them, Eric had set another glass of lemonade in front of him. "This one is straight up I take it?"

Eric placed one hand around the back of Nick's neck while the other gave him a brotherly pat on the face. "It's going to be okay, little brother."

"I don't understand, Eric. I saw her body. You found me down by the river soaked to the bone the next morning. I had to have carried her ..."

"Shhhh." Eric stole a quick glance toward the doorway. "Keep your voice down. Now think about it." He wrapped a protective arm around his younger brother, just like when they were kids. Eric had been the one to cover for Nick when he was ten and broke their mother's favorite antique vase. He had even covered for him when he wrecked Dad's Porsche. Nick hadn't been a reckless youth, just adventuresome. "Dagger is wrong. It couldn't have been Rachel. Maybe you should finally get some therapy, Nick. You need to come to terms with what happened. It was an accident."

Nick took a sip of orange juice, his mind drifting to that night five years ago. Wistfully, he murmured, "I wonder if there are people out there hoping I don't remember?"

"Remember what?" Edie asked, appearing in the doorway carrying a vase of fresh cut roses. She set the vase in
the middle of the table and continued to rearrange the stems.
The brim of her straw hat was turned up and her white sundress had a smudge of dirt on the pocket. "Let's not keep
secrets, boys," she smiled, pouring herself a cup of coffee
and taking a seat across from Eric.

Eric explained, "This whole thing that Dagger brought
up is playing havoc with Nick's head. I suggested he make
another stab at seeing a therapist. Maybe someone special-
izing in repressed memories."

"You two talk like I'm not even in the room." Nick
pushed his glass away, slouched back, a fist propped under
his chin.

Edie reached across the table, not quite able to reach
Nick's hand. "That's not true. We're family, Nicky."

"Maybe you can convince him," Eric said.

She tapped a well-lacquered nail against her coffee cup.
"Actually, I agree with Nick. If he's having problems with
over-imbibing now, won't it get worse once he starts to
remember?"

Eric scowled. "You're supposed to help, Edie."

"I am, Sweetheart." She placed her hand over Eric's.
"But really, do you believe Dagger? All he has is an earring
that could be owned by thousands of other women. Do you
really think that it was Rachel that was seen being murdered? Come on." She flashed her green eyes from Nick and
back to Eric. "I say give it up. Forget about it. Dagger's
investigation will go nowhere. Don't you think Rachel
would have tried to contact someone over the past five years

if she were still alive?"

"Just get her talking about her childhood. I want to know where she was born, where she grew up, what her parents did for a living." Sheila's voice was even more demanding and vicious over the phone. "Find out what schools she went to. It obviously wasn't a finishing school. She didn't even know which fork to use last night."

Worm pulled the phone away from his ear slightly. "You don't have to yell Sheila. I'm not deaf."

"Where are you meeting her for lunch?"

"The Patio." Worm looked around at the tables dotting the sidewalk, shaded by the canopy overhang. The sidewalk cafe offered outdoor seating for those wishing to mingle with nature.

"How tacky," Sheila muttered.

A turquoise motor scooter pulled into a parking space near the front entrance. Worm eyed the driver dressed in black leather with a black leather vest zipped over a short-sleeved, white, scooped shirt.

"Oh, my."

"Oh, my, what?" Sheila mimicked.

"Uh, sorry. I was distracted by a motorcycle with great, uh, pipes."

"Well, pay attention."

The driver pulled off a turquoise helmet, sending more than a yard of brown-and-gold-streaked hair tumbling down her back.

"Oh, my god. Save me."

"Now what!" Sheila demanded.

"You won't believe who just pulled up on a motorcycle dressed in leather."

Sheila's voice perked up. "Dagger's there?"

"No. It's Sara."

Sara carried her helmet under her arm. Dagger had bought her the motorcycle a month earlier. She was afraid of his big Harley and didn't feel comfortable driving his cars even though he felt she was ready to take them out on her own. Instead, he bought her a small Honda to drive to and from the stores during nice weather.

Worm was just ending his cellular call when she walked up. Several men seated at the outside tables stared at her approvingly.

Worm said, "I didn't know you owned a bike."

"Have you been waiting long?" Dagger had coached her on a strategy and how to keep her guard up around Worm. She took a wild guess that Worm had just received last-minute instructions from Sheila.

"No, just got here myself." Worm smiled broadly. "You look soooooo different in leather. I mean, without a dress on. I mean." His face turned the carrot color of his hair.

Sara smiled and walked into the restaurant. They were greeted by a woman in black pants and a tuxedo shirt. She led them along red brick flooring to the mezzanine level in back of the restaurant.

The walls were painted to look like a quaint eighteenth-century New England village. Wrought iron railings and an abundance of hanging plants gave the room an outdoor ambiance. Sara had seen the restaurant before, had had a cup of tea last summer in the outside patio. But she had not been inside. She had tried to coax her grandmother to join her on trips into town. But Ada Kills Bull had rarely left the reservation land except to sell her fresh vegetables and canned goods at the roadside vegetable stand Sara had built at the entrance to the reservation. Cars would line up for two blocks on both sides of the street just to buy the home-grown vegetables, canned goods, and herbs.

Sara marveled at the light posts strategically placed throughout the restaurant and the large chalkboard where the daily specials were written. Her eyes were as wide as a child's on Christmas morning. She had eaten out with Dagger before, but each new restaurant found her in awe of the decor and furnishings.

"You've never been here before, I take it?" Worm patted his bristle-stiff hair in an attempt to tame it. In his youth he had been called 'matchstick' because his bright orange hair always grew straight up. That, and his bony physique, made him look like a lit match. He was almost relieved, once in high school, that his friends started calling him Worm instead.

"No." Sara studied his face. Though freckly, it was smooth, like a baby's skin, which made him look younger than his twenty-three years. He was eager, with an inquisitive face and a sweet smile. Just knowing he had to work with Sheila filled Sara with pity for the young reporter. She wondered if Leyton Monroe had a strict dress code. Worm seemed overdressed even for Sheila Monroe's gofer.

They no sooner ordered than Worm began his laundry list of questions. "So, Sara, where were you born? I've always been interested in life on a reservation."

"And why is that?" Sara slowly stirred her iced tea.

"I don't know for sure. Maybe it's a throwback from when I played cowboys and Indians. I always felt bad for the Indians." He blushed when Sara didn't respond. "That was a lame answer. I guess you hear that a lot."

A group of waiters and waitresses started clapping and converged on a table where they presented a woman with a cake. They led the group at the table in a rendition of *Happy Birthday*. Sara was surprised when everyone in the room started to sing.

"Does this happen often?" Sara asked.

"A lot of restaurants do it now. It's really kind of embarrassing."

Over lunch, Sara sprinkled the conversation with vague answers to Worm's questions. Yes, she grew up on a reservation somewhere near the Canadian border but after her parents died, Grandmother moved her to South Dakota, then Wisconsin. They eventually settled in on the tiny reservation land in Cedar Point her grandfather had owned. She told him she was home-schooled. She soon turned the conversation to Worm, as Dagger had suggested.

"Did Sheila tell you about Rachel Tyler?"

"About her being alive? Yeah. That was some bombshell Dagger dropped on Mr. Tyler. Did he believe Dagger?"

"No." Sara swirled pasta around her fork. The salad was crisp with a tangy Italian dressing. She especially liked the black olives, something she had never eaten before until

Dagger started introducing her to different foods. "What was really interesting," Sara continued, "was that Sheila didn't believe him."

"Why is that interesting?" Worm pushed his empty plate away and grabbed the dessert menu.

"I had always heard she was such a great reporter. I would have thought the entire concept of Rachel Tyler being alive would have sparked her nose for news."

Worm laughed, placing the menu down and settling back in his chair. "Sheila doesn't like news stories where she has to do a lot of legwork. She likes grunts like me to do the work and she gets the by-line."

Sara set her plate to one side and watched a group of high school-aged youths filter into the restaurant. She found herself wondering what it would be like to feel part of a group, to be able to shop with close female friends and share laughs like this group was doing. These were things normal friends did. But she had to remind herself, she wasn't normal. When her grandmother was alive, she had been the one to shore up Sara's confidence, to remind Sara that she was unique. And no matter what she may have missed out on in life, she experienced more than anyone could ever dream of. Now she had to find that strength within.

"Sara?" Worm touched her arm.

Pulling her attention back to Rachel, Sara said, "I'm sorry. I was just thinking that I can give you some of the details and you can follow up on them, write the story, and take the credit."

"Fat chance." Worm leaned his elbows on the table, his eyes darting around the restaurant. He leaned closer to Sara and whispered, "Leyton Monroe will always make sure his daughter gets the credit for everything. It's a nowhere job. But it's the biggest newspaper in the city, owned by one of the richest men in town who owns six additional newspapers across the country."

"Is that so important?"

"Is it important?" He laughed, settling back in his chair again and digesting the significance of what Sara had said. "Actually, no. I was always taught in school the most important thing is the facts."

Sara placed a hand on his arm and peered into his eyes. "Don't tell Sheila you are working on the story. Write it up and present it to Leyton Monroe's biggest competitor as an example of your investigative techniques."

"I don't know." Worm stared at Sara's hand, then placed his on top of hers. "As long as I'm employed by Leyton, anything I work on belongs to *The Daily Herald*."

"Only if he or Sheila commissioned you to work on it. At least that's what Dagger told me." She slowly slipped her hand out from under his. "If what we find out confirms that Rachel Tyler was alive up until last Thursday, and if we find her killer or killers, this could be a breaking story for you, Worm."

Worm looked at her in a way that made Sara feel uneasy, not leering, not the way Nick had looked at her, but just different.

"Would you like to go out Saturday night?" Beads of perspiration worked his glasses down the bridge of his nose. He pushed them back up.

Sara looked away, clasped her hands in her lap.

"It's Dagger, isn't it? You're in love with him."

"Dagger understands me and that's not an easy thing to do."

"It's okay. He's good-looking, brilliant, mysterious. All the things women are attracted to. I'm just a nerd."

Sara smiled and returned her hand to his freckled arm. "Nerd is just another name for an intelligent, focused, serious professional."

Worm considered what she said, nodded to himself as though agreeing with some of her assessments. Then he smiled broadly. This time when he touched her, it was a brotherly pat.

"You're right. I'll do it."

18

Padre walked up to the front door of the townhouse where deliverymen were carrying in washers and dryers. Inside the unit Dagger claimed was the crime scene, he saw two men in bib overalls installing the vent for the dryer. No one paid any attention to him. He was dressed like any vacationer with his floral shirt hanging out over his madras-print shorts and deck shoes sans socks.

As Dagger had suggested, Padre took several vacation days so he could work on the case. If anyone at the precinct knew he was working on the Rachel Tyler case, word would get to the press quicker than you could say murder.

He had covered the beach area, and Maria, the desk clerk, had been right—none of these townhouses was occupied. Matter of fact, the water hadn't even been turned on until this weekend.

All the wooded property belonged to the Dunes Resort, so there were no nearby residential houses or streets running alongside which might produce a witness from early Thursday morning.

Dried twigs crunched under his shoes as he walked

west, away from the townhouses. He stopped and looked out on the lake where sailboats dotted the horizon. It was a beautiful view. No wonder the rental charges were anticipated at five hundred dollars a night.

"Sure thing, Padre," the police sergeant said to himself. "You can afford a two-week vacation here. Bring the wife and kiddies." He turned his gaze to the side view of the buildings.

They could have carried the body out the front door to a waiting car, tossed the body in the trunk. But then, what about the rug? If it were stained the way Dagger described, they would have had to get rid of it, probably use a large truck.

If they opted to carry her out the patio door and down to a waiting boat, they would still have needed to get rid of the bloodstained rug. Unless the body was still wrapped in the rug.

Padre turned and followed a path along a bluff, walking slowly and looking for a fresh gravesite. They may not have had time to dig a grave after they killed her but they could have dug it beforehand. He wiped a forearm across his damp forehead and was thankful he wasn't wearing his heavy blue jeans.

The underbrush was thick with wildflowers and shrubs. Nothing looked trampled on, disturbed, or moved. Bending down, he pulled on a number of plants to make sure they were real. Over the years he had learned to expect just about anything from creative felons.

Up ahead he could hear laughter, children's voices. As he neared the end of the path, he saw an inlet filled with paddleboats and large inner tubes. A slide emptied out into the pond.

Padre rubbed his stomach. The aroma of grilled hot dogs and hamburgers filled the air. It was time to take a break. Besides, he might find a witness. It was worth a try.

"Are you sure you weighted down the body before you dumped it in the lake?" Luke asked. He waited until after the waitress delivered their sandwiches before speaking. "You fucked up when you killed the woman. Then we left that earring behind. You two make this whole operation look like amateur night. Now I had to go and promise that we'd get the earring back."

Mince shoved a wad of French fries into his mouth. He chewed and smacked his lips while he spoke, causing the craters on his face to appear inhabited, the critters frantically looking for a way out. "You know this Detective Dagger who has the earring?" Pieces of French fries dropped from his mouth and onto his plate. He replaced it with a corner of his roast beef sandwich and took a slurp of his Pepsi.

They were huddled in a booth in the far corner of the restaurant. Joey placed the newspaper on the seat and cocked his head to eyeball the petite waitress' rear as she walked away. He said, "He's just like any other two-bit private dick. They don't know what else to do and nobody will hire them so they hang out a shingle." Joey's eyes followed the waitress around the room. She had firm breasts and a small waist. He licked his bottom lip and mentally peeled off her clothes.

"Hey." Luke snapped his fingers in front of Joey's eyes. "Pay attention. This is pay dirt. You might be able to redeem yourselves." He leaned his elbows on the table, his massive biceps struggling under his short-sleeved Henley. The waitress came back with the check and smiled at him. To most women, Luke resembled a beefy Paul McCartney because of his, what women call, bedroom eyes. But he didn't return the smile and waited until she left before speaking again. "We need to get the earring back. This will eliminate any proof of who the victim was." His cellular phone rang and he scooted out of the booth.

Once Luke left the table, Joey asked, "We're not going to tell him?"

"No. It's our only edge. Just look?" Mince gazed out the window toward the entrance where Luke was talking on his cellular. "If we're in this together, why does he shut us out when he talks to Tyler?"

"You're right. How do we know they aren't cooking up a way to cut us out all together?"

Their glares were dangerous, conspiratorial, each untrusting since they had been double-crossed more than once in their lives. This time, they had their best ace in the hole—they still had the body.

"Is he going to work with us?" Dagger spread the blueprints out on the coffee table. His black denim shirt had the sleeves ripped off, the sides split open to just above his waist. These were his easy-to-maneuver-in work clothes.

"Yes," Sara said. "Worm left the restaurant with very little information about me and all kinds of leads and questions about the case."

"YOU'RE LATE, YOU'RE LATE, AWK." Einstein flew over to Dagger's desk.

Sara stroked the macaw's back. "Miss me?" Einstein bobbed his head up and down. "I brought you something." She handed him a thin branch from an apricot tree. Einstein wrapped one foot around the branch and brought it up to his beak.

"COMPANY, COMPANY. AWK."

Einstein held onto the branch with his toes as he eyed Simon curiously. "MR. POSTMAN. AWK."

"Hey, there, Einstein." Simon reached out to touch the macaw and was met with a gentle nip from his beak. "Whoa, take it easy," Simon laughed. "Jittery guy."

"You know better than that, Simon. Einstein is pickier than a prom queen at a homecoming dance." Dagger leaned over and whispered to Einstein, "Say you're sorry."

Einstein held his foot up and waved the stick like a peace flag. They all laughed.

Dagger shooed Einstein to his room. "What have you found out, Simon?"

"You're gonna love this."

Dagger explained to Sara, "I asked Simon to put out a few feelers about Rachel and Robert Tyler. Simon knows more people in town than anyone else."

"Yeah, and I charge triple-time on Sundays." He leaned his hefty body against the desk. "Well, at first I heard all about the pretty model swept off her feet by a millionaire widower. He flooded her hotel rooms with yellow roses whenever she was on a shoot. They were featured in every tabloid paper you can think of. She had dated the Prince of Belgium or something, went to the Oscars with some heart-throb actor. But when it all came down to it, Robert Tyler was the one who captured her heart. It was a picture perfect couple."

Dagger sat on the arm of the leather sofa, arms crossed. "Why do I hear a BUT coming?"

Sara added, "I have to say it sounds too good to be true."

A rolling thunder of laughter started deep in Simon's chest. "Oh, I guess you can say that. The down and dirty word from the streets is—Rachel and Eric Tyler were knockin' boots two days before her wedding day."

19

"Eric Tyler?" Dagger laughed.

Sara's dark eyebrows scrunched over in thought. Puzzled, she turned to Dagger and said, "Knocking boots?"

The two men chuckled. Dagger explained to Sara Simon's delicate terminology for sex.

Sara blushed. "Two days before her wedding? What happened to the sweet, flawless model? I thought she loved Robert?"

"That's the flaw I was telling you about." Dagger asked Simon, "What's the word on the street? Did she marry the old man for his money?"

"She was always seen wearing designer clothes and jewelry and driving expensive sports cars before her marriage," Simon replied. "So it's hard to confirm if she was after his money. Most agree she liked to live in the manner to which she had been accustomed."

* * *

Worm rubbed his eyes. He had been searching the Internet for any information on Rachel Tyler. There were still fan clubs out there holding out hope that Rachel was still alive. Several close-up shots of Rachel filled the screen. She had the longest lashes Worm had ever seen, and the mole below her right eye seemed to be her trademark. He could picture her being a high school prom queen, maybe the princess of a European monarchy, probably the secret love of every serviceman whose locker was plastered with pin-ups. Worm printed out the pictures.

No matter how beautiful he thought Sara was, no matter how unique her exotic features, Rachel was even more beautiful. She was tall and willowy, with long, corn-silk hair. Her eyes were the color of jewels, and her lips heart-shaped, pouty. Despite all of her country girl charm and prom queen sweetness, she had a certain look in her eye and a slight parting of her lips in the perfume ads that screamed out sultry, sexy. And her eyes smoldered with every dirty little thought reserved only for a girl from the wrong side of the tracks. Yet she wasn't. She could be all things to all men. And she had touched Worm where no woman had ever touched him before. He had to find out everything he could about her.

He let the phone ring, regarding it as a pain-in-the-ass interruption. But soon relented and was immediately sorry he picked it up.

"Sheila, you told me to find out everything I could on Sara."

Worm's modest apartment was just off Taft Avenue, above a flower shop owned by his uncle. Furnishings were a mixture of hand-me-downs from his mother and aunts. Friends have joked that his décor was early flea market. Worm moved the phone to his other ear and separated his notes on Rachel.

"So? What did you find out?" Sheila demanded.

"I'm still working on it. Since Sara was home-schooled, there are no high school records. Her parents died when she was six. Just let me work on this at my own pace. It isn't easy trying to trace someone who uses an alias."

"Alias? Maybe she's a fugitive."

Worm could hear Sheila sucking on a cigarette, blowing the smoke out in a huff.

"Not a fugitive, Sheila. But Native Americans have a given name. You know, like Little Foot or Big Bear. I did find out her grandmother's name so I'll have a place to start."

"When are you going to see her again?"

"Tomorrow."

"Are you coming back to the office?"

Worm pulled his glasses off and rubbed his eyes. He signed off AOL and accessed his word processing program. "Have too many leads to follow, Sheila. I'm sure Linda can get your coffee. Gotta go." Worm hung up and smiled. He opened a new document. At the top of the page he typed:

RACHEL TYLER
The Death of America's Sweetheart

20

Dagger drove up the long driveway to the house, the wind riffling through his long hair, the beam from the motorcycle's headlamp bathing the tree-lined road in a spray of light. Sara hadn't answered the intercom from the front gate so she was either in the shower or not at home. He didn't like the fact that the gate had been left open.

He drove into the garage, noticing briefly how bright Einstein's aviary was. The timer on the fluorescent bulbs should have decreased the light in the room. Right now, the lights should be completely off except for a nightlight. It was close to midnight and way past Einstein's bedtime.

Maybe Einstein was sick and Sara was with him, that's why she couldn't answer the intercom. But if that were true, why was his skin tingling? Why did it feel as if the hairs on his arms were standing on end?

The garage door closed as he made his way up the side-walk. From the outside, everything looked in order. The electric blinds on the windows were closed. Everything was quiet. But something didn't feel right. Slowly, he pulled his gun from his ankle holster and opened the kitchen door.

Lingering odors from the shrimp and steak Dagger had grilled earlier hung in the air. A coffeecake was sitting on a rack on the counter. Dagger touched the cake. It was cool. He listened for music, the running of shower water. Nothing. What bothered him most was that he didn't hear Einstein.

He kicked into mercenary mode. Clicking off the safety on his Phoenix Raven .25 semi-automatic pistol, Dagger pressed his back to the wall and slowly made his way to the living room. A man sat at his desk going through the drawers.

"Hold it right there." Dagger leveled his sight on the man. "Hands up and back away from the desk."

The pudgy-faced man at the desk regarded him briefly, then went back to his work.

"Are you deaf?" Dagger yelled.

From behind him, a voice said, "You first."

Dagger felt a searing pain across the back of his head. Then everything went dark.

The gray hawk circled the Tyler mansion one last time, passing the East Wing where Edie was arguing with the nanny on why Eric Jr. shouldn't be taken out of his bed when he cries at night. Robert Tyler was reading at his desk, steam drifting up from a cup next to the phone.

The hawk landed on the railing outside Nick Tyler's room. The air was cool, a welcome change from the humid temperature during the day. From a side window which was cranked open, residuals of a strong floral odor could be detected by the hawk's keen scent. It bowed its head, one eye scanning the dark recesses of the room looking for movement. Nick wasn't home. There were no signs of the three men who had met with someone in this house a couple days ago.

Satisfied that everything was secure, the hawk opened its wings and glided off the balcony. Its wing beats were long and powerful, and in a matter of a few minutes, the reservation was within view. Flying over the skylights, the hawk noticed the lights on in the aviary, saw several figures in the living room and heard voices, loud and threatening. It sensed danger, smelled blood, heard sounds of distress.

Landing outside the opened second floor balcony door, the hawk changed shape and Sara stepped nude from the balcony and into her bedroom. She dressed quickly, opened her dresser drawer, and felt for her Sig P-245 compact pistol. The voices grew louder and she heard books clattering to the floor. Stealing a glance outside her bedroom door, past the catwalk and down into the living room, she saw Dagger. His hands were tied and the rope looped around the catwalk railing. He was suspended like some calf prepared for slaughter. Blood was trickling down the front of his tee shirt.

Sara recognized the men. The balding man with the cratered face and the thin, beady-eyed lech were the ones who had killed Rachel. The third man, the one the size of a football player, had been at the Tyler mansion the day of Nick's party. The brute now loomed over Dagger.

"I'm going to ask you one more time, where is the earring?"

"Go to hell."

The football player jammed his fist into Dagger's stomach producing a painful groan.

Sara wanted to flee, to shift back into the hawk where she could escape danger. But the cold, solid feel of the gun in her hand gave her a sense of security. And Dagger was in danger.

Sara saw Einstein fly over to a perch by the birdbath. "WHERE'S THE EARRING. AWK."

"Einstein," Dagger yelled. "Shut up!"

The football player shifted his attention to the macaw. "What's your name, bird?"

"AWWWKK, EINSTEIN'S THE NAME, BRAINS IS MY GAME. AWK." Einstein paced nervously, tap dancing on his perch, his head weaving and bobbing.

The man laughed. "Is that so? Well, why don't you tell us where the earring is?"

"IN THE BOX. AWK."

"Einstein, I told you to shut up!" Dagger moaned.

The large mass of muscles glanced quickly around the room and immediately spotted the box on the table. He lifted the lid, then smiled. "Well, what do you know? That parrot is an Einstein."

"You know," the balding man said, "that damn bird's worth at least five thousand dollars. It's a scarlet macaw. Might even be an endangered species." He made a move toward Einstein.

Sara stepped onto the stairway. "I wouldn't touch him if I were you." She pointed the gun at the big man closest to Dagger, the one who seemed to be in charge.

The big man barked, "I thought you checked the upstairs rooms."

"I did."

"Obviously not good enough."

Sara placed both hands on the gun. "I just learned how to use this so please forgive me if I miss an arm or a leg and accidentally hit your head, heart, or other vital parts of the anatomy." Smiling sweetly, she slowly moved the gun to the man holding the earring.

The football player chuckled. "Well, well. Aren't you a fine looking piece of ass." Turning to the thin man he said, "Go get that bitch."

Sara's steady arm fanned the gun over to a new target—the rope tied around Dagger's hands. To Sara's enhanced eyesight, the target was no farther than a foot from her. She fired once, cutting the rope and sending Dagger sprawling to the floor. She called out his name as she threw him her gun.

The men watched in amazement as Sara swung herself over the railing and twenty feet down to the living room floor with the agility of the wolf.

"Hey!" The bald man let out a cry as a bullet tore through his shoulder and embedded in the door to Dagger's bedroom. That left it two against two.

The thinner man leered as he circled Sara, looking for the right opportunity to get in a good hit. Sara had a feeling he had more than murder and mayhem on his mind. There was a glint in his eyes, a scent of sweat, musk, a man in heat. And all it did was motivate her, anger her at how they had torn her house apart, how they had hurt Dagger.

He made a dive for her and came up with a handful of thick hair. Sara drove a knee into his groin, turned and high kicked her foot, planting it on the side of his head and sending him sprawling over the sofa and onto the coffee table.

When the intruders made a run for it, Sara started to take off after them. But Dagger grabbed his stomach and doubled over.

"Dagger, are you okay?" She turned quickly and helped him to the love seat.

"I'm fine. You have to follow them, Sara. Find out where they are staying."

"But you should see a doctor."

"Go now," Dagger ordered, wiping his mouth with the back of his hand.

"AWK, GETTING AWAY, GETTING AWAY." Einstein squawked.

With rapid wing beats, the gray hawk kept pace with the car carrying the three men. This part of town was void of streetlights but it wasn't too dark for the hawk to see.

They are heading in the direction of downtown, Sara reported.

Startled, Dagger practically fell off the couch. *Jezzus, Sara, can you give me a little warning? It sounded as if you were right behind me.*

I'm sorry. It's not like I can ring a doorbell.

Neon lights bathed the street below in psychedelic colors. The car had entered Interstate 65 and was headed north. The hawk focused on the car and tried not to be distracted by the lit billboards.

They are making a phone call. I can hear the dialing.

"Yeah, I'm here," she heard a deep voice say.

It sounds like the man who was beating on you. He isn't saying whom he's talking to. He's only reporting that he has the earring.

When are they going to hand it over?

All he mentioned was meeting someone tomorrow.

Traffic came to a halt as blinking construction road signs reduced the expressway to one lane.

Uh, oh.

What is it, Sara?

Construction. The car is at a standstill. There's a long line of trucks.

Come on home, Sara.

Don't you want me to try to get the earring back?

No. They don't have the real one. I planted a fake.

Sara dabbed antiseptic onto the wound in the back of Dagger's head and on his face. "Follow my finger." She moved her index finger left to right and watched his eyes. His temples pulsed, jaws clenched. "I think you have a concussion."

"No. I've had a concussion before. Believe me, this is just a bump on the head."

"How did they get through the locked gate?"

"Probably jammed the code. I'll have to reprogram it. They must have parked their car behind the garage because I didn't see it when I drove up." He winced as he stretched his arm. "Listen, the night of Tyler's party, did you notice how many of the Tyler men were smoking cigars?"

Sara thought for a moment. "All three of them, I think. I didn't go in the smoking room but I'm sure I saw them go in. What are you getting at?"

"You have to look at everyone as a suspect."

"You don't think Nick had anything to do with Rachel, do you? It was his brother who had the affair with her."

"Just keep your eyes and ears open when you are in the Tyler house." Dagger looked at the empty bookshelves and the books cluttering the floor. "I'll clean this up tomorrow." He turned his attention to the landing outside of Sara's bedroom and the steep jump. "How the hell did you jump down from there without breaking a leg?"

"I guess the same way I was able to shoot the rope from your hands."

"Shit, I thought you were going to shoot my hand off." Dagger tried to touch his sore chin but Sara slapped his hand away.

"I saw the rope as if it were only a foot from me, magnified, the eyesight of the hawk."

"And I suppose the jump over the railing was more than human skill." Dagger smiled. "There's no end to your talents."

Einstein flew into the aviary and returned a few seconds later, landing on the couch between Sara and Dagger. The macaw dropped a cheese curl in Dagger's lap.

"Oh, he's so sweet." Sara cuddled the bird. "Are you mad at Einstein for spouting off?"

"You are supposed to be asleep." Dagger took a bite of

the cheese curl and fed the rest to Einstein. "I knew he'd repeat everything which is why I put the fake earring in the box."

Sara leaned back against the cushion and thought about Robert Tyler. "He must be in on it. How else would those guys know about the earring?"

Dagger shrugged out of his bloodstained shirt and tossed it on the floor. He ran his fingers through his head and winced. Now he understood what it meant when people say their hair hurts. He could feel every hair in his head. Turning he propped a pillow under his head and stretched out on the couch.

"Actually, we just proved that Robert Tyler has nothing to do with the killers. Someone at the party heard that we had an earring. When Tyler was here this morning, he saw where we kept the earring. But those goons didn't go right for the box. Instead, they started to tear the shit out of this place looking for it."

Sara saw a videotape sitting on the coffee table. "What is that?"

"That's from our surveillance camera at the gate. Skizzy should be able to get some pretty good pictures of those three guys off this tape, better likeness than those composites I gave him."

21

The next morning found Dagger nursing his headache with several aspirin and an ice compress. "No one saw anything?" Dagger stirred his coffee with deliberation as he spoke with Padre on the phone.

"This is a pretty spiffy resort. I'm sure glad my employer is paying for my room."

Dagger laughed. "Just keep the room service down to a minimum."

"Seriously, Dagger. Did you give any thought to the possibility that they placed Rachel's body on a boat and wrapped an anchor around her feet?"

"My witness didn't see any boats."

"But it was dark out. Maybe the running lights on the boat were turned off."

"No. On a clear night with that moonlight shining, it would be hard for anyone to miss a boat."

Dagger opened the hand towel and emptied the unmelted ice into the sink. He winced and pressed a hand to his ribs.

"Are you going to get those ribs taped up?" Padre asked.

"They're just bruised. I'll be fine."

"I'm going to make another walk around, talk to a few people, maybe check to see where the hotel stores excess furniture. Maybe with luck I'll turn up a bloodstained white rug."

Robert Tyler followed Dagger into the kitchen and placed a box on the table. "I thought this might help. There were quite a few things of Rachel's I just couldn't bring myself to discard. There are some photo albums and even her high school yearbook." He eyed Dagger's bruised and battered face. "Are you okay?"

Dagger told him about the three men who had paid him a visit last night. Then he showed him the composite pictures. "The night of Nick's birthday party, do you recall any of these men being on the premises?"

Robert shook his head slowly, his frown creating tiny lines around his mouth. "These men had something to do with Rachel's murder? And you think they were in my house?"

"Don't jump to any conclusions. We think they are involved somehow and might be looking for something in your house. I didn't say they know any of your relatives and I definitely don't want you going home and accusing anyone. I just want you to be aware of any suspicious characters."

Robert studied the pictures again, then set them on the counter.

"What about your pre-nuptial agreement?"

Robert pulled papers from his inside suit pocket. "Basically, Rachel would receive a lump sum of twenty million dollars if we divorced before our third anniversary. Then it increases to one hundred million if we divorced after our tenth anniversary."

"It increased the longer you stayed married?"

"Yes."

"So it would have been to Rachel's advantage to stick around."

"Except Rachel was never after money," Robert said emphatically. He walked over to the screened door. Sara was outside watching Einstein fly around the yard, the bright feathers painting the sky. "You never clipped his wings?"

Dagger joined him at the door. "I couldn't do that to him. I used to take him to the forest preserve to get some fresh air. But this place is more wide open. We still have to keep an eye on him. Hunters sometimes trespass. I have found nets and animal traps out there." Dagger watched for a moment and then rushed past Tyler and out the door. He stood on the porch and let out a long, piercing whistle. Einstein had flown out of range, out of eyesight. Something he knew he shouldn't do. The moment the shrill whistle cut through the air, Einstein came charging out of the trees and landed obediently next to Sara.

"Sara," Dagger called out. "Don't let him get too far." Dagger walked back inside. "Sara's training him to answer to the whistle she has hanging around her neck. Then she can take him out when I'm not home."

"That bird is almost like having a kid." The circles

under Robert's eyes made him look haggard. His chin seemed to sag from the weight of his frown and his shoulders slumped like those of a man beaten and down for the count. He helped himself to coffee and sat down.

"You don't know the half of it," Dagger huffed. Gingerly, he sat his battered body down and pressed a hand to his ribs.

After a minute of silence, Robert clasped his hands in front of him and asked, "Where has Rachel been for five years?"

Dagger opened a notebook and started writing. "What do you remember about the last day you saw Rachel? According to the original police report, she had lunch with you at the yacht club, then went shopping alone. You were to meet her at the boat for a night cruise but you had a meeting."

"Right. I told all that to the police. Rachel was a little upset with me so she went by herself."

Carefully, Dagger touched his face. Propping one hand under his chin, he felt the coarse stubble and wondered how painful it would be to shave today. The noise alone would probably sound like scraping a knife on a blackboard. He touched his swollen cheek, ran his tongue over his teeth to check if any of them loosened during the night.

"I don't mean to have you rehash everything you said previously, Mr. Tyler. I'm looking for what wasn't said. How was Rachel mentally that day? Preoccupied? Agitated? Was her anger toward you unlike her? Maybe something had happened and she was taking it out on you."

"I guess you could say she was agitated but I assumed it

was at me, but now that I think about it, she was agitated before I even told her my meeting would take longer than expected. I offered to take her sailing the following night but that didn't appease her. I had to cancel dinners and even vacations before and she'd always taken it in stride."

Dagger checked the police report and jotted down notes. "Your daughter-in-law and Eric returned that day from a trip. Did you see them?"

"No. Eric called me at the office to tell me they had returned from our Ty-Island Resort in the Cayman Islands. Eric and Edie had purchased some oceanfront property to build a home. They were meeting with the builder and also checking with our resort manager at Ty-Island. Eric usually makes the trips to our resorts to check things out. I'm getting too old for all that traveling."

"And they both said they hadn't seen Rachel."

"Right."

Dagger placed his pen down and pressed his fingertips to his eyelids. It was a relief not to have the sunlight glaring in his face. His head was pounding and he knew the pain reflected in his eyes probably made him look as haggard as Robert.

The grieving widower was looking for answers. Dagger knew from past clients that loved ones go into a grieving limbo, living life just going through the motions. And that was what Robert was doing now—just going through the motions.

22

"I have to make an appointment to see my own father?" Sheila threw the pieces of the check on her father's desk. "Daddy! How could you? You paid Dagger to string me along? I thought you loved me?" Her green eyes flashed and angry tears welled. She sank into the chair in front of Leyton's desk.

Leyton pieced the check together and pursed his lips. "He told you."

"Of course. And he loved every minute of it."

"Naturally. A gentleman would never have hurt you that way." Leyton pulled a cigar from his humidor, leaned back, and lit the cigar in celebration.

"I thought my own father would never treat me like some bargaining tool. Dagger was my whole life. And you paid him to drag his feet, to never commit."

Leyton sat forward, surprise masking his face. "That's what that ingrate told you? That's bullshit. I paid that idiot to NOT stand you up. I had to pay him to MARRY YOU."

* * *

Sheila stood in the living room of Sara's house and gazed up at the steel catwalk, the high ceilings and skylights. "What a grotesque building," she whispered. Curious, she walked over to the doorway into the aviary.

"AWWWKK. WICKED WITCH." Einstein let out a long, loud scream that sounded as if he were being attacked. He fluffed his feathers as though his entire body were shaking in fright.

"Shut up, you ball of fur. I'm certainly not thrilled to see you, either."

"That's feathers." Sara stepped around Sheila and peeked in on Einstein.

"What?"

"Ball of feathers, not fur. Dagger should be home any minute." Sara gathered her hair, lifting it off her back briefly. Its thickness felt as heavy as a rug.

"No problem." Sheila strolled around the living room surveying its contents, mentally examining the decor.

Sara walked over to Dagger's bedroom door and closed it before Sheila had a chance to extend her browsing. She wondered how Sheila managed to find pink shoes, blouse, suit, jewelry, all in the same color.

Sheila looked from the closed bedroom door to Sara and recognized the shirt Sara wore as being one of Dagger's. Sheila's gaze drifted up to the second floor. She peeled off her suit jacket and tossed it on the couch

"Would you like something to drink?"

"No. I'll wait. You go do your planting, baking, or opening mail, whatever it is you do." Sheila dismissed her with a wave of her hand. She made her way over to Dagger's desk and peered not too discreetly at the notes and papers.

Sara knew there wasn't anything important left on the desk. It was when Sheila placed one foot on the bottom stair leading up to Sara's bedroom that Sara lost her cool.

"If you don't mind, the rest of the house is off limits."

Sheila's well-shaped eyebrows arched in surprise, and then a self-satisfied smile played at the corners of her mouth. "Well, well. Seems the sugar-and-spice persona was an act after all."

Sara folded her arms and leaned against Dagger's desk. "Sorry if I get territorial." Sara could see Sheila's eyes light up, knew she thought Sara was referring to Dagger. "But this is MY house. I only buzzed you in at the gate because you are Dagger's ..." Sara chose her words carefully ... "friend. If you want to wait for him, you can do so on the couch. If not, I suggest you wait in your car."

Sheila's back straightened, causing her to imitate her father's patented stare down his nose at an insubordinate. "I believe this is also Dagger's place of business and he has an open door policy."

A voice bellowed from the kitchen. "My business is by appointment only. Clients rarely know where I live." Dagger stood in the doorway. "What are you doing here, Sheila?" He tossed his car keys in the basket on the oak-paneled bar.

"HELP ME, HELP ME, AWK," Einstein yelled when he heard Dagger's voice.

Sheila turned, her face flushed, but she recovered quickly. "Dagger, Darling." She rushed to him but he walked past her to the aviary and let out a soft whistle. Einstein flew over and clamped onto Dagger's arm. Einstein opened his beak and spread his wings in a threatening stance. Sheila kept her distance.

"I need to talk to you." She looked back at Sara and added, "Alone."

Sara took Einstein from Dagger. "We'll go outside."

Once they left, Dagger glared at her. "Don't ever come here without calling first and don't EVER unleash your condescending tone on Sara again."

"I have to call your beeper number to talk to you? I'm treated better than that by my maid. I have to have you followed just to find out where you live." She slammed her purse on his desk but then noticed his face. "Dagger, Sweetie, what happened?" She reached over to touch his bruised cheekbone.

Dagger pulled away and sat down at his desk. "What the hell is so important that you had to disrupt everything and everyone in this house?"

Sheila slid one hip onto the corner of his desk. "Nice try, Chase Dagger. You know damn well why I'm here. Daddy said that check was to pay you to marry me. And I want to know if that's true."

Dagger leaned back in his chair and stared at her. He didn't know what he ever saw in Sheila. Yes, she was nice to look at, but so was a '57 Chevy.

"Sure, whatever he said." Dagger checked the phone messages on his desk.

"I don't believe you."

"I'm sure your father has never lied to you before."

Sheila was silent for awhile. Then, in a hurt voice she asked, "Have you?" She placed a hand on his arm. "Ever lied to me? Did you mean it when you told me you loved me?"

Dagger's head started to pound. He looked up and wondered what it was going to take to get through to her. "If you remember correctly, Sheila, I never told you that I loved you. YOU have said that I love you. YOU have made comments like how nice that WE love each other so much. YOU proposed to me. YOU set a wedding date without even consulting me."

She smiled seductively, batting her eyelashes. "But you never once protested, Sweetheart." Sheila looked at the huge aviary and up at the cathedral ceiling high above the catwalk. "That aviary is big enough that Einstein and I won't get in each other's way. We can be happy here, Dagger. Let me make an offer to Sara and I'll buy the house from her as my wedding gift to you."

"Oh, god." Dagger rocked back in his seat and leveled a look of disgust at her. "You are unbelievable. This is reservation land. You don't just BUY it. You think money is the answer to everything?"

"No." Sheila settled both cheeks on the desk, crossing one leg over the other, exposing her shapely legs. "Love and great sex is the answer to everything."

"You can get both anywhere, can even buy it if you pay the right price."

Sheila held up her hand, admiring her engagement ring. "Only a man that truly loves me would buy me an exquisite ring like this."

"My point exactly." Dagger stood up in an attempt to maneuver Sheila to the door. "I didn't spend a penny on it. A client who had a cash shortfall paid me with that ring."

Dagger chalked it up to his swollen cheek that he was unable to see Sheila's hand before it connected with his face.

"She must have had some right hook." Simon handed Dagger a brown envelope as he watched Sara dab an alcohol gauze onto Dagger's bleeding cut.

"Maybe you need stitches." Sara grimaced at the fresh blood oozing from Dagger's wound. Sheila had managed to reopen it when she slapped him.

"WICKED WITCH, WICKED WITCH, AWK." Einstein flapped his wings.

"Your fiancee did this?"

"Ex-fiancee. And let's not talk about her. Is this from Skizzy?" Dagger pulled out the pictures and printouts on the men believed to have killed Rachel and broke into Sara's house.

"Those are them, huh?" Simon peered over Dagger's shoulder at the pictures.

Dagger read from the computer printouts. "Luke Gabriel, aka John Gage, John Galloway. Suspected arms smuggler, kidnapping. Also suspected of passing counterfeit bills. Never served time. Was arrested once for driving without a valid license." Dagger held up the second picture and report. "Maury Genova, aka Manny Genteel, nickname Mince."

Simon chuckled. "I can understand the nickname. His face looks like he's been in a fire. It looks like head cheese."

"I think he was the trigger man. He has a list of misdemeanors as long as my arm. Been in trouble since the age of thirteen. Served three years in a correctional institution for petty theft, destruction of public property. Then nothing for several years. He changed his line of expertise to armed robbery." Dagger flung his picture on the desk in disgust. He picked up the last of the papers. "Joseph Callahan, aka Joe Keller. Another rotten youth sob story with a string of misdemeanors. He graduated to deviate sexual assault. Unfortunately, the women refused to press charges. He met Manny in the correctional institution. I'm sure they blame society." He lined up the pictures on his desk. "The question is, how did they get involved with Rachel?"

23

Padre finished his coffee and studied his notes. The verandah outside the lobby of the Dunes Resort was spacious and ornate displaying large urns of potted plants. A couple walked past dressed to the nines. Her brimmed hat matched her floral dress and his suit was a cross between a tuxedo and a Park Avenue power suit. They glanced at Padre long enough to run their gaze slowly down his pane-checked shirt, khaki pants, and deck shoes.

As they turned to leave, he looked down at his attire and shrugged. All day he had run into people dressed to the teeth, even if just for sunbathing. Many recoiled from him as though he were some derelict begging for money, until he showed them his business card. He had tried to remain as discreet as possible, but hotel security soon latched onto him. It was bad publicity for someone to be questioning their guests about an alleged murder on the grounds of the Dunes Resort, especially since he was out of his jurisdiction. So Padre accepted their offer of a free dinner and a hasty check-out. But he wasn't quite ready to go.

"You stay with Papa. I'll be right back." The young

mother kissed her son and walked back into the lobby. The boy, about four years old, pulled away from his father and walked over to the railing, captivated by the workmen in the courtyard who were cutting the evergreens into the shape of animals.

"What are they doing?"

Padre looked over to see the boy standing a foot from him, his tiny finger pointing toward the courtyard, his dark eyes round and wide in fascination.

"They just carved that evergreen into the shape of an elephant. Do you see its big trunk?"

The boy turned and shook his head. "An elephant?" he repeated.

"Are you on vacation?" Padre asked. The sergeant had two boys of his own but it had been years since they were this boy's age. When the youngster nodded again, he asked, "What did you like best about your vacation? The water? The boats? Or maybe you built a sand castle on the beach?"

The boy handed a small green truck to Padre. "The snowplow."

"Snowplow?" Padre examined the truck. It looked more like a piece of farm machinery. Even his boys when they were young liked trucks. "I don't think we have snowplows here yet. It doesn't snow until November."

"There." He pointed off in the distance.

Padre could barely see the yellow metal roof through the trees. He could only assume it was a maintenance shed. Thoughts clicked in his head. Maybe the killers didn't have to go far to hide the rug.

* * *

"Anybody here?" Dagger ducked under a sign hanging low over the doorway of Harbor Rentals, a Lake Michigan icon for the past eighty years. The owner had refused to sell his property to the neighboring Cedar Point Yacht Club. But over the years, the Yacht Club has come to rely on the many resources Harbor Rentals had to offer.

Wood flooring creaked under Dagger's feet. Through the large picture window he could see the sun setting, casting a streak of light across Lake Michigan.

A gray-haired man straightened up from his sanding bench and cast an eye in Dagger's direction. A gleaming pipe fit snugly in the side of his mouth, spouting puffs of smoke. He wore a navy blue sweater with patches on the elbows even though the July temperatures were still hovering around eighty-five degrees. The sparkle in his eyes and the sunburned face reminded Dagger of *The Old Man and the Sea.* The office was located on a converted houseboat and docked right at the entrance to Cedar Point Harbor. The odors of fish and fuel fought for dominance.

Sailboats, motor boats, and charter fishing vessels dodged the jet skis at the entrance to the marina. Boaters walked the piers carrying coolers, fishing gear, and clothing.

"Howdy," the old man said. "What can I get ya?"

Dagger handed him a business card. "I was hoping to speak to any of the crew on board Rachel's Dream about five years ago."

"That's a long time."

"I know. But you look like a man who keeps halfway

decent records." Dagger examined the old wheel the man was sanding. Its smooth lines and texture testified to the old man's patience and attention to detail. The sign above the showcase of antique boat wheels and fishing poles said *Salty's Antiques.* "Are you Salty?" The old man nodded, pulling a file folder from a cabinet behind the desk.

"I remember that day," Salty offered. "Beautiful woman. Never did find her body, though, did they?"

"No."

"Why the interest now?" Pleats of flesh rested on his eyelids as he peered at Dagger inquisitively.

"You know bureaucrats."

"Ahhh, and the insurance company wants to make sure she's not cooling her heels on some beach somewhere. But I would think that her life insurance would be a drop in the bucket for Tyler."

"It's a little more complicated than that."

"Here we go." Salty's leathery hands ran down the rental agreement to the crew names. "We have a lot of turnover in this business, I hope you realize." He puffed vigorously on his pipe in thought. "Grant Oakley quit about two years ago. I think he went off to one of those islands in the Caribbean to work on a cruise ship. But Pete Foster, he's still here." Salty took his pipe out of his mouth and pointed it toward the picture window. "That's him putting Calcutta to bed."

Dagger walked along a shaky pier and past several slips until he came to the forty-foot sailboat. "Can I come aboard?" he called out. "Salty said I could find you here."

"Who's asking?" Pete peered out from behind dark sunglasses tethered to his head by a neon green strap. His torso
was bronzed and muscular and his hair bleached blonde by
the sun.

"Chase Dagger." Dagger handed him his business card.
"I need to speak to you about the disappearance of Rachel
Tyler."

Pete checked his watch and popped a beer can. "Off
duty," he announced. "Do you want one?"

Dagger declined and sat down on one of the bench seats.
He tucked his sunglasses in his shirt pocket and leaned forward, elbows on his knees. He found his ribs and stomach
felt better in this position.

"I read the police report so I won't take up too much of
your time." Dagger waited until Pete finished tossing the
bagged garbage on the pier and took a seat across from him.
"According to the police report, neither you nor your fellow
crew member heard Rachel call for help."

"That's right." He took a long swig from his beer, his
gaze turning briefly to the cut on Dagger's cheek.

"Is it customary for you to not radio for help when you
run out of gas?"

Pete took another long swallow of beer. "Sure.
Especially when the person hiring you tells you not to."

"So you had no wind and no gas and you decided to
anchor for the night."

"Mrs. Tyler said her husband would be taking a small
boat out to meet us."

"So everyone fell asleep and when you woke up, Mrs. Tyler

was missing. What did you think?"

Pete shrugged, crumpled up his empty can and tossed it into a five-gallon bucket nearby. "Old man Tyler picked her up in the middle of the night. We didn't know anything was wrong until the Coast Guard showed up the next morning."

"That was around six o'clock?"

Pete nodded.

Dagger studied his hands, picking at a sliver of wood on his index finger. "Can I tell you my scenario?"

Pete stared at Dagger with his baby blues blinking slowly.

"I think the crew had a few too many beers and passed out. That's why you didn't hear the splash. That's why you didn't hear her call out for help." Dagger studied the man's Nordic features, a sure attraction for any woman with a heartbeat. "Or maybe," Dagger suggested, "you gave your buddy enough booze to pass out and you and Mrs. Tyler had a party of your own."

Pete flashed a quick grin, winky winky. "Now, that wouldn't be nice, would it?"

"It certainly would be difficult to admit to the police much less to Robert Tyler. And maybe you had a little bit of decency in not wanting to smear the reputation of a dead woman." But Dagger was certain it would take more than decency for Pete to keep a secret. "Or maybe the price was right."

"Never know."

Dagger pulled out his wallet and counted out a thousand dollars. "Let me know when I've hit the right price." When Pete didn't respond, Dagger kept counting.

Once Dagger's offer totaled five thousand dollars, Pete picked up the money and recounted it. "It wouldn't be the first time I was hired to take care of more than just the sails."

"Hired?" Dagger pushed a stray hair away from the open wound on his cheek.

"She gave me a thousand dollars. Those nails left marks on my back for a week." He grinned broadly again, and rubbed himself. "She was hot."

24

Padre grabbed a flashlight from his car and made his way on foot down a dirt path to the maintenance shed. He kept thinking of the story Dagger told him about the witness. Padre had a hard time swallowing that story. From Padre's perspective after surveying the townhouse yesterday, there was no way anyone could have seen the murder through the patio windows unless he were standing right on the deck or hanging from a mast in Lake Michigan. But, as in the past, Dagger would let him know only as much as he wanted him to know.

Padre followed the flashlight beam to the maintenance shed. Broken pottery, bricks, and logs cluttered the area. He shone the flashlight through a dingy windowpane and could barely make out the outline of two snowplows. The boy had been right. He had seen snowplows in the summer.

He fumbled his way to a barn-type door. A large, rusting padlock held the door shut. After knocking it a few times, the rusting padlock snapped open.

"Gee, someone left the door open," Padre laughed.

Gravel littered the floor. The smell of gasoline hung in

the air mingled with a musty odor. The warehouse was crammed with maintenance equipment strewn about without any sense of order.

He followed footprints which dotted the dust and grime in a path from the door to a side room. A large cabinet hung on the wall with a sign saying SNOW SHOVELS.

He opened the cabinet and found more than snow shovels. He found a rolled up carpet. Laying the flashlight on a shelf, Padre dragged the rug from its hiding place and dropped it on the floor. Starting at one end, he kicked at the rug and it started to unroll. Grabbing the flashlight, he shined it on the white rug, which was stained with what looked like blood. Bending down, he pulled at some of the stained fibers and held them in front of the beam.

"Damn." He flipped open his phone and called Dagger.

"I don't know why the hell we have to do all the drudge work while Luke sits back at the hotel making phone calls." Mince pulled onto the gravel road leading to the maintenance shed. He pressed a hand to his right shoulder and winced. "Goddamn flesh wounds hurt worse than if the damn bullet went through me. It should be Luke out here lifting up this heavy rug."

"He said we left the loose ends so we have to get rid of them," Joey reminded him. "And the rug is one big loose end."

"Any idea what we're supposed to do with it? We can't burn it."

"Bury it. I brought shovels and there are a lot of woods

south of here. We don't need to dig a trench too deep."

Mince jammed the brake pedal. "Hey, did you see that?"

"What?"

"I thought I saw a light on in the shed."

Mince turned the headlights off and killed the engine. Quietly, they exited the truck and made their way down the path.

"TELEPHONE, TELEPHONE, AWWWKK." Einstein poked his beak between the bars of the grated door.

"You are just dying to answer it, too, aren't you, Einstein?" Sara located the portable phone. It was Padre.

"Dagger went to the marina," Sara told Padre.

"I think I found the rug."

"You did?"

"Well, it's A rug, and it's blood-stained, so I'm assuming it's THE rug."

"Do you have Dagger's cellular number?"

"Wait a minute," Padre whispered. "I hear something."

"Padre?" Sara thought she heard a moan and then a thud. The phone was disconnected. "Padre?" Sara hung up the phone, her heart pounding. The Dunes Resort was an hour's drive away. She dialed information for the Michigan City Police Department while she ran up the stairs to her bedroom. Stripping out of her clothes, she explained to the dispatcher that a Cedar Point police officer might be in danger and gave them the name of the resort. She didn't have time to call Dagger. It would be easier and quicker to communicate with him telepathically.

Sara stepped nude onto the balcony and leaped into the air. The hawk's rapid wing beats helped it reach an altitude above the trees almost instantly.

Dagger?

Dagger almost lost control of his motorcycle. "Sonofabitch!" He careened around a corner and down a sidewalk near an outdoor café sending dinner patrons running for cover.

I'm sorry. I did it again?

I'll get used to it, eventually.

Padre's in trouble.

Where is he?

Sara explained Padre's phone call and how it sounded as if someone had surprised him.

We can't get there in time, Sara. I'll place another call to their police department. Make sure they realize the urgency. Where are you now?

I'm not sure. I'm following the shoreline so it shouldn't take too long. Once I get there, the wolf will have a better sense of smell.

Be careful, Sara. Remember what we talked about. After his call to the police, Dagger described to Sara his meeting with Pete Foster.

And this was never revealed in the police report?

No.

Dagger, have you tried calling Padre's cellular phone?

Yes. There's no answer.

After a few moments of silence, Sara said, *I can see the*

resort. I'm going in for a closer look. The hawk glided over
the resort, seeing the lights around the pool, courtyard, and
the streets outlining the property. It searched for police cars
and spotted them parked in front of the hotel. Then it looked
for the maintenance shed where Padre had said he'd found
the rug.

*I'm here, Dagger. I don't see an ambulance, only police
cars parked by the entrance.*

I'm about twenty minutes away.

Dagger prayed nothing serious happened to Padre. Mile
markers flew by and he passed several unmanned police
cars, parked for the sheer purpose of slowing traffic. The
helmet was hot but it was a necessity when driving at night.
Bugs were too numerous and some too large to leave one's
face unprotected.

It wasn't until his fingers started aching that he realized
he had a vice grip on the handlebar. Subconsciously he was
thinking the worst about Padre. He approached the exit for
the Dunes Resort. He was ten minutes away.

Gliding over the maintenance shed the hawk searched
for movement. Its acute eyesight made the area below look
bathed in daylight, every detail illuminated. It circled the
shed twice. Convinced it was unseen, it swooped down and
shifted into a gray wolf.

Immediately, its sense of smell detected danger. Lifting
its head, the wolf listened, trying to block out distant sounds

from the pool, the squirrels and cicadas, the four-legged creatures, and the horns from offshore boats.

Convinced that no two-legged creatures were close by, the wolf scurried up to the shed door and immediately picked up the scent. It followed the scent of blood down to the shoreline.

Dagger, where are you?

Dagger flinched and swore under his breath. *I should be there shortly, barring any unforeseen speeding tickets. Have you seen any police?*

Not yet. I haven't found Padre yet, either.

What looked like a pile of rags bobbed just off shore. The wolf kicked up sand as it rushed toward the water. It immediately saw that the pile of rags had arms and legs.

Oh my god. I found him, Dagger.

Is he alive?

The wolf ran into the water and grabbed Padre by the back of his shirt, dragging him on shore. Then it raced toward the hotel, through the gardens sending patrons running for cover. It stopped as it neared the entrance and let out a loud howl. Police officers standing near their cars looked over.

The wolf turned and ran, stopped and howled again. It repeated this several times until the officers decided to follow. It heard the officers ask each other if they were following a wolf or a dog. One officer pulled a gun but another told his partner to put his weapon away.

The wolf ran up to Padre's motionless body and howled again. It moved into the thicket as the cops approached. It watched as the cops tried to resuscitate the man.

"Was he attacked by the wolf?" one of the cops asked as he pulled his gun again.

"No, he's been shot. The wolf just might have saved him."

One officer called for an ambulance and within moments, the beach was turned into a crime scene area with spotlights, wooden horses, and onlookers.

The wolf edged its way into the underbrush as the crowd grew. Fearful of humans, it retreated farther into the darkened forest, shifted into the hawk, and from the safety of high branches, watched with anticipation at the activity below.

I don't know if he's alive, Sara cried.

What's happening?

Sara explained what the police were doing. She heard one of the officers say Padre was breathing. *He was shot, Dagger. And they left him to drown.*

The Harley coughed and sputtered as Dagger weaved around the wooden horses that had been set up. He was stopped before he could get any closer.

"You're going to have to park your bike someplace else." The fresh-faced kid with a name badge that said LANSING, tried to sound authoritative in a uniform that was too big for him and a holster that was starting to slip down to his hip bone. He hiked the gun belt up and kept his hands on his hips, which to Dagger looked more like an attempt to keep his gun belt from pulling his pants down around his ankles.

Dagger whipped a business card in front of the rookie. "I'd like to speak to the officer in charge. I think I might know the victim." He rushed past, forcing the teen-cop to run to keep up.

"That would be Sergeant Duranski. He's the guy with the big head, literally."

The crowd parted as Dagger pressed forward. Sergeant Duranski wasn't hard to find. He did have a big head and a wide face to go with it. But he had a large enough frame to carry it, almost seven-feet tall.

When Officer Lansing introduced them, Dagger had to crane his neck to look Duranski in the eye. This was no country-bumpkin, small-town sheriff. His eyes narrowed with suspicion at Dagger, and when he opened his mouth to speak, there was enough space between his front teeth to drive a truck through.

Dagger gave a quick look at the body on the beach and told Duranski the victim was Sergeant Jerry Martinez of the Cedar Point Police Department.

"How did you hear about this, Mr. Dagger?" Duranski turned Dagger's business card toward the light.

"Just Dagger will be fine."

Duranski grunted in response. "You're the fella that called. How the hell did you get here so quick?"

Paramedics arrived with medical equipment and a stretcher. The two men moved away to give them room. Dagger explained how Padre was helping him with a case, how Padre's phone call had been disconnected, and why Dagger had reason to believe Padre was in trouble. Dagger watched the paramedics strip off Padre's shirt. The bullet was in the chest, but fortunately had missed the heart.

"Listen," Dagger said to the paramedics, "Cedar Point Hospital has a trauma center and a helicopter. You can be there in the same amount of time as it takes to get him to your hospital."

"We already called them," one of the medics said, never turning away from his work. The technician had the fastest hands Dagger had ever seen. "He's stabilized," the paramedic announced. "But we have to get him to the trauma center quick." He turned to his female partner. "Find out the chopper's ETA."

Is he going to be okay? Dagger heard Sara's voice in his head.

He's stabilized but they don't know yet. I just hope he makes it to the hospital in time.

"Lansing," Duranski called out. "You and Sizemore find out if anyone saw or heard anything." To Dagger he said, "You realize, he may be Cedar Point's cop, but his attempted murder is my business. So I WILL be at Sergeant's Martinez's bedside to get his statement."

"Of course." Dagger drifted away from the beach toward the maintenance shed. Shadows jumped as he followed a footpath. An owl hooted up in the trees.

Where are you going, Dagger?

I'm going to take a look at the maintenance shed. He heard the trees rustling overhead and assumed it was the hawk. The large door gaped open, the interior dark. Nudging the door with his elbow, he entered.

"Something in here of interest?"

Turning quickly, Dagger almost hit Duranski with the

flashlight. "Are you looking to give me a coronary?"

"Didn't mean to startle you. I get a little suspicious when strangers start sticking there nose into my territory." He ran his tongue over his piano-key teeth, almost losing it in the large gap. Duranski had to duck through the doorway. He clicked on a flashlight of his own, a heavy-duty light with a beam as wide as he was tall. "How long you been a P.I.?"

"About five years. I've known Sergeant Martinez almost as long. He's a good detective."

"Any reason why you're checking out this shed?" Duranski followed close behind.

"When Padre called my house, he told my assistant where he was. She made the first call to your station. I just wanted to check this shed out." The beam illuminated the walls, bouncing off the heavy equipment. It rested on a bare spot on the floor about fifteen feet by twenty feet, swept or brushed clean. "Looks like something rested here," Dagger said. He opened the cabinet marked SNOW SHOVELS. Some shovels hung from nails, others leaned against each other. None were hanging on the left side of the cabinet, as if they had been moved aside to make room.

"If I find out you're holding out on me," Duranski warned, "I will be more than happy to show you one of our best cells."

25

Early Tuesday morning, Sara pulled up in front of Skizzy's Pawn Shop just as the truck engine coughed and died. "Darn." She struggled to place the gear in neutral but to be on the safe side, also put on the parking brake.

"Are you alone?" Skizzy poked his head around Sara and checked both sides of the sidewalk and across the street. "Hurry, hurry." He closed the door behind her and refastened all the locks and chains.

Sara set a cooler on the counter and a bag saying, "I brought you some home-grown vegetables I froze and some pickles and stewed tomatoes I canned. You should get the vegetables into the freezer right away."

Skizzy peeked inside the bag. "This what I think it is?" He smiled, his face forming cherub cheeks, as if he hid ping pong balls in his mouth. "Warm fry bread and fresh coffee."

"I made the fry bread this morning." Sara followed him down the staircase to his workroom. Skizzy was wearing the same camouflage pants and stained tee shirt he had worn during her previous visit. She wondered why he would wear military clothing if he was so suspicious of anything to do with the government, including the military.

"I've already swept the building for listening devices. Big Brother didn't sneak in here during the night." Skizzy wasn't smiling.

"Do you do that every morning?"

"Yep, every morning. And if I go out for any reason, I do it again when I return. Can't trust them. They are clever, yes sir." He thumbed through pages of computer printouts from the telephone numbers Dagger had given him. "Where is Dagger this morning?"

"He spent the night with a sick friend in the hospital."

"Well, tell Dagger I highlighted all the repeat calls and who they were to. Do you have something to put this in? They have telescopic equipment that can read from miles away."

Sara blinked and stammered, "No. Do you have an envelope?"

"Sure, sure." He opened a large brown envelope and blew into it, tipped it upside down. "Can't even trust bugs. Did you see that episode of X-Files where the government has outfitted bugs with audio and visual equipment for spying?"

Sara smiled. "No, I must have missed that episode." She felt sorry for him. To be that neurotic had to take its toll. And she wondered if Skizzy trusted anyone besides Dagger.

"Well, I'm sure you heard about those longhorn beetles that have been infesting some trees in Chicago." He leaned closer, his voice conspiratorial. "Chinese espionage." He nodded, agreeing with himself.

* * *

"I hope you don't mind meeting me here." Eric Tyler nodded to the waitress that he wanted a refill on his coffee. He and Dagger were seated in the restaurant at the plush Cedar Point Yacht Club.

Dagger could see fishing boats headed out toward the breakwall. Kids were already casing out their lounge chairs at the pool.

"Actually, Eric, I think you will prefer that we meet here rather than at your office."

Eric looked puzzled. They ordered breakfast, and once the waitress left, Eric said, "You were saying?"

"This is about Rachel Tyler."

Eric smiled but his eyes were cold steel. His hair looked as plastic as a Ken doll's and his reaction seemed prepackaged. Absorb Question A and sift through files for appropriate reaction.

"My father has been despondent ever since you dropped your little bombshell. He has told me he refuses to go to the police, doesn't want the publicity." Eric stirred his coffee slowly. After several moments of contemplation, he said, "You know this all sounds ludicrous."

"How did you get along with her?"

Eric checked his watch. The waitress delivered their breakfast and refilled their coffee cups. His cell phone rang. He spent two minutes on the phone. "Sorry about that," Eric said. "Where were we? Oh yes, Rachel. Well, what can I say? I was engaged to Edie when Dad married Rachel. I guess you can say we got along like brother and sister. One big happy family." He took a stab at his eggs and chewed slowly.

He was a lot different from Nick. Nick was more relaxed, laid back. Dagger could picture Nick partying til all hours and saying the hell with it the next day when he was supposed to show up for work. But Eric seemed more regimented, serious, all business. He was definitely more like his father.

Dagger rubbed the sleep from his eyes and tried to push thoughts of Padre out of his mind. Dagger had dozed in the visitor's lounge most of the night. Padre had a restful night and the prognosis was good. The surgeon had reported that most of the bullet had hit the gold cross Padre wore around his neck. Only a fragment of the bullet had entered his chest. But the thought that the man responsible might be sitting across from him made Dagger's blood boil. He was in need of sleep and tired of waltzing the two-step with Eric.

Although this was a sensitive subject, Dagger wasn't in a sensitive mood. "Did your father know you had an affair with Rachel?"

Eric choked on his toast and took a long swallow of water. "Excuse me? Where did you hear that ridiculous rumor?"

"Around." Dagger chewed slowly and watched the tinge of red creep up from Eric's starched shirt collar to his forehead.

The room was starting to fill up with society fat cats clad in ascots and nautical blazers. Attractive young women clung to the aging fat cats' arms, some dragging along young children.

"Well, it's bullshit." Eric pushed his plate away. "Let me guess. Nick got drunk and ran off at the mouth. Truth is, Nick was the one with the hots for Rachel. Not me."

"Nick would have been a little too young for Rachel. Maybe seventeen?"

With a shrug of his shoulder, Eric said, "You know how those raging hormones work. I was totally faithful to Edie. We were getting married. But I don't even think Nick would have touched her. She was Dad's fiancee. We Tyler boys do have scruples."

"Where were you the night Rachel disappeared?"

Eric's gaze swept swiftly around the room before resting on Dagger's face. "If you must know, I was trying to catch up on paperwork in my office. This is completely useless. Unless you have a police shield to show me, I don't owe you any explanations. Now, if you don't mind." Eric checked his watch again. "I have an appointment."

"Look at you. I give you one simple assignment and you screw it up." Dagger held a bunch of flowers and searched for a place to put them. He settled for the water pitcher.

Padre laughed. "What did you do? Steal those off the candy striper's delivery cart?" He winced as he reached for the controls.

"I'll get that." Dagger pushed the button to raise the bed so Padre was in a sitting position. "I was glad to hear you were awake and moved out of ICU so quickly."

"That's my insurance company for you. By this afternoon I'm sure they'll want me released."

Dagger opened the blinds and walked past the empty bed that had been tightly wrapped in stark white sheets and a blue bedspread. He pulled a chair close to his friend. Padre's color looked better. He had lost a lot of blood and was lucky to be alive. Padre would have died if it hadn't been for Sara and her unique talents.

"That Sergeant Duranski stopped by early this morning to question me. Nice guy. Kinda like a Grizzly Adams."

"Listen, Padre ..."

"Hey, don't start with that blame game. I wanted to help out."

"The doc says your medal may have saved your life."

"Yeah. God came through again." He pushed away the breakfast tray which contained a bowl of half-eaten oatmeal. "That Sergeant Duranski said something about a wolf finding me on the beach. What the hell is that all about?"

"That's what he told me. It was probably a dog though. Those country bumpkin cops wouldn't know a wolf from a dog if it bit them." Dagger held up the photographs of the three men. "Any of these men look familiar?"

"The two on the right."

Padre had identified Mince and Joey. "Just two?"

Padre nodded and explained how he had found the bloodstained rug. "I'm sure they came back to get it."

"Well, they got it. It could be anywhere. They could have weighted it down and dumped it into Lake Michigan or hauled it off to an incinerator somewhere." Dagger told Padre about his conversation with Eric Tyler.

"And you think he's lying?"

"Of course."

Padre looked over at the machines that were beeping his heart rate and blood pressure. "That damn thing is annoying. Unplug it. With my luck I'll spend the afternoon waiting to see a flat line."

Dagger reached over and pulled the plug out of the outlet. Immediately a voice came over the intercom and a face appeared on his television screen. "Excuse me, gentlemen. Please plug that machine back in." A pudgy face framed in tight curls smiled at them from the screen.

"Skizzy is right," Dagger muttered as he stuck the plug back in the socket. "Big brother AND sister are watching."

"Thank you," the smiling face replied just before it disappeared from the screen.

Padre continued, "I heard them talking, Dagger. They said something about the body. I was in and out of consciousness and I wish to hell my memory was better. Things are kinda muddied."

"That's okay. It will come to you. Just concentrate on getting better."

"The hell with that. I want you to fill me in. And don't leave out a thing."

26

Dagger returned home around two in the afternoon to find Sara sitting at his desk pouring over the list of phone numbers.

Sara asked, "How is Padre?"

"Making surprising progress. He's a tough old bird." Dagger pulled his shirttail out of his pants and wiped his face.

"AWK." Einstein fluffed his feathers and squawked from a branch in his tree.

"Not you, fella. Padre."

"AWK, SPREAD UM."

"Mail come yet?"

"No." Sara looked up from the reports. "You doubted the possibility that there was anything to investigate."

Dagger smiled. Sara was right. He leaned against the front door frame and stared out at the yard with its perennials in full bloom and welcomed the rain shower he barely beat home. He was silent for a while, thinking of Padre, Rachel, and exactly how dangerous Rachel's killer or killers were.

"It isn't your fault Padre got hurt, Dagger."

Dagger turned away from the door. "I admit I didn't think this was going to be a big case. But I also didn't realize how dangerous it could be. That was my fault."

The cool from the air conditioning felt great. Standing in the doorway to the aviary, Dagger told Einstein, "Little too cool out here for you, Mister. You better stay here in your sauna."

After grabbing a glass of iced tea, Dagger retreated to his bedroom and closed the door. Thirty minutes later he emerged showered, shaved, and wearing gray pants and a Henley shirt. He shook is long, wet hair like a dog just in from the rain. It fell in loose waves, leaving his shirt water-spotted. On the coffee table was a plate containing a ham sandwich and a stack of Dagger's favorite mild peppers.

"Thanks." He sank onto the sofa, his lack of sleep and sore body taking it's toll. "Einstein's napping?"

"Yes."

Even with the sound-proofed door closed, Einstein could still be awakened by a phone call or loud noise. Macaws were naturally light sleepers.

Sara carried the pages of phone numbers from Skizzy over to the table. Dagger got a whiff of sunflowers when she sat down and wondered what it would take to get her to give up the few sack dresses she still owned. Maybe they could have one big bonfire and burn the rest of them.

"Did you have any trouble with the truck?"

"Not really."

"Not really?" Dagger had taught Sara how to drive a stick shift and the drive to Skizzy's was the first time she had driven his truck by herself.

Sara played with the hem of her dress and studied the scars on her knuckles.

Dagger chuckled. "How many times did you kill the engine?"

"A couple."

"You'll get the hang of it." He pulled the reports onto his lap. "What have you found?"

"One number was called repeatedly for several months after Rachel disappeared. Then the calls were once a month for the first year and then nothing until a couple of weeks ago."

"Who was it to?"

"The Carmelite Retreat. It's a rehabilitation institute in upper Michigan. When I checked the address, it is the same as The Abbey, one of the Tyler resorts."

"I don't understand." He read the addresses on the reports, then looked at the printout from the Tyler web site listing Tyler properties. "I wonder ..." Dagger phoned Robert Tyler.

"The Abbey is our property near Boyne, Michigan," Robert explained. "Why do you ask?"

"Have you ever heard of the Carmelite Retreat?"

"No. Should I?"

"According to the report I have, Mr. Tyler, The Abbey was purchased by the Carmelite Monks about six years ago."

"That's impossible. I would have known that."

"Would you? Who besides you has the authority to sell Tyler properties?"

"Just Eric. But he would never have done it without

my consent."

"Are you sure about that?" Dagger listened to Tyler's breathing, imagining what other secrets Eric had kept from his father.

"Let me check into this." Tyler's voice had an edge to it. He was a man who insisted on control, who prided himself on being on top of things. And who would never accept betrayal from anyone, especially a son.

"I only have one word of advice," Dagger cautioned. "I'll give you the phone number for the retreat. Act as if you are aware they purchased the property. And don't let Eric know that you found out about the retreat."

"May I ask why you are interested in The Abbey?"

"Not yet. Let me know what you find out first." Dagger hung up.

"Good cookies," Simon mumbled as he washed down the chocolate chips with milk. "Sara is some cook, Dagger. Gotta watch yourself. She's going to be a good catch for some guy."

Einstein could be heard in the aviary screeching, "AWK. WANT A COOKIE. AWWWKK."

"Thanks for that reminder. But that's why I have a locked gate by the street—to keep the suitors out."

"Yep," Simon winked. "Gotta keep her for yourself." Simon cocked his head to one side and sized up Sara's body, which was alluring even in the sundress. "Good set of hips there for childbearing." His eyes twinkled. Sara gasped.

"Ease up, Simon. Sara isn't used to your gutter mentality yet. Now how about telling me what you've found?"

Simon wiped crumbs from his grinning face. "Well, old Eric has a bit of a gambling problem. He likes to play the ponies and is a regular at those private poker parties they have at the downtown hotels in Chicago. They move 'um around, you know, so the cops can't find them. He also frequents those casino boats under a fictitious name. Bets five thousand bucks a hand. Rumor is his debts at one time totaled five million." Simon chuckled, took a sip of coffee. "Between his gambling and his wife's expensive taste, they were in some dire straits."

"How long ago was that?" Dagger asked.

"He's been a good boy for a while. Must have won some of it back. His worst financial problems were about six years ago."

"Six years ago?" Sara asked.

"That would make sense," Dagger said. "Eric sells one of the Tyler resorts without his father's consent. He uses the money to pay his debts."

"And you think the old man's wife might have found out about it and college prep boy Eric bumped her off?" Simon chuckled. It started deep in his thick middle and erupted into a roaring laugh. "Yep. Those rich people sure do have their problems."

Worm heaved the file box onto the coffee table. "This is really exciting." He pushed his glasses up on his nose and beamed proudly.

From the aviary, Einstein stared curiously at the visitor. His head dipped and swayed as if sizing up Worm.

"Wow, is he beautiful." The reporter made a move toward the aviary.

"Don't get too close," Sara cautioned. "He won't bite but he tends to nip strangers, which might startle you." Sara turned to the macaw. "Einstein, this is Sal Wormley." She handed Einstein a Brazil nut. "Try to be quiet."

Einstein wrapped his toes around the nut and flew off to the top of the tree.

"So Einstein was Sheila's competition? Dagger made a wise choice." Worm laughed. He settled in on the couch and started pulling papers and a book from the box. "Where is Dagger?"

"He had to go out of town for a few hours."

"I have copies of all the press clippings during Rachel's modeling career. I also went through her high school year-book which you gave me. They didn't come any sweeter than Rachel Liddie. She was prom queen, sweetheart queen, Miss Teen, you name it." Worm's eye's drifted up to the cat-walk and the skylights spanning the ceiling.

"Was there ever any negative publicity about Rachel?" Sara sifted through some of the copies Worm had laid out on the coffee table.

"Nothing. She wasn't a temperamental artist, always sweet, caring. No nude photos, no scandalous affairs." Worm dug down to the bottom of the box and pulled out a file folder. "Her parents still live in Indianapolis, but Dagger told me not to approach them."

Sara closed the door to the aviary. Einstein immediately

flew to the door and clamped onto the bars. He screeched his dislike for being imprisoned. It was an ear-piercing clatter of bird-eze. "Einstein, we have company."

Einstein wrapped his feet around the top bar and hung upside down, training one beady eye on Worm. A sound crept from Einstein's throat, sounding much like a purr.

Sara reached through the bars and stroked Einstein's head. "Asking him to keep quiet is like telling a fish to stop swimming."

"He's smart. No wonder Dagger named him Einstein." Worm showed Sara several photos of a tropical beach with tanned women in floral skirts and bikini tops, another scene of a market square with the women holding up straw purses. "See anyone familiar?"

Sara studied the photos. The blonde was definitely Rachel, with her long legs and blue eyes. "Was this a photo shoot?"

"Yes, in Australia. This was about a year before Rachel met Robert Tyler. I found the others in a French magazine called *Shutter*. It's comparable to our *People* magazine. It catches the celebrities at play. One of the photos was from Monte Carlo and another from the Riviera. I'm trying to get the originals so we can get a better enlargement."

Sara studied what seemed like two vacation photos. A blonde woman was standing beside Rachel, but Sara didn't recognize her. The woman could pass for Rachel's sister.

27

Dagger felt an eerie presence in the room, as if the Carmelite Retreat were haunted by years of unsettled spirits. He had learned by browsing the framed newspaper clippings in the lobby that the hotel had been built on an old Indian burial ground.

The ornate décor had been tamed down since its resort days. The walls were a muted color, the crystal chandeliers replaced by wall sconces dimly lit. The furniture was a drab brown, matching the robe of the monk who had greeted him at the front desk.

Dagger had accepted the offer to use the Tyler jet and had been assured the pilot could be trusted to not inform anyone of their destination. Even the flight plan had stated they would be flying to Detroit, not Boyne, Michigan.

Robert had confirmed that The Abbey had been sold six years before. He had been unsuccessful at convincing Dagger to let him tag along. Dagger felt it best if Robert didn't arouse any suspicions on the homefront.

Outside the windows, Dagger could see patients being walked or wheeled through the gardens. The only thing that added color to the lobby were the fresh floral arrangements on the tables.

"Mr. Dagger, I'm so sorry to keep you waiting."

Dagger turned to see a round-faced man, a lone curl brushing the top of his otherwise balding head. He introduced himself as Duncan, stuck a pudgy hand out, and shook Dagger's fingers. Duncan spoke in a whisper so when Dagger responded in a normal tone, his voice seemed to echo off the lobby walls.

"I have only about a half-hour before my flight leaves," Dagger admitted.

"Of course. Follow me."

Duncan led Dagger to a room on the third floor overlooking the gardens. It was the size of a suite, probably one of the more expensive rooms. It had been Rachel's for the last five years. Sunlight streamed in through the tall windows, giving a warm glow to a room draped in yellow-flowered curtains and bedspread. There were no photos on the dresser, no keepsakes, mementos. Only a book of poems by the bedside. In the closet hung a few dresses, sweaters, some canvas flats.

"Nurse Reynolds tended to Ada Matthews," Duncan said.

When Dagger had shown Rachel's picture to Celia Flaherty, the guest services manager, she had identified the woman as Ada Matthews, a woman brought in by her brother, Sean, five years before. Supposedly the brother had her in a hospital for a few months. When she lapsed into a coma, the doctors recommended she be placed in a private home. Calls were made weekly by the brother for an update on his

THE GOOD DIE TWICE 181

sister's condition, but when he had to go out of town, Ada's sister, Pamela, made the weekly calls. Six months later Ada had come out of her coma but didn't recognize her sister or even know her own name. After several more months of visits and attempts at hypnosis, her sister stopped visiting. They had only left instructions to be contacted if there were any signs of change in Ada's condition.

Dagger had also shown the guest services manager the pictures of the three goons who had broken into Sara's house, but the manager couldn't be sure if any of them was the so-called Sean Matthews.

"Father Duncan? You were looking for me?" Nurse Reynolds had graying hair that was pulled back severely in a tight bun. Her eyes sagged at the corners, though her mouth was in a continuous smile, pleasing, grandmotherly.

"Yes, Mr. Dagger has a few questions about Miss Matthews."

Once Duncan left, Nurse Reynolds opened the curtains wider and straightened the bedspread as if expecting company. She appeared jittery, opening and closing the dresser drawers, flitting from the dresser to the table.

She seemed to gloss over Dagger's appearance. He wondered if his all-black clothes, ponytail, earring, and the grunge-looking stubble made her uncomfortable. It wouldn't be the first time he had that effect on the older generation who still remembered the Capone days. Dagger's choice of dress seemed to grant him all the best tables in Italian restaurants.

"Please, have a seat," Dagger coaxed. He took a seat on the bed.

"I'm told you are with an insurance company?" She sat down on a yellow love seat near the window and clasped her hands.

"I'm trying to determine how Ra ... Miss Mathews got from the retreat to Cedar Point, especially since she had no recollection of who she was or even that Cedar Point was her home." Dagger fanned the poetry book looking for notes, some hint of when Rachel might have begun to get her memory back.

"I really can't say. She made casual conversation but would always seem puzzled and confused when we tried to encourage her to remember. Since it caused so much distress, we tried not to pressure her."

"You were her nurse during the entire five years?"

"Yes. I was her physical therapist."

Dagger showed her the pictures of Joey, Mince, and Luke. "Do you recognize any of these men?"

She lifted the reading glasses, which were hanging from a beaded chain around her neck. "Oh, my, it's been so long; I really can't be sure."

"Take another look," Dagger urged.

Nurse Reynolds studied each of the pictures intensely. Shaking her head, she handed him first Joey's and then the remaining pictures. "Definitely not them. But Celia saw him more than I ever did."

"Unfortunately, her memory isn't too keen." Dagger wanted to say that her memory wasn't too great either but pissing off Nurse Reynolds wasn't going to win her over. "Maybe you remember specific features. Was he short, tall, scars?"

"He was tall, that much I remember."

Dagger handed her a picture of Eric Tyler. "What about this man?"

She lined all the pictures up in front of her. After a few moments she confessed, "If you were to put these men in a line up, I wouldn't be able to swear to anything." As an afterthought, she added, "But don't give up on Celia. She's one of those whose light bulb comes on at the most unusual time. Two weeks from now at four in the morning, she'll jump out of bed with the answer."

"Unfortunately, I can't wait that long." Dagger handed her his business card and asked her to keep it handy should she remember anything else.

Nurse Reynolds sighed heavily. "Ada was a beautiful young woman. It was a pity her family couldn't visit her more often."

"No one came to claim her belongings after she left?"

Nurse Reynolds shook her head. "When she was first brought in her sister supplied her with a few summer and winter things, a coat, perfume, nothing more."

"Was there any time before she disappeared when she seemed to remember her past?"

"No."

"To your knowledge, did she write to anyone prior to her disappearance?"

She thought a moment, "No. That is one thing I would have noticed since I'm the one who sifts through the mail before it is picked up. Ada didn't even have a diary."

"What did she talk to you about?"

"Normal things. The weather, the flowers. She liked

thumbing through catalogs, looking at clothes. And she liked poetry."

Something didn't seem right, Dagger thought. Rachel had to have remembered. How else would she know to call Robert? How else would she know her way back to Cedar Point?

"When did you first notice she was missing?" He placed the pictures back in his pocket.

Nurse Reynolds pulled her glasses off, leaving them to dangle again. "She usually went to her room right after dinner to watch television or read but the next morning she didn't come down for breakfast."

"How would someone get off the grounds if they wanted to leave?" Dagger gazed at the property outside the windows. There weren't any fences. Vendors came and went. Cleaning vans, produce, groceries. Visiting hours ended at eight o'clock at night.

"What time does the last vendor leave?"

The nurse shrugged. "Could be laundry, which leaves around midnight each day."

"And what company is that?"

"Sierra. We contacted the sister when we first discovered Ada missing but her sister told us Ada had arrived home safe and sound."

"Can you describe Ada's sister?"

"Why," Nurse Reynolds smiled, "she looked just like Ada."

28

Dagger rubbed the sleep from his eyes and staggered to the kitchen. He didn't get back into town until after nine, then stopped over to see Padre in the hospital. Having missed dinner, he wasn't in the mood for breakfast. Instead, he grabbed two pieces of cold pizza and a can of Pepsi and took a seat at the kitchen table.

Sara joined soon after, fresh as the morning dew, her hair long and shiny. No sack dress today. Instead, she wore bright yellow capri pants and a yellow and white flowered top. "Yuk," Sara said as she eyed Dagger's choice of breakfast food. She popped a bagel into the toaster and poured a glass of orange juice. "How was the plane ride?" She spread cream cheese with salmon on her bagel and slid onto the seat kitty-corner from Dagger.

"Pretty posh. Nothing like a company jet. You should try it sometime."

Sara shivered. "No thanks. I'm afraid of flying."

It took several seconds for him to realize Sara was serious and to find the absolute humor in her fear of flying. He laughed, his eyes twinkling. Shaking his head, he reached out and slipped his hand behind Sara's neck, wanting for a brief moment to kiss her on the forehead, but thought better of it. Simon's voice kept echoing in his head … "Brother and sister? Right!" Dagger instead released his grip and took a swig of his Pepsi.

Sara said, "Well, I'm sorry. There's something scary about sitting in a metal tube and letting someone else handle the controls."

Dagger explained his visit with Nurse Reynolds.

"And she didn't recognize any of the pictures?"

"No."

"And what about the woman who posed as Rachel's sister?"

"That's just it." Dagger wiped his mouth with a napkin and tossed it on his empty plate. "She says she looked just like Rachel."

"You're kidding!" Sara rushed to the living room and Dagger followed. She showed Dagger the pictures Worm had of Rachel and a woman who could pass for her sister. "These are some of Rachel's vacation photos."

Einstein flew over to the perch in back of the sofa. He playfully hung upside down by one foot and held a fruit tree branch in the other.

"What are you up to, buddy?" Dagger asked as he carried the pictures to the sofa and sat down. He used a magnifying glass to examine the picture closer but it was of little help.

"Worm is going to see if he can check the studio that made the copies to see if they still have the original."

Einstein chattered away with a relentless stream of ear-piercing screeches.

Dagger turned his attention to the box on the coffee table where he had placed Rachel's earring after Luke and his boys stole the duplicate. He held up the earring and studied it. The branch fell onto the cushion behind him so Dagger picked it up and handed it over his shoulder at Einstein. But the macaw was more interested in something else.

The earring was large and black, almost the color of a Brazil nut and it was probably the biggest one Einstein had ever seen. Without any forewarning, Einstein swooped from the perch, snatched the earring in his beak and flew up to the catwalk, where he perched on the railing.

"Einstein, no!" Dagger jumped from the couch.

Sara ran to the kitchen and returned with a large can of cheese curls. "Einstein, look what I have for you." She shook the can.

Einstein cocked his head to one side. With his toes he grabbed the earring from between his beak and examined his treasure.

Sara opened the can and held up several cheese curls. "I'll trade you, Einstein. That earring doesn't taste good at all. Come on. You know these are your favorite."

Einstein gnawed on the earring, mentally weighed the offering Sara held up, and gnawed with his beak again.

"EINSTEIN." Dagger snapped his fingers. "No more Baywatch."

Einstein looked sharply at Dagger, stared at the trophy and released his grip. He returned to the perch in back of the couch.

"TREAT."

"Here you go." Sara held out her hand and Einstein gently picked up the cheese curls.

"You broke it, Einstein." Dagger held up two pieces— the backing and the stone that Einstein had gnawed free from the prongs holding it in place. He turned the dark stone over. "That's funny. The black color doesn't go all the way through. It doesn't look natural."

Sara asked, "What's wrong with it?"

Dagger rubbed his fingers across the stone. "The bottom of the stone is pink." Dagger took the stone outside to the garage where he gently dabbed paint remover on it. After washing the stone thoroughly, he returned to the living room and showed it to Sara.

"It's beautiful!" Sunlight glistened off the many facets of the gem. The stone was a soft pink color. Sara held it up and marveled at its clarity. "I think I read about this once."

Dagger was fascinated with Sara's knowledge, attributed mainly to the abundant reading materials her grandmother supplied for her in her home schooling. The bookshelves were stocked with encyclopedias and almanacs. And having been such a recluse growing up, all Sara really had was her grandmother and her resource books.

Sara handed Dagger the stone and retrieved one of her books. After several minutes she found what she was looking for. "This is a pink diamond. It is the most expensive and rarest diamond in the world." She pointed to a picture on the page as she explained, "They are produced in Australia, and a one-carat diamond has been valued at over one million dollars."

"One carat?" Dagger whistled. Einstein followed suit with a piercing whistle of his own.

"Einstein, shhhh," Sara coaxed.

The macaw fluffed out the feathers on his head and accepted another cheese curl.

"Damn." Dagger sat behind his desk and typed on the keyboard. "This sucker has to be at least fifty carats. And the mate is on her body, wherever that is." He accessed the Internet and typed in *diamonds* and *Australia* and let the system do a search.

"Do you think it's real?" Sara asked.

Dagger skimmed through the results of the search. There were travel web sites for Australia and literally thousands of web sites on diamonds. "I'm going to have to narrow the search." He went back to the SEARCH line and typed in *pink diamond*, using the required quotation marks. It came back with several hundred hits. The eighth one caught his eye. "I think I found something."

Sara peered over his shoulder. The web site materializing on screen described the history of the Williamsburg Collection, a stunning choker necklace of twenty pink diamonds with a huge oval diamond suspended from the middle. The matching oval earrings were identical to the one Dagger had sitting on his desk.

"It can't be the same," Sara gasped. "Can it?"

Dagger scrolled down the page, reading, "The complete set is valued at four hundred million dollars. It had once belonged to the Duchess of Williamsburg and is displayed at the Argyle Museum in Argyle, Australia."

29

Dagger did his best thinking with a hammer in his hand. The framework was in place for the Florida room; the cement was set. The pre-fab structures available these days saved time and money. Dagger had twelve windows on order and was nailing the frames for the windows to the studs. Sweat trickled down his tanned chest. He lifted his baseball cap, ran his forearm across his forehead, and tugged the cap back down.

He had called Padre to fill him in on his trip to the retreat. Padre had one of his men tailing Eric, but so far Eric Tyler hadn't done anything the least bit suspicious.

There wasn't too much daylight left and the mosquitoes would soon be searching for someone to nibble on. With each whack of the hammer, Dagger added up pieces to the puzzle. Did Luke or Eric pose as Rachel's brother? Could Luke by chance been in Australia around the same time as Rachel? Sara had called the museum curator and left a message on the recorder. Dagger wasn't sure what time it was in Australia but he had a feeling their time zone placed them one day ahead of Indiana.

He caught a glimpse of Sara behind the screened patio door. Her young eyes looked tense, absorbed. It was classic Sara. One bare foot was curled on top of the other, one hand was clenched, the other had found its way to her mouth, probably a fresh knuckle that hadn't been chewed on yet.

"What's wrong, Sara?" Dagger had to catch himself sometimes. According to Simon, the inflection in Dagger's voice sounded more like he was asking, 'What's wrong, now, Sara.' Having her around was like owning a cat. She would slink around corners, silently watching him. Was easily startled if Dagger made too sudden a move.

Dagger gathered up his tools and tossed them in his toolbox. He was ready for a shower anyway. Sara backed away when he entered through the patio door. He went right to the refrigerator and grabbed a beer.

"Worm called. Sheila asked him to check on who owns the title to my property."

Dagger took a long pull from his beer and shrugged. Sara kept chewing on her knuckle. The thumb and index fingers on her right hand looked deformed from the swollen bumps. She pulled her hand away and clasped both tightly. Dagger didn't understand it. There were times Sara could be so confident and bold, like when Luke and his guys broke in. Then there were times she looked and acted like a helpless twelve-year-old.

"She did say she was interested in buying the place. But it's not for sale." He turned saying, "I'm going to take a shower."

Twenty minutes later Dagger found Sara sitting on the living room floor surrounded by reference books. He pulled his damp hair back behind his ears and peered over her shoulder.

"What are you looking up?"

"Titles and trusts. I don't have a title to this property," Sara confessed. "It was in grandfather's name."

"I'm sure your grandmother left it to you in her will."

"She didn't have a will." There was a hard edge to her voice, which wasn't what Dagger was used to.

"Sara, why didn't you say something?" He reached over to pick up one of the books.

"I can handle it." She pulled the book from his hands and tossed it on the stack.

"Okay." Dagger retrieved another beer from the refrigerator and plopped down on the couch, draping his legs on the coffee table. Simon had told Dagger he was too hard on Sara, expected too much, and in subtle ways made her feel useless and ignorant. Even Einstein was quiet, as if he sensed an undercurrent in the air and was ducking for cover.

Sara had a law book pulled onto her lap as she leaned against the couch, legs crossed at the ankles, layers of thick hair drifting over her arms and down the front of her dress. Her lips moved as she read like a third grader struggling with the pronunciation of strange words. One knuckle was making a subtle move to her mouth. Dagger could be a cold-hearted bastard sometimes, but at this moment, for the first time, he understood the phrase heart-wrenching. He pulled his legs off the coffee table and rested his elbows on his knees.

"I don't even understand legal mumbo jumbo, Sara. The bottom line is, either someone can buy it out from under you or it reverts back to the Interior Department or the Bureau of Indian Affairs or the specific tribal council."

Sara remained silent, studying the words on the pages in front of her.

"Sara, this isn't like you. Stop being a baby."

He regretted it the moment the words spilled out of his mouth. She turned on him with fire in her eyes, shoved the books off her lap, and stormed upstairs to her bedroom.

"Jezzus … women."

30

You certainly have my attention, Mr. Dagger," came the accented speech of J.C. Kinnecutt, the curator at the Argyle Museum in Argyle, Australia, the heart of diamond mining. Dagger pictured him gray-haired with bushy sideburns and a pipe sticking out of his mouth.

It was nine in the morning and they were on a conference call in Skizzy's basement. He was videotaping the diamond Dagger had found and transmitting it over the Internet to Mr. Kinnecutt's office.

Dagger asked, "What can you tell us about the Williamsburg Collection?"

"It is made up of the finest quality pink diamonds ever discovered," J.C. began. "It has a delightful history. Amory Beaumont was a diamond hunter commissioned by Britain's Duke of Williamsburg to find a fitting gem for the Duchess. Beaumont discovered a mine in Perth, Australia in 1851 and brought back a seventeen-hundred-carat diamond. The Duke refused to let the diamond out of his sight and insisted the finest cutter from Amsterdam be sent to Australia to cut and polish the gem. It took the cutter close

THE GOOD DIE TWICE 195

to a year to finish the job."

J.C. spoke quickly, the excitement in his voice growing as he continued. "In the meantime, Beaumont was instructed to return to the mine and blow up the entrance to keep others from finding a diamond bigger and making the Duke's diamond pale in comparison. But the Duke was a clever chap. He sent his men to make sure Beaumont didn't make it out of the mine. He didn't want someone else commissioning Beaumont."

Skizzy made a few more adjustments. "Are you ready?"

Dagger stood, legs apart, hands on his hips. He had tried to apologize to Sara for last night but she acted as if it never happened. She could be a lot more forgiving than he could.

The sounds of squeaking wheels could be heard over the computer microphone. Sara leaned forward, mesmerized by the technology that allowed someone thousands of miles away to see a diamond lying on a swatch of black felt right in front of her.

An image of the diamond appeared on the screen. There was unexpected silence from the curator. "Good lord," J.C. moaned. "Um, listen. Can you get one of your experts out your way to check ... no." J.C. hesitated. "Show me more of the earring. And can you zoom in?"

Skizzy rotated the camera, giving the image an almost three-dimensional look.

"Wait now. Let me load my photos." Within a few minutes the computer showed a split screen, a picture of the earrings from the Argyle Museum records and the image of the earring lying on Skizzy's table. "I don't believe this." J.C. gasped. "It has to be the most excellent forgery I have ever seen."

Dagger crossed his arms and rested a fist under his chin. The jewelry on the screen looked identical and someone went through a lot of trouble to make a duplicate. Rachel couldn't have died because she had a duplicate. She had to have had the real ones. "J.C., how do you know yours are genuine?"

"Well," J.C. cleared his throat, "I guess I just know. It has been in a locked display case under constant video surveillance. You don't just leave a four-hundred-million-dollar collection unprotected."

"Four hundred million?" Skizzy gasped, his eyes jerking to the monitor and back to the earring on the cloth.

"I'm investigating a murder, J.C. And I think the earrings had something to do with it."

There was the longest silence while J.C. digested what Dagger had said. Skizzy straightened up from where he hovered over the camera. Sara remained mesmerized by the images on the screen.

"Let me check something out," J.C. said. "I'll be right back."

Dagger paced the length of the room. The ceiling was low and another few inches and his head would be scraping the support beams. Metal shelving lined the walls and Dagger couldn't help but notice some of the bottled water was dated six years ago.

"Gentlemen," J.C. said as he returned to the microphone, "do you have the other earring by chance? And what about the necklace?"

"No and no." Dagger jammed his hands into his pants

pockets and glanced at Skizzy. What had J.C. been doing all that time? Checking out the authenticity of his set? If so, J.C. was remaining non-committal.

"J.C., when was the last time the Williamsburg Collection was out of its display case?"

J.C. explained how the jewelry was used during a photo shoot five years before. The collection was returned to the museum immediately. "Matter of fact," J.C. added, "I believe I have a picture from the photo shoot." Papers rustled in the background and a minute later, J.C. returned to the computer. "Yes, here she comes."

Within a few moments, a picture of Rachel appeared on the screen wearing a white glittering evening gown and the Williamsburg Collection.

Dagger's mind started to play out a scenario. Maybe Rachel was unaware she had the real ones. Or maybe she did steal them and tried to cut her partners out. He stared at the fresh, innocent face on the monitor. Rachel Tyler did not look like a thief.

J.C. stammered a bit, cleared his throat and started again. "I beg your silence for a short time until I can come to the states and see the diamond for myself. I am embarrassed to say that our country would be in a rather awkward situation if it were to get out that the Argyle Museum has lost one of its most prized possessions. Of course," he cleared his throat again, "not to mention the loss of my job. It isn't something that would look tidy on a job resume."

31

"I want my money, NOW." Mince tossed the paper on the table and stalked over to the window. "Tyler is late."

"I'm meeting Tyler alone. I think it's better that way." Luke gathered up the papers and dumped them in the garbage. "You two go downstairs and have a drink. Give me about thirty minutes."

"I don't like that idea," Mince protested. "We're in this together and I want to hear every damn word that's said."

"Yeah." Joey's dark eyes flashed. Apart, neither one would take on Luke, but together they felt stronger, more confident, more cocky.

Luke jammed his hands on his hips and scowled. "I'm not even supposed to have hired you two but if you want to be the ones to explain to Tyler how you fucked up and killed that woman, be my guest."

"We're working on it," Joey sneered.

"And we also have another offer for Tyler," Mince added. "So we ain't going nowhere."

There was a knock at the door. Luke regarded the two men briefly, then opened the door to Edie Tyler.

* * *

Edie paced, billows of cigar smoke drifting up to the ceiling fan in Luke's hotel suite. She stopped, glared at Joey and Mince, and then jammed the cigar into the ashtray.

"I have better ways to spend my afternoons." She dropped down onto the love seat, crossed her legs, and draped her arms on the armrests. "Exactly why should I pay you two idiots anything?"

Joey followed the curve of her calf up the shapely legs exposed by the long slit up the side of Edie's white skirt. "Because we went through a lot of trouble and our time is valuable."

Edie laughed, and flashed her green eyes at Luke. "You hired them, you fire them."

Mince sat on the edge of the couch toying with a nail clipper. He patiently worked from one finger to the next, not paying much attention to Edie but watching more intently on Luke's reaction. Nail clippings were flying.

"Do you mind," Luke scowled. "Do that in your own room."

Mince shrugged and shoved the nail clipper back in his pocket. He looked quickly at Joey whose gaze had reached Edie's cleavage.

"Well, Joey and me," Mince started, "we figure our time and silence is worth about a hundred thousand each."

"WHAT?" Edie shot out of the love seat and looked quickly to Luke who shook his head.

"Ten thousand each," Luke said evenly. "That was the agreed upon price."

Edie reached for a cigarette and tapped the end of it on the coffee table before accepting a light from Luke. She glared at him and blew out the first puff of smoke in his face. "You need to fix this problem ... now."

"Fix this problem?" Joey laughed and walked over to retrieve two beers. "What do you think we are? A flat tire?" He handed a beer to Mince.

Mince took a long swig. "Joey and me, we got something more valuable than that earring." The two conspirators grinned.

"Like what?" Edie demanded.

Mince peered at her over the rim of his beer can and announced, "We still got the body."

"What the hell are you doing out of the hospital?"

Padre walked into the living room holding his arm against his chest. "I told you. Insurance companies are turning hospitals into drive-thrus."

"Here, have a seat." Dagger offered to help him to the sofa but Padre refused.

"Quit fussin'. You remind me of my wife." A gauze bandage could be seen at the nape of his opened shirt collar. The old scar on his cheek was healing nicely though his face was shallow from a loss of weight.

"I'm surprised you have so much color."

"Liar. I'm as pasty as a dead carp. But at least the bullet missed all vital organs. Once I got the water out of my lungs, I was practically back to normal."

Padre caught sight of Einstein under the shower in the

aviary. Peering up toward the catwalk, he asked, "Where's Sara?"

"Why is it everyone asks where Sara is? What is it with you guys?"

"What? You think we want to look at your ugly puss?" Padre laughed and then studied Dagger's face. "How are your ribs?"

"Getting better." Dagger lifted the lid on the box and showed Padre the earring.

"Damn, it sure looks different in pink." Padre sat down on the edge of the couch and examined the gem while Dagger explained what they had learned from J.C. Kinnicutt. "Four hundred million?" Padre whistled.

"Somewhere out there is the other earring and the necklace."

"Was she wearing the necklace the night she was murdered?"

"No." Dagger thought back to the night at the Dunes Resort. Sara had only mentioned the earrings. The necklace wasn't something she would have missed.

Padre smiled. "Busy tonight?"

Sara looked around at the crowded tables at the Seaside Cabana, a cocktail lounge in the Driftwood Hotel. She could make out dark shadows moving restlessly behind tables and booths in darkly lit corners.

A waitress in blue shorts, white halter top, and sailor's cap stopped by the table and gave Nick an approving stare, her eyes layered in heavy lashes that seemed too long to be real. He smiled back and ordered a beer for himself and a glass of wine for Sara.

She gave Sara a casual glance and asked, "Do you have some I.D., Hon?"

"She's okay. Trust me," Nick said, smiling his patented Tyler smile. The waitress smiled back and offered no resistance.

The room smelled of stale smoke and a variety of perfumes and aftershaves. A large fish tank bubbled behind Sara, and she turned to admire the colorful species darting from one side of the tank to the other.

With her elbows propped on the table, Sara began to chew on the knuckle of her index finger. She should have just eaten dinner and gone home. She didn't want to stop for a drink with Nick but she thought she might get more information. Now she felt trapped, a peculiar sensation spreading over her body. She could feel eyes on her. Her knuckle stung, cracked open, and started to bleed.

"You okay?" Nick grabbed her hand. "I didn't think that salad would fill you up." He dipped a cocktail napkin in a glass of water and dabbed at the cut.

Glancing quickly around the room, Sara could see every female in the place had her eyes on Nick. Anyone who could read a magazine or newspaper at some time in his or her life had seen his photo in ads or in the society pages. Nick turned and flashed his dimpled smile at a table of young women who had been staring for the past ten minutes. His tan looked rich and caramel-colored against his stark white shirt.

"How are things at home?"

Nick said, "A little strained. Ever since … well, you know." A strand of blonde hair drifted down his forehead. Even a hair out of place didn't deter from his looks. He resembled a cross between Brat Pitt and a young Robert Redford.

"Is there a problem here?" The waitress' lashes fluttered as she placed a hand on Nick's shoulder. "Oh my." She stared at the bleeding callous protruding from Sara's knuckle. "I'll see if I can find a bandage."

Once she left, Sara asked, "You seem especially bothered by the news about Rachel." She stared at the beer, and how quickly Nick had downed it. "I would guess that your step-mother's disappearance five years ago has bothered you more than you let on. Want to tell me about it?"

The waitress returned with a bandage and an antiseptic wipe. She smiled at Nick and said, "Guess you'll have to kiss it and make it all better."

"Owww." Sara winced as the alcohol touched raw skin.

"That's okay. I'm blowing on it." He held her hand close and blew on the exposed area. Once he placed the bandage on, he examined her other knuckles closely. "My shrink would say you have a very nervous habit. Most people bite their nails." He held onto her hand longer than needed.

She slowly pulled it from his grasp and studied those annoying bumps. "I guess habits are hard to break." She slipped her long hair back behind her shoulder and sat up straight, as if some etiquette school matron had just slapped a ruler against the back of her chair. The women in the room would probably die if they knew she would rather be curled up on her couch in one of her sack dresses and a good book than properly attired in a cap-sleeve loose-knit sweater and skirt, sitting across from the most eligible bachelor in probably the entire Midwest.

"When did you start seeing a therapist? Five years ago?"

Nick stared at her through the dark glass of his bottle. "You've been hanging around a private detective too long. Might be dangerous to your health. You be careful."

Sara wasn't sure if that was a threat. The words may have seemed like it, but his eyes didn't. She wondered if maybe Nick were warning her against someone else.

She tried a different approach. "Do you think your brother had anything to do with Rachel's disappearance?"

"No, oh no." His mind seemed to drift, blinking back the memories. "No, there's only one person at fault, Sara." He took another long pull from his beer bottle, completely forgetting the waitress had brought him a glass.

Sara felt sorry for him. Nick knew something. And what about Eric? Two siblings afraid that a young wife would take their inheritance? Sara doubted it. At least she didn't believe it of Nick.

"Penny for your thoughts." Nick tapped a metal object on the table. It was a room key for the Driftwood Hotel.

Sara stared at the room key. "I, uh …" Caught off guard, her face flushed, but more from anger than embarrassment. "A little presumptuous of you."

Puzzled, Nick looked at the key and shrugged. "Not at all. I just need a peaceful night away from the zoo every now and then." He flashed that movie star smile again. "Besides, according to Sheila, Dagger is pretty protective of you and he's the last person I would want to tangle with."

Sara stared at the key. Maybe, since Nick had already been plied with liquor, he might open up more if she agreed to help him to his room.

"Okay, Nick." Her voice was a whisper, her eyes innocent. "Let me help you to your room."

32

"You sure you're up to this?" Dagger pulled his truck to a stop and killed the lights.

"Never felt better," Padre grinned. "Just don't walk too fast.".

Fog snaked its way from the forest preserve behind them, crept through the underbrush, and curled around their feet. They made their way down the road toward the lake and stood in front of the townhouse where Rachel had died. The moon played tag with a sky full of clouds.

Dagger turned on his flashlight, throwing a wide beam on the shoreline. They ambled side-by-side down the beachfront. "Let's think about this. Rachel never lets on to anyone that she regained her memory. She returns to Cedar Point to ... do what?"

The beam caught a wave as it drifted toward them, lapping onto the sand, and depositing a stream of foam. Dagger stopped and watched as the wave lazily retreated. The air had a damp chill to it and off in the distance lightning lit up the clouds.

"She probably wanted to tell her husband she was

alive," Padre offered.

"True. And she called him first. Records show the call came from a pay phone at the truck stop off Exit 4 on the toll road."

"And she probably wanted to get the jewelry from where she had hidden it."

The two men continued their search of the shoreline in silence. They were searching for the other earring Rachel had worn the night she died.

"How much time did you say elapsed between the time the murder was reported and you came down to the townhouse?"

"Ten minutes."

Padre thought for a moment. "Doesn't seem like enough time to move the body and replace the rug. She had to have been wrapped in the rug and dumped in the lake."

"I'm not about ready to have Sergeant Duranski call out his divers."

They found a bench and Padre sank down onto it. "Let me just rest a minute." Dagger joined him and the two sat and listened to the thunder rumbling off in the distance.

They had been walking east, away from the Dunes Resort since Dagger figured the killers, if they were to dump the body, would want to do it away from the prying eyes of the resort patrons.

"You know," Dagger started, leaning back, arms stretched across the back of the bench, "this is just too long of a walk for those guys to carry the body away from curious eyes and be gone before I got down here. Are you sure you didn't find a fresh grave anywhere?"

Padre scoffed and massaged his chest where the wound was still tender. "If the shoreline is too close to the Dunes Resort, I would think the surrounding woods would be, too."

"Well, the only other option is they never moved the body."

Thunder rumbled softly, then gradually grew as the winds carried the sound eastward. The two men pondered the possibility and slowly turned toward each other, their minds on the same wave length.

The two men climbed the stairs to the townhouse where Rachel had died. Padre said, "When I stopped by, the washers and dryers were being installed. But the desk clerk said the units might not be occupied until the middle of August."

They made their way around to the back of the townhouses. The beam from the flashlight rested on the back door.

"Here, hold this." Dagger handed Padre the flashlight and fished around in his pocket for his lock pick.

"I'm not seeing you do this, you understand."

"You don't see a thing, Padre. You were never here." He heard the tumblers click and turned the knob.

"This is really stupid, Dagger. Don't you think the delivery men would have smelled a dead body in this heat?"

"Maybe there's a crawl space and the killers did a John Wayne Gacy number on her."

Except for the décor, each of the units was identical, until they reached the third unit.

"Damn, look at the size of this living room." Dagger

flashed the beam across a large fireplace, entertainment center, and wet bar. The kitchen was the size of one you might find in a downtown restaurant.

Padre snapped his fingers. "I remember. The desk clerk said each building had a hospitality room, one unit that would be shared by all and could be reserved for private parties. Look, it even has a pool table."

Dagger walked down an aisle past the laundry room to a storage room. "Well, here's something the other units didn't have." He pointed to a walk-in freezer.

Padre pulled out his handkerchief and carefully flipped on the light switch. "The refrigerators in the other units weren't plugged in, yet this baby is humming to beat the band."

The room contained empty stainless steel shelves and probably served as a pantry. The floor was covered in stark white tile and the two men checked for blood or any other signs of foul play.

"You ready?" Padre asked, his fingers itching to open the freezer.

Dagger smiled. "Let's do it." The freezer door had been padlocked. Dagger used Padre's handkerchief to hold the lock while working the pick through the tumblers. Once it snapped free, he grabbed the large freezer handle, pulled it down, and yanked the door open.

A plume of frosty air billowed through the doorway as if seeking warmth. But it didn't block their view of the body lying on a wooden crate. Her dress was stained red, her blonde hair flowing around her head.

"Wow." The word escaped Padre's throat like crinkled

foil. "I guess your client wasn't imagining it."

Her beauty was frozen in time, her blue eyes locked open in childlike wonder, and her skin tinged in blue. Rachel Tyler was no longer a missing person.

Dagger unfastened the matching earring from Rachel's ear and turned it over. "Now we found the second earring to the collection. All we need is the necklace."

Sara sat on a chair in Nick's hotel room and watched Nick finish his drink and struggle out of his shirt. He fell across the bed giggling, flung the shirt down on the floor. Crawling across the bed, he anchored himself against the headboard. Smiling at Sara, he patted the bedside next to him.

"I don't bite." He blinked lazily, his eyes glazed, speech slurred.

A hotel room in Tyler lingo was a one-bedroom suite on the top floor with a spiral staircase leading up to a loft. The air conditioning purred, drowning out the sound of the light rain pelting the windows.

"Why do you blame yourself, Nick?" Sara was attempting to continue the conversation Nick tried to avoid in the cocktail lounge. She watched his eyes search the room as if he were getting his bearings. She tried another approach. "Did the therapist help?"

Nick laughed. "Sucker cost Dad a hundred bucks a half hour. She wanted to, he changed his voice to a high falsetto, 'fixate on my obsession about my mother and how it might affect my sexual orientation'." A giggle erupted and Nick rubbed his hands over his face, inhaled long and deep. "The minute she heard I had done some modeling, she thought I was gay."

"So, you never did tell her about Rachel."

Nick shook his head. "Couldn't. No. I didn't want to remember."

"What about hypnosis?"

"Didn't want it."

Sara moved to the bed and sat facing Nick. "Know what I think? I think you didn't need hypnosis to remember." She brushed his damp hair from his forehead. "I think that night, or at least parts of it, are so clear you are trying to make them as buried as the parts you don't remember."

Nick grabbed her hand and brought her fingers to his lips. "God, you are beautiful."

Sara slowly pulled her hand away and clasped his between her two hands. His skin was warm, the hair on his arms blonde against his tanned skin. She watched his lids become heavier and close.

Unexpectedly Nick whispered, "God, she was beautiful."

"She?" Sara asked. "Rachel?"

"I couldn't believe it when I saw her there. She looked like she was asleep, lying on the floor." Nick closed his eyes tightly, pressed his fingers to the corners of his eyes.

Sara thought she saw tears and when he opened his eyes, she saw that they were red.

"I thought I must have done it. I was lying on the couch, actually," he giggled again, "fell off of it. I had been to a party and had a few too many brownies." More giggles erupted. "But then I felt the blood on the back of her head when I tried to help her up. She wouldn't move."

Sara felt Nick's hand tremble and heard his voice crack, the tears coming to the surface. She turned and sat next to him, tried to put her arm around him. Nick scooted down on the bed and wrapped his arms around her, his head on her chest. She tentatively touched his back, not quite sure what his intentions were. But she felt his body shudder and only when she heard the stifled whimpers did she realize he was crying.

She cradled him in her arms, tears coming to her own. Whatever Nick thought he did that night, he was incapable of removing Rachel's body on his own. But why should there have been a body? The crew members said she was on the boat.

"Nick?" She stroked the back of his head and waited for the trembling to stop. "Nick? According to your father, Rachel disappeared off the yacht. How could she have been dead on the living room floor?"

"No," Nick mumbled against her blouse. "Dad paid them off to say that. The next morning I was lying on the grass by the pier, my clothes all wet. I must have carried Rachel's body down to the water, probably weighted it down."

Sara thought for a moment. She gathered her hair with one hand to pull it out of the way and went back to stroking Nick's head. Dagger had shown the picture to Pete, one of the crew members. He recognized Rachel's picture and had claimed to have partied all night with Rachel. Someone was lying.

"Think back, Nick. I know everything is fuzzy but somehow, in your condition, I doubt you could have carried

Rachel's body out of the house and all the way down to the pier on your own. And just the fact that she just showed up again proves that she didn't die the first time."

"That's a lie. Dagger is wrong."

"I don't think so." She wanted to tell him she was the one who saw Rachel that night, that she knew absolutely sure Rachel had been alive. Instead she said, "Maybe what you think you might have dreamed was real and what was real might have been a dream. It's just a matter of sorting it all out in your head. He was silent. Sara could feel his body relax, his breathing slow and even. Was he asleep? Did he not hear a word she said?

Slowly Nick sat up, raked a hand through his hair, and stared intently straight ahead. He had the strangest look on his face, eyes suddenly clear.

"There was something else." His head twitched, as though the mind was trying to cast off stray cobwebs. "Rachel did talk to me. I remember she bent over me on the couch, kissed me on the forehead and said 'sweet dreams'. I found that so strange because I remember looking over and also seeing her still lying on the floor."

33

Sara checked the rearview mirror before pulling out. She didn't feel comfortable driving Dagger's '64 Mustang convertible. He said it was worth a lot of money, a classic, and she didn't feel that confident yet behind the wheel.

She pressed a button and the motorized convertible top folded down. Once it was secured, Sara pulled the Mustang out into traffic. The earlier storm had moved through leaving a humid wind which felt good rustling through her hair. Once she left the downtown lights the sky lit up with millions of stars.

She used her cellular phone to call Dagger but got the irritating busy signal when either the call was out of range or the cellular service lines were tied up. Next she tried calling Worm at home to see if he had been able to identify the girlfriend of Rachel's who could pass for her twin sister.

Sara placed the phone back in her purse and checked her rearview mirror. Small pinpoints of light were growing a little too quickly. Maybe it was her imagination but she could swear a truck had followed her from the hotel.

She maneuvered the Mustang along a road that wound

through the forest preserve. She picked up the phone and tried Dagger again. Finally, she got through.

Dagger said, "We hit the jackpot tonight." He proceeded to tell her where he and Padre found Rachel.

She told him about her conversation with Nick. "I don't think he had anything to do with Rachel's disappearance but it has been tearing him up. You should have seen him tonight, Dagger." Sara watched as the truck's lights filled the rearview mirror. "Oh, my."

"Sara?"

"I think someone followed me from the hotel."

"Where are you at?"

Sara turned down a frontage road and slowed down. The truck turned, too.

"I just turned down the road that runs alongside the stone quarry. The truck followed."

"I'm not too far away. Hang in there, Sara."

Dagger never let his foot off the gas pedal as he exited the toll road. He had left Padre to wait for Sergeant Duranski and a couple of representatives of the Cedar Point Police Department. Padre had a plan, so Dagger left him to work it out and hitch a ride home with one of the detectives.

"Sara, talk to me. What's happening?" He didn't like the dead silence. He approached the forest preserve from the opposite direction and could see the fence surrounding the vast emptiness of the quarry. Dagger reached into the glove box and pulled out one of his spare pistols. This one was a Bersa Series 95 .380 automatic. Lightweight, pocket-size, with an overall length of only six-and-a-half inches.

Yellow eyes peered out from the underbrush and then scurried across the road. Dagger swerved to avoid hitting the raccoon.

"Sara?" Dagger tried again. He wasn't getting a dial tone so he knew the phone line was still open. Now it wasn't necessary. Up ahead he saw a blue truck with a cap pulling off the road. Dagger tossed the phone on the seat and gunned it. His truck fishtailed around the corner and skidded into the road behind the blue pickup.

He almost missed the turnoff the pickup had taken and had to backup, tires screeching. Racing down the unmarked path, Dagger pulled up alongside the pickup just as it rammed the Mustang through the fence. Dagger jumped out of his truck. He watched in horror as the Mustang with Sara inside soared off into the blackness, down into the quarry.

"SARA." His scream echoed through the quarry. The driver of the truck fired a shot at Dagger, then backed the pickup out onto the road and disappeared in a cloud of dust and gravel.

Dagger dove toward the edge of the quarry and grabbed onto the mangled fence. Several hundred feet below he could see the light from the headlights of the Mustang and then an explosion as the car crashed onto the floor of the quarry.

Dagger yelled, "NO," and buried his face in his hands. He rolled away from the carnage and lay on his back, the palms of his hands pressed against his eyes. "God, Sara. What have I done?" The smell of dirt and wet leaves filled his nostrils. The crackling fire sounded distant and then the smell of melting metal filled the air. And there was something else. A rippling, a sound like a huge flag flapping in the breeze. Dagger stared up at the sky and turned his head in time to see the gray hawk flying out of the quarry and landing on a huge branch overhead.

Dagger blinked quickly. "Sara?"

I'm sorry about your car, Dagger.

Dagger rolled onto his stomach. His quiet sigh of relief swelled to uproarious laughter. He could feel tears welling so he covered his face and laughed even harder. "Damn, I envy you." He pushed himself to a kneeling position.

Dagger, I can't shift back. I don't have any clothes.

The detective stared at the hawk, it's brilliant blue eyes that pierced the haze.

"Well, Sweetheart," he chuckled, "I think you have a problem."

"See, you still beat me back." Dagger placed a cup of tea on the coffee table for Sara, who was drying her hair with a towel. She had already showered and changed into shorts and an oversized shirt. He was amazed. The entire ordeal didn't appear to have even phased her. "Come here," he whispered.

Sara dropped the towel on the bar stool and combed her hair with her fingers. She tentatively approached, only to have Dagger pull her toward him and wrap his arms around her. Her hair smelled of oranges and bananas and her body no longer shook when he touched her. He broke the embrace and held her at arm's length. "You scared the hell out of me."

She smiled timidly and repeated, "I'm really sorry about your car."

"No problem. I'll get another."

She sat on the couch gathering her legs under her. And as she sipped her tea Dagger told her about the second earring. He lifted his shirt collar and used it to wipe the dirt from his face. The shirt smelled like smoke, and pieces of damp leaves still clung to the fabric.

"Padre had us lock everything back up and then he called Sergeant Duranski in on the case since we found the body in his town. And if he found me standing there with a dead body and a lock pick in my hand, what we found in the freezer would not be admissible in court. So Padre was going to tell him the back door was unlocked and we were suspicious of the locked freezer."

"When are you going to tell Mr. Tyler?"

"Padre will tell him in the morning."

34

Robert Tyler was up early the next morning. After Padre had called about Rachel, Robert couldn't take his eyes off Rachel's portrait. He wanted to lash out at someone, wanted to line up the family members and find out what role everyone played in Rachel's disappearance five years ago. But another part of him didn't want to know, didn't want to think that any member of his family could be that cold and vindictive.

Padre told him Dagger would be stopping by with news about the earring he had found at the murder scene. Robert couldn't think of anything else after Padre hung up. It was bad enough someone in the family might be a prime suspect in Rachel's murder. Now, he had to wrestle with the thought that his beloved Rachel was involved in a robbery.

Eric entered the dining room dressed for his usual weekend round of golf. "Coffee fresh, Dad?"

"Hmmm?" Robert, lost in thought, pulled his attention from the portrait hanging on the wall. "Oh, yes. They just brought the coffee out." He watched his elder son load his plate with a sample of everything on the buffet table. Eric

jammed a celery stick in his mouth and carefully maneuvered his overflowing plate to the table.

The wall of windows in the dining room displayed a sky
of fast-moving clouds, residuals from last nights storm.
Behind those clouds was a blue sky and a promise of clear
skies for the remainder of the day.

Robert's chest tighten as he studied the white stripe in
Eric's hair and how much his son resembled his mother,
Theresa. Nicholas, on the other hand, took after Robert's
side of the family. But Eric had his business drive; Nick had
his mother's wanderlust.

Although Robert had promised Dagger he wouldn't
bring up the subject, he thought a subtle mention couldn't
hurt. "With everything that has happened, I thought I would
take a few days off, maybe go up to The Abbey."

Eric's coffee cup hovered, his eyes held Robert's gaze.

"The Abbey?" Edie echoed from the doorway. She
glanced at Eric as she walked to the buffet table, her white
sandals clicking along the solid oak floor. "But that place is
so dark, Robert. If you want to get away, there is no place
like one of the islands." Edie surveyed the buffet table and
settled on a plate of fresh fruit and a blueberry scone.
Sitting down, she glared across the table at her husband.

Nick arrived dressed in tennis whites and looking well-
rested. "Well, it's unusually quiet in here." He poured himself a glass of orange juice, grabbed a bagel and cream
cheese and sat down next to his brother.

"And where were you last night?" Edie tried to turn the
subject to Nick.

Nick eyed her over his glass of juice. "I stayed up most

of the night talking to a friend."

Robert checked his watch and was relieved when Lily appeared with Dagger trailing behind.

Dagger waited for Lily to leave and smiled at the curious stares from the Tyler brood.

"Well, well." Edie was the first to speak. "Don't you usually hi-jack planes on Saturdays?"

Edie had once commented that Dagger's appearance ... his penchant for wearing black clothing combined with his long hair, dark eyes, and a deep summer tan that failed to fade in the winter, must make people want to change planes when they saw him boarding.

"That's Tuesdays. Airports are too crowded on weekends."

Robert rose and shook Dagger's hand. "Coffee?"

Dagger declined. He noticed that the only person who seemed relaxed was Nick. Maybe his soul-searching talk with Sara last night cleared the fuzziness in his memory even more. Dagger would be curious to get Nick in a one-on-one.

"Let me guess." Eric dabbed a napkin to his mouth. "Someone spotted Rachel hitchhiking last night."

Robert's face turned ashen and Eric made an abrupt apology.

"Please have a seat," Robert offered.

"I can't stay. I just thought you might be interested to hear about the earring I found at the crime scene." He dug into his pants pocket.

"Not that again." Edie sank back in her chair.

Dagger set the earring on the table.

"Wait." Edie sat up. "I thought the earring was black?"

Dagger said, "Cleaned up rather nicely, don't you think?"

"My god," Robert said as he picked up the earring. "What is it?"

"You are looking at a pink diamond."

Edie's face turned pasty white. Her fingers twitched and Dagger could sense she was itching to touch it. Typical female? Would Sheila's reaction been the same? As if trying to distance herself, Edie pushed away from the table, stood, and gripped the back of the chair.

"Where on earth would Rachel get a pink diamond?" Edie turned to Robert.

"Don't look at me. I didn't buy it for her."

"It's fake," Eric said, picking up the diamond and holding it up to the light. His gaze shifted to Dagger. "Right?"

Dagger smiled. "No. Rachel went through a lot of trouble to camouflage these. And where there's one, there should be another." He let that statement hang in the air.

Nick grabbed for the earring and felt the weight. "Dad?" He turned toward his father. "Do you think this is why Rachel disappeared five years ago? Maybe she was hiding out from whomever she stole it from."

Robert steepled his fingers in thought. "Rachel would never have done something like that."

Dagger should have been busy watching to see whose imaginery wheels were churning, whose eyes resembled the proverbial deer in headlights. Instead, he found himself gazing at Rachel's portrait and then Edie who was standing just in front of it, back up to Rachel's picture. Then a sudden thought struck him.

Dagger picked up a picture of Edie lying on his desk and scanned it into the computer. Using computer graphics, he changed her short red hair to long blonde. The thought had struck him when he saw Edie standing next to Rachel's picture. Except for the hair and eyes, there was some resemblance. They couldn't pass for twins but they had the same nose, bone structure. It wasn't unusual for close friends to dress alike, wear their hair the same.

The first call Dagger had made was to Worm. He asked the reporter to search Rachel's yearbooks and pictures from college for a classmate by the name of Edie Winthrup.

Sara had mentioned that Edie wore contacts. Dagger changed the eye color of the image on the screen to blue. He printed out the color picture and held it next to the picture of Rachel.

"Damn." Dagger picked up the phone and called Robert.

"Mr. Tyler, tell me again everything Rachel said to you when she called."

"Not again."

"You have to face the fact that the Williamsburg Collection was stolen and the last person who had it was your wife."

"I just can't …" Robert inhaled long and deep. "Damn, I can't believe this is happening."

Dagger gave Tyler a few moments. Finally, Tyler repeated what he remembered from the night Rachel called.

"Are you sure? Maybe there was something she said which you thought unimportant at the moment."

"Wait. Yes, I remember now. She asked if I still had the kangaroo."

"The kangaroo?"

"Yes, and I don't for the life of me know what it means."

Dagger told him it might be a clue as to where the necklace is and he should spend the time thinking back on everything Rachel had said, done, purchased, whatever might jog his memory. After he hung up, Dagger grabbed the picture of Rachel and composite of Edie and left.

The ivory elephants danced on the wall as the front door rattled.

"WORM, I KNOW YOU'RE IN THERE!"

Worm cast a look of disgust at the door and mumbled, "Go away." He hadn't expected Sheila to actually camp out on his doorstep. He read his last entry on the monitor and added another sentence, his long fingers dancing across the keyboard.

Padre had kept him updated on the discovery of Rachel's body and he wanted to get that portion of the story written while it was still fresh in his mind.

Sheila banged on his door again.

"I'LL BE RIGHT THERE," Worm yelled. He gathered up all his notes littering the table, floor, couch, and shoved them in his briefcase. He added Rachel's yearbook, which he had just started to check through for an Edie Winthrop, just as Dagger had requested.

"WORM!"

"All right, already." Worm picked up his notes on Sara and tossed them generously around the living room. "Oops." He closed out the document on the screen of his laptop.

Straightening the elephant wall hangings, Worm checked his flushed face in the mirror before opening the door.

"It's about time." Sheila charged past Worm.

"What's the problem, Sheila?" He closed the door and watched with amusement as she surveyed his furnishings.

"Who do you think you are to just call and leave a message that you'll be working at home, not one but two days in a row?" She tossed her purse on the couch and went immediately to the papers on the table. "You don't answer the phone, don't return phone calls." She cast a cursory glance toward him. "Don't keep me updated."

"When I have something to report, you'll be the first person I call."

"Wonderful." She jerked a chair out from the table, saw the threadbare seat and nicked wood and thought better of it. Her head swiveled from side to side, checking the ceiling, the floor, her feet, as if half-expecting something to crawl up her leg. "You know, we pay you a pretty good salary. Can't you find a better apartment?"

Worm ignored her and sat down, shuffled some papers together, pulled out a notepad. He had no plans on offering her anything to drink. After a few moments of silence he asked, "Don't you have something better to do?"

Sheila spied Sara's name on a document lying on the

coffee table and smiled. She settled on the couch and started reading.

"That doesn't reveal much." Worm checked his watch. He had a meeting with the editor of the Porter County Tribune to show him the story he was developing.

"You're right." She tossed the document down with disgust. "Maybe I picked the wrong man for the job."

Worm picked up the discarded report and added it to another pile. "If you think someone else can get faster results, then by all means." The words caught in his throat. This was not the time to act cocky, especially since he didn't have another job yet. He leaned forward, hands mapping out a story on their own, part of the genes from his mother's Italian side of the family.

"You know, Sheila, I'm kinda between a rock and a hard place here. If I stay in the office, I get sidetracked. When I work at home, I've got this family thing going." His hands swayed to the left, then the right, back and forth. "Part of the agreement of paying such low rent is I gotta help my uncle in the greenhouse on the weekends. If I try to work on this," he pointed to the short pile of notes on Sara, "then I have my Mom calling asking why 'donna you help Uncle Maggio'." He forced a smile. Sheila wasn't smiling. Now the hands splayed open, palms up. "What's a guy to do?" He glanced at her white shorts and sleeveless top. "You look great. Going to the yacht club?" Compliments with Sheila always worked.

"Yes." Sheila smiled, her fingers fidgeting with the neckline of her sailor collar. "Fashion show brunch." She checked her watch and stood. "I'll let you get back to your family duties." She turned back when she reached the door. "And Worm, the telephone is a wonderful invention. Use it."

35

"Remember me?" Dagger lifted his sunglasses and looked at Pete Foster, who was hosing down a forty-two-foot Bayliner.

"Digger?"

"No, Dagger." He placed his sunglasses back on the bridge of his nose. "I need to show you a couple of pictures."

Pete turned the water off and dried his hands on his cut-offs. He followed Dagger to a shady spot by Salty's office. "It was time for a break anyway." Pete nodded toward the houseboat. "Want something to drink?" Dagger declined. Several minutes later Pete returned with a can of lemonade.

"Is this Rachel Tyler?" Dagger showed him Rachel's picture with her blue eyes sultry and blonde hair flowing.

"I thought I confirmed this last time you were here."

"Look again." Dagger handed him a picture of Edie, her hair blonde, contacts blue.

Pete looked at the picture and grinned his surfer boy grin. "Is this some test?"

"They look alike to you?"

Puzzled, Pete looked at the pictures again. "They aren't the same woman?"

"Nope. The only difference is the mole. Did the Rachel you bumped pelvises with have a mole?"

Pete held up both pictures, searching first one face then the other. "No, come to think of it, she didn't." He handed the pictures back. "All you really had to do was check for my skin under her nails." The surfer boy grinned again.

"Of course," Dagger smiled back. But he wasn't smiling at what Pete said. He remembered that Edie had those long, art deco nails. Rachel didn't like sculptured nails and never wore anything but clear polish on her short nails.

Edie pushed her way into Luke's room, tugging at her sunglasses and shoving them in her purse.

"What? No hello?" He closed the door, folded his arms across his chest just below the bright yellow word *Aruba* on his shirt.

"Where is it?" She found the black earring on the coffee table. Taking off her shoe, she brought the heel down on the earring, shattering the plastic into bits and pieces.

"What the hell did you do that for?"

"No wonder Dagger didn't follow you after you took the earring," Edie said. "It's just costume jewelry, for crissake. Rachel was wearing the real ones." Edie smiled slowly. "She was clever enough to camouflage the damn things."

"She had them all along?" He scraped the black fragments into his hand and dumped them in an ashtray.

Edie dragged one lacquered nail across her lower lip. "I don't lie about diamonds." Edie told Luke about Dagger's visit.

"Well, he obviously knew we'd be after it so he made a fake one. I told you before, he isn't anyone you should take lightly."

"We need the mate to the earring, Luke. And what about the body? Someone is going to stumble on it." She paced in a tight circle, pulled her hat off her head and flung it on the couch. Her nondescript navy suit was toned down so as not to draw attention. She had left the expensive pearls at home and the hat was an attempt to somewhat conceal her identity. When you're one of the Tyler brood, you are easily recognized.

"Where are your goons hiding the body?"

"Just calm down." Luke stopped her in mid-stride, placed his large hands on her back and massaged her neck. "I'll get both earrings. It's your job to find the necklace."

She pulled away and continued pacing. There was a time when they would have left a trail of clothes to the bedroom or not even made it to the bedroom. But when it came to money, neither one wanted to be sidetracked.

Edie said, "I tore that damn house apart five years ago. And I questioned her family and friends til I was blue in the face."

"Well, search the house again."

"Like I haven't? Our chances of finding it are …" Edie glanced toward the opened patio door. "What on earth is that?" The gray hawk stared back at her and ruffled its feathers.

"It's a fuckin' bird. Now pay attention."

The gray hawk leaped from the railing and flew off.

"Just do your part, Edie. Dagger would be stupid to keep the diamond at his house. But we've been following him. I think I might know who he gave it to."

36

"What a bloody long plane ride." J.C. Kinnecutt gulped the glass of water Dagger offered him and settled back against the cool leather. His pale blue eyes took in the chrome and black décor and airiness of the house. "Nice digs."

J.C. had called Dagger from the airport, got directions to Sara's house, and rented a car. He had yet to check into his hotel because his priority was to see the diamond earring. His white shirt was soaked. J.C. pinched the fabric between two fingers and fanned it away from his body.

The curator was younger than Dagger anticipated. The picture he had formulated in his mind of a gray-haired gent with bushy eyebrows couldn't have been farther from the truth. J.C. was tall and slender with a head of thick blonde hair. He guessed him to be in his early forties only because of the crinkles around his eyes and the hint of gray at his temples. No wedding ring but a nice Rolex watch. He even had great taste in cars since J.C. had rented a Porsche.

"What on earth do you have in there?" J.C. walked over and stood in front of the closed Plexiglas door. Einstein was on one of the high tree branches napping. "A lovely bird. You just have one macaw in that big room?"

"Yes. Einstein and I both like to have a lot of space."

Rubbing his hands together, J.C. returned to the sofa saying, "Let's have a look at the darling."

When Dagger removed the lid to the box and pulled out the earrings, J.C. gasped and quickly pulled a narrow black box from his pocket.

"You have both earrings now?"

"Yes." Dagger sat on the leather love seat. He watched J.C. pull a cap off the pointed end of his instrument. A red *Ready* light was flashing. "What are you doing?"

"This is a thermal tester. There are some new fakes going around called moissanite. Can fool some of the best experts. Only one problem. Moissanite conducts electricity whereas diamonds don't." The *Ready* light stopped flashing and J.C. pressed the pencil-thin point to the diamond earring. The word *Diamond* lit up. He spent several minutes studying each earring, then peered through a loupe for the final examination. He groaned like a man in his last seconds of orgasm. "I can't believe it."

"They're real?"

"My god." He set the loupe down. "Absolutely."

Dagger picked up the black box which could be mistaken for a beeper had it been three inches shorter. He scratched a finger across his jaw bone and eyed his visitor. "I can only assume you already tested the set you have back at the museum."

"Practically had a coronary when I saw the results. But it still didn't tell me if what you had was genuine."

"What if someone didn't have one of these nifty things?" Dagger asked, holding the black box up. "How would he be sure?"

Smiling, J.C. opened a small case. It was the size of a shaving kit. He retrieved a stone and a pair of tweezers. "Do you have matches?"

Dagger walked over to the wall of bookcases where Sara kept a long butane lighter for lighting candles. He stood in front of J.C. and pressed the button, sending a flame out the tip.

"Good, now if you could hold the flame under this stone." J.C. held the tweezers over the flame. "Not too close or we'll have soot on the bottom."

"What does this do?"

"This particular stone I brought is a moissanite. When it comes in contact with a flame that is at least two-hundred-and-fifty degrees centigrade, it changes color to a bright yellow." Within twenty seconds, the colorless diamond changed color. Next, he held the flame under the earring. It didn't change color.

Dagger turned the flame off and set the lighter on the coffee table. He settled into the leather love seat, crossing one ankle over his knee, right elbow on the armrest. "Tell me, J.C., how does someone get valuables out of your country without Customs noticing?"

J.C. stared longingly at the earrings. "All anyone has to do is fill out a declaration form listing what they are taking out of the country." He chuckled, adding, "And lie a little."

"What about airport searches?"

"They only do them randomly," J.C. replied.

"Perfect for a model. They have suitcases of costume jewelry."

"Absolutely. And Customs will just rely on the declaration. That and a pretty smile from a gorgeous filly will get her through Customs quicker than you can say," J.C. admired the earrings again, "diamonds."

"You can come out now." Dagger announced. Sara slowly made her way down the stairs from her bedroom. "I thought you might be slinking around somewhere. You didn't want to meet J.C.?"

"He seems to know his diamonds."

"Yes, he does. He's going to stick around town for a few days in the hopes that we find the necklace."

"He was pretty adamant about taking the earrings with him."

"Guess he was afraid of letting them out of his sight. I should really give them to Padre to put in the police department vault but for some reason, even I don't trust them out of my sight."

Sara crossed her legs and sat on the floor, elbows on the coffee table. "Was that Worm who called?"

"Yes. He checked records from Rachel's college days and did find an Edie Winthrop listed. And Pete remembered that the woman on the yacht that night did not have a beauty mark."

"So you think Edie wore a wig?"

"Probably." Dagger carried the earrings to his concealed room for safekeeping. He returned and sifted through papers on his desk, sat down and switched on his computer. As it hummed, clicked, and did all its other computer machinations, he watched Sara play with her hair, grabbing narrow clumps and braiding them. "And besides," Dagger added, "Edie was the only one who went tearing out of the house after my visit this morning."

The gray hawk had waited up in the trees to follow the first Tyler who left the house. Edie had gone straight to Luke's hotel. Eric and Robert, on the other hand, kept their golf date.

"Are you going to tell Nick about Edie? She obviously is the one who convinced Nick he killed Rachel. And where do you think Eric was when all this was going on?"

"Lot of questions, young lady." He looked over at her, the intensity in her eyes as she busied her fingers. It was a welcome alternative to her chewing on her knuckles. "I already know Eric was at the office the evening Rachel disappeared. He worked late trying to catch up on paperwork. And I don't think we should break it to Nick just yet. I can't predict what his reaction might be, and there's a good chance he could screw up the entire investigation."

"But Edie would have needed help getting Rachel to a hospital and then to The Carmelite Retreat."

"That's her buddy, Luke, I presume."

"Hmm." She busied her fingers some more until she had ten thin long braids on each side of her head.

Dagger shoved a fist under his chin and stared at the young woman, the fingers working over, under, over, under. Her bright eyes staring vacantly. He finally asked, "What's happening in that head of yours?"

Sara shrugged. "I just remember the report Skizzy ran of the phone calls made from the Tyler house before and after Rachel's disappearance. Some were to Australia."

"Luke helped to steal the diamonds so he was probably still in Australia."

Over, under, over, under. Sara's fingers worked faster. "Maybe."

Edie pushed open the door to Robert's bedroom and slid in, closing the door softly behind her. Through the opened patio doors she could smell a variety of perennials from the gardens below. She went directly to a large cherry wood armoire in the corner.

When Rachel first disappeared, Edie had searched through every box of jewelry Rachel owned, every secret hiding place Edie knew of, and every wall safe. It wasn't difficult to discover the combination. Robert uses his wedding anniversary, a major mistake most people make. They either use a birth date of a family member or some other significant date.

Edie had made one major blunder. When Rachel returned from her photo shoot in Australia five years ago, Edie had called her in the limo five times, insisting that she come right home, hysterical that she not let her suitcase out of her sight. She had under-estimated Rachel's intelligence. But more seriously, she under-estimated her integrity. Edie could never keep a cool head when that much money was involved.

Being a Tyler had its advantages: prestige, name recognition, an enviable mansion to live in, access to a resort in just about any country. Unfortunately, Edie's pre-nuptial entitles her to only the money her husband earns, not what was held under corporate purse strings. And with the way she and Eric spent money, there wouldn't be enough to keep her in pearls let alone diamonds.

"Dammit, Rachel. Where did you hide it?"

Edie pulled out a stack of sweaters and set them on the bed. Then she started to press on the back wall. Most custom-made armoires were designed to specific recommendations. By using her best bedroom techniques, Edie had the cabinetmaker spilling every secret known to man and then some. She found out Rachel had requested a secret door in the back wall.

Suddenly, a door sprung open. Excited, Edie shoved her hand inside the compartment but felt empty space. "Damn!"

"Looking for something?"

Edie screamed and lurched back from the armoire. Lily stood in the doorway, a look of disgust clouding her face.

Pressing a hand to her chest, Edie explained, "Just looking for Eric's favorite golf sweater. He thought his father might have it."

"Didn't mean to startle you but I usually don't expect to find anyone in Mr. Tyler's private bedroom." She braced the door open and waited. Reluctantly, Edie left.

37

"What have you got, Coffey?" Padre spoke into the walkie-talkie. Detective Ben Coffey was seated on the rooftop of the Dunes Resort with a pair of binoculars aimed at the road leading down to the beachfront townhouses.

"I've got a white sport utility vehicle headed your way. It looks like one Luke Gabriel behind the wheel. He's alone."

"Okay, let's get ready boys." Sergeant Duranski unfolded his body from the floor of the townhouse. He gave Padre a stern look. "Hope that friend of yours is right."

"He's rarely wrong."

Duranski's bulky shoulders shrugged. "All the private dicks say that."

Padre and Dagger had it all pre-planned. After Dagger dropped the pink bombshell on the Tyler dining room table, it was his hope that someone would go racing out to the Dunes Resort to check the body for the other earring.

Duranski and his men were quite comfortable in the center unit with its wrap-around couch and entertainment center. They had rigged a surveillance camera in the storage room which housed the walk-in freezer. The monitor was sitting on the kitchen counter, ready to display whatever occurred in the adjoining storage room.

Lansing stood and pulled on his utility belt. He stared intensely at the monitor. The walkie-talkie blared again. "All yours," Coffey announced.

The SUV's engine died at the rear of the building. The blinds were closed. Luke wouldn't be able to see in. They waited and watched, careful not to move, not to make a sound. If Luke had a key to the back door, there was a chance he also had a key to the door leading into the kitchen where the men were waiting.

They heard a rustling at the back door, a key being inserted, the door handle turning. They could hear the door squeak as it opened, heels click against the tiled floor. On the monitor, the lights in the storage room flipped on and the cops watched as Luke unlocked the freezer and entered.

Dead bodies shouldn't bother Luke. He had seen his share. But there was something about seeing Rachel's body that briefly saddened him. She was beautiful, even in death. He was sorry he ever hired Joey and Mince. Luke would have been able to get Rachel to tell him what they wanted to know. A woman that beautiful would do anything to keep from having her face marred. He would have had her chirping like a bird.

Luke checked Rachel for the second earring. There wasn't one. A search under the body, on the floor, then the storage room itself, proved fruitless. It didn't take long for

him to find the silk scarf, bright yellow with splashes of
scarlet roses. He inhaled deeply from the fabric balled in his
hand and his eyes narrowed. Luke slammed the door to the
townhouse and stormed back to his SUV.

"I thought Edie's scarf might come in handy." Dagger
popped open a beer can and handed it across the
bar to Padre.

"Oh, no," Padre protested. "The doctor wouldn't be too
happy about that."

"WHAT'S UP, DOC. AWK." Einstein flew over to
the couch.

"Hey, Einstein. How's the feather flying?" Padre
laughed as Einstein gave a good impression of a colorful fan.

Sara set a cup of hot tea in front of Padre and said, "This
is my grandmother's secret recipe."

Padre asked Dagger, "How did you get Edie's scarf?"

Dagger glanced at Sara and smiled. "Let's just say a little bird flew in and stole it from her."

"Right," Padre chuckled. "However you got it, it was the
perfect touch. About now I'm sure Luke is tearing into Edie
accusing her of stealing the other earring."

"You want him to think Edie is working behind his
back?" Sara scooted onto the bar stool and rested her elbows
on the bar, a fist pressed against her cheek, one pinky finger
working its way toward her mouth. The bar was nestled in
the corner of the living room. The black marbled top reflected the ceiling lights.

"Definitely." Dagger took a long pull on his beer, his gaze resting on Sara's fist. "Nothing like partners thinking they are being betrayed. All the dirt settles at the bottom."

Padre's eyes blinked wearily and he finished his tea in one long gulp. "At least Duranski has more faith in you now."

Dagger shrugged. "Like I care."

"You have to keep guys like him on your side, Dagger." He pushed the cup away and scooted his stool away from the bar.

Sara pulled her fist away from her face and clasped her hands in her lap. "Padre, do you have a way of finding out where people were at any given time?"

Padre looked at Dagger, then Sara. He stood and turned sideways to face Sara, his body leaning against the bar. He had a smile of amusement, the kind that he usually reserved for school children who would ask him curiosity questions during a precinct tour.

"Sure. If he was serving time somewhere, or the guest of a jail cell awaiting bail, maybe search through charge card receipts. It would give us some idea. Why do you ask?"

Dagger eyed her curiously from the serving side of the bar, his feet apart, arms crossed. He watched her fingers intertwine, as though they battled each other for territorial rights. 'Shall we stay here? Head for the mouth?' Sara seemed to take control and they remained in her lap.

"Just curious if Luke really was in Australia and exactly when Edie met him."

"AWK, AUSTRALIA, KANGAROO." Einstein flapped his wings and danced on the perch.

Padre cast a curious gaze toward Dagger. "Guess I could do a little more checking. In the meantime, old man Tyler needs to figure out what Rachel meant when she said 'kangaroo'. Is it animal, mineral, or vegetable?"

"He's going to have to do a more thorough search of the house." Dagger walked Padre to the door.

"KANGAROO PAW, AWWWKK."

Sara jumped off the bar stool. "Okay, mister. It's bedtime." She clapped her hands and Einstein flew off the perch and into the aviary.

"KANGAROO PAW, KANGAROO PAW."

"Kangaroos don't have paws, Einstein." Sara watched him fly onto one of the branches and peek at her between the fronds. She switched on the nightlight. Before turning away, she cast a quizzical gaze at the macaw. Sometimes things Einstein said didn't make sense ... until much later.

After Padre left, Sara went upstairs to her room. Dagger knew she wouldn't be going to bed. About four times a week he would hear her patio door slide open. He just wasn't sure if she was going out for exercise or to keep in practice.

Curiosity got the best of him. Dagger grabbed his binoculars and went upstairs. Her bedroom smelled of fresh flowers and subtle perfume. In the dark he could barely make out the rattan chair nestled in the corner and the fern hanging from the ceiling.

He sat on the floor, elbows on the cushioned window seat, binoculars in hand. Focusing the binoculars, he spotted the gray hawk gliding in a slow circular pattern. The night-vision binoculars lit up the night and were strong enough for him to see the detailed wing panel and tail banding.

Dagger sat mesmerized by the grace and power of the large bird. And then, as it swooped closer to the ground, it shifted into the gray wolf. Dagger's mouth literally fell open. The wolf was unbelievably fast as it tore off for the open land. And then something he thought he would never see happened. The wolf shifted back to Sara as she ran nude toward the river, her long hair flowing behind her, her hips and legs firm and shapely. She twirled like a dancer giving him a full view of her firm breasts.

"My god. What a body!"

Almost as quickly she shifted back to the gray hawk and rose swiftly, its body outlined against the full moon. To have the speed and senses of the wolf and the hawk was something Dagger couldn't fathom. Then what he realized made his face flush. Sara had the eyesight of the hawk. She could see at night and she could see distances he could only imagine. She could probably see him! He dropped the binoculars just as Einstein alighted on the bed.

"WHAT A BODY. AWK"

"Hey, where did you come from?" He chased Einstein down the stairs and into the aviary. "Sara is too good to you. She left your door open." Dagger pulled the grated door shut and watched as Einstein settled in on his favorite branch.

38

Skizzy pulled the bat close to him and crept from the back room. He wasn't sure what woke him, if it was a noise or just the sense that something wasn't right. His heart pounded behind his ribcage and his hands were beginning to slip off the bat. He gripped it tighter and entered the front of the store.

If there were intruders, why didn't the alarm go off? Did he check the locks on the door earlier? He should have checked them one more time, he thought. Silently he stood listening, waiting for his eyes to adjust. The blinds on the front windows were closed. The street light outside the store had burned out months ago and the city had yet to fix it.

It was difficult to distinguish the shadows, some short, some tall. He thought he saw a shadow move so he gripped tighter on the bat. "Who's there?" Skizzy yelled. "I've got a gun and the silent alarm went off. Police should be here any minute." It was a lie. He didn't have a loaded gun, knowing full well there was a risk of his being shot with his own weapon. And he didn't have a silent alarm to the police or alarm company.

He took another step into the room. Another shadow moved. Maybe his eyes were playing tricks on him. He didn't feel a breeze from a broken window or an opened door. And he would have heard glass breaking. But thieves are clever, a voice in his head said. Should've checked the door one more time last night, Skizzy thought.

A shadow moved.

"Hey!" Raising his bat, Skizzy felt a blow from behind.

"I called you right away," Simon told Dagger. Nodding to the two paramedics leaning against an ambulance, Simon added, "You know, Skizzy ain't gonna let anybody take him to no doctor."

Dagger had pulled on his clothes and driven over as soon as Simon called at six in the morning. Simon had stopped for coffee at the bakery across from Skizzy's Pawn Shop. That was when he noticed the door to the pawn shop ajar. Skizzy would never leave the door open. When Simon stepped inside, he found Skizzy bleeding and lying in a pile of broken glass.

Dagger combed his hair back with his fingers and pulled up the collar of his black pullover. His temples pulsed as he clenched and unclenched his fists.

The morning air was damp and wisps of steam floated above the street where cool air met the warm pavement. The sun was burning through the haze on the horizon as a passenger train rumbled along the tracks at the end of the street.

"Hey, buddy," a rotund paramedic with a doughy face

called out. "You better get to your friend in there and talk him into letting us treat him."

Dagger turned to Simon and said, "Give Doc Akins a call and see if he can get over here quick. If he can," he looked toward the paramedics, "send them on their way."

Once Dagger pushed the door open he saw Skizzy on the floor holding a large piece of glass.

"Get away. Get out of here," Skizzy yelled, lashing out with his makeshift weapon while streams of blood obstructed his eyesight.

"It's me, Skizzy. It's Dagger."

"My god. What have they done to my place, Dagger?"

Dagger knelt beside his friend and examined the gashes on his face and head. "Who did this to you?" He used the alcohol wipes and gauze pads the paramedics had given him. Skizzy's skin was pale and his hands shook.

"They rifled through every crevice in the store looking for it. Pulled all the jewelry out of the case, used the guns to break the showcases. But they didn't get downstairs."

Simon stuck his head in. "Doc is on his way."

Skizzy grabbed the glass shard again. "Who's there?"

"It's okay. It's Simon. And Sara's here, too," Dagger said.

Sara carried a cardboard tray of coffee and juice. "Skizzy, what happened?" She set the tray on the windowsill and pulled her tote bag off her shoulder.

Dagger tried again, "What were the men looking for, Skizzy?"

"No telling what they did, what they planted. Government men probably, planting bugs."

"Drink this, Skizzy." Sara held up a carton of orange juice. She guided the straw to his mouth.

Simon announced, "Here comes Doc."

A lanky man with pointed features stepped into the shop. His silver-streaked hair and youthful face made it difficult to tell his age. But he dressed preppy and wore wire-framed glasses. Doc Akins taught veterinary sciences at the local college. He had turned from people to animals. But his former patients still had a way to reach him and he helped them whenever possible.

Skizzy grabbed Dagger's arm. "No doctor, no. You know what those doctors do. He'll plant a computer chip in me." Skizzy became more agitated the more he talked. His tee shirt was soaked with blood and the cuts on his arms had slivers of glass in them.

Simon grabbed a broom and started to sweep the glass out of the way while Dagger told Skizzy about Doc Akins.

"Doc had his license taken away for giving pot to cancer patients to relieve the effects of chemo. He's a good guy, Skizzy. Just let him take a look at you, clean your wounds, stitch them up."

"No shots. There's stuff in those shots. People get injected with viruses."

Dagger grabbed Skizzy by his bony shoulders. "Calm down." He waited until he had Skizzy's full attention. "Okay, no shots. But if he needs to, let him spray some of the cuts to numb them."

"Okay if I close the door?" Doc pushed the door closed and locked it. "I don't want any of my cop fans sneaking a peek at my business."

Skizzy looked at Doc with renewed interest.

Doc nodded to Dagger. "Let's get him off the floor to some place more comfortable. We should get him out of these clothes so I can see where all the injuries are."

Skizzy's body shuddered as he was helped from the floor. "They ripped them up. Tossed everything out of my drawers looking for something."

Dagger handed Sara some money. "Logan's is open twenty-four hours. Go pick up some underwear, shirts, pants, tennis shoes. Pick up some food there, too. It looks like they dumped everything out of his refrigerator."

"Cut the labels out of the clothes," Doc said.

Dagger looked at him with surprise and shifted his gaze quickly to Skizzy, who furrowed his brow quizzically at Doc. Skizzy was even skeptical of those who seemed too good to be true.

As if to assure the injured man, Doc added, "I'm monitored constantly, Skizzy. I can almost feel their eyes on me, always checking to see whom I'm meeting for lunch, what books I'm buying, what calls I'm making. I have my own methods now and I don't blame you for not trusting me. I find it difficult to trust people, too. Especially those who think they understand or sympathize with me."

"Yeh, they try to think they're your new found friend, yeh." Skizzy's body was racked with chills as he sat on the ripped couch. Cushions had been cut and the stuffing pulled out.

"You're going into shock, friend." Doc pulled the gauze pads from the wounds and opened his gym bag.

Dagger could hear Simon in the shop area sweeping up

more of the glass and cleaning up the showcases. Dagger's
jaws ached from clenching them, and he tried to take deep
breaths to ease his growing anger.

 While Doc cleaned the wounds, Dagger tried again to
get Skizzy to tell him what had happened.

"How many men?"

"Two. You know how light I sleep. I heard something."
Skizzy took a sip of the orange juice. "No way they could
have gotten in, not with the alarm and all those locks. I gotta
get a new alarm. Maybe get rid of the windows. Never heard
an alarm. Can't afford a new one." Skizzy peered out from
under the washcloth.

"We'll get something. You wanted an alarm more high
tech anyway, Skizzy. Now what about the men. Did you get
a look at them?"

"No, not good. Just an outline. One guy about my height
and weight. The other guy flabby. Uglier than sin. Damn, I
thought I was ugly."

He was getting his sense of humor back, Dagger
thought. "What were they looking for, Skizzy?"

"An earring. Hell, I got a showcase of jewelry. Take your
pick, I says. But they didn't like what I had."

Doc sprayed one gaping wound and threaded a surgical
needle. "Need a few stitches here, Skizzy. This is going to
pinch a bit but I'll try to get it done as quickly as possible."

Dagger righted the garbage can, and using latex gloves
from under the sink proceeded to clean up the mess on the
floor. He tossed food and broken bottles from the refrigerator into the garbage. Skizzy was going to need new plates,
glasses and cups. The more devastation Dagger saw in the

cabinets, bathroom, living area, and the shop, the more Dagger's anger grew. He began to toss broken glass into the garbage with such force, he was sounding like a one-man demolition team.

Simon yelled, "Hey, what are you doing in there?"

Dagger dragged the garbage can into the shop and set it next to the one Simon was filling.

"Maybe Skizzy should just find another place. He'll never trust this one to be safe."

Dagger shook his head. "He'd never go for that. He has too much equipment here, and you know how Skizzy is about strange places. He'll be gutting the wallboards looking for listening devices." Dagger flung chunks of broken wood into the garbage. He stared out toward the street. The ambulance was gone but one police car was still there. Skizzy wouldn't file a report. Dagger had no idea what the cops were waiting around for.

Dagger glanced at the surveillance camera anchored from the ceiling. The tape had been removed from the player behind the counter. The alarm hadn't sounded. It worked intermittently and was definitely in need of replacement. Dagger's fist clenched and unclenched along with his jaw.

"I don't like that look," Simon said, resting the handle of the broom under his chin. "Nope, that is a black cloud look."

"I'm okay," Dagger snapped.

Simon went back to sweeping, the corners of his mouth turned down. "Like hell, you're okay," he snapped back.

"Don't worry."

Simon stopped his sweeping and glared at Dagger. "I'll damn well worry if I want to, you stubborn ass." The broom started moving again, dust clouds swirling, glass clinking. The air was tense and after a few minutes of silence, Simon said, "My sister still has some showcases from her days as a jewelry shop owner. They are just collecting dust in her basement."

Dagger looked at the shelves hanging from the walls. "I've got some bookcases and furniture from my old office I can give him."

Simon brushed a hand through his sweat-soaked hair. Dagger peered into the back room. Doc was using tweezers to remove glass from Skizzy's arms. Skizzy's face was clean though bruised and swollen and he sported more gauze pads and bandages than a price fighter.

"Any idea who did this?" Simon asked.

"Oh yeah." Dagger's muscles tensed as he ripped a damaged shelf from the wall and flung it on the floor. "I've got a damn good idea."

From a restaurant next to the bakery, Mince and Joey sat and watched the commotion at the pawn shop.

"Did you see the girl?" Mince asked, fingers spreading the slats of the blinds.

"Yeah. How the hell did she get out of that Mustang?" He checked the cuts on his hands. Skizzy had fought like a tiger and they had to use his own bat to smack him around. Mince with his bum shoulder was of little use.

"I saw it go over the edge."

"Me, too." Joey peered through the blinds as the police car pulled away. "Mince, we gotta keep this to ourselves.

Luke finds out what we tried to do to the girl ..."

"Yeah, I know."

The blinds snapped shut.

Dagger and Simon spent all morning at Skizzy's. Simon borrowed a moving truck and transported his sister's and Dagger's furniture. Dagger made a sweep of the premises and everything in it and assured Skizzy he didn't detect any monitoring devices of any type.

Sara washed and folded the clothes she had purchased for Skizzy after cutting out all the labels. She didn't understand why Skizzy thought he could be tracked with labels, but she would have to save her questions until she and Dagger were alone.

Skizzy had been adamant about Sara's not purchasing food at the health food store. She thought it would be safe. Skizzy said the government preys upon the weakness of the people who latch onto the latest fads, gets them comfortable while the government taints the food or codes the labels. So she had stopped at home to pick up canned goods and meat from the freezer. She also had purchased storage containers and emptied condiments, coffee, sugar, flour, and other staples into the containers so the bar-coded bottles would not be kept in his house.

Sara offered to stay with Skizzy while he napped. She spent the time putting the undamaged merchandise into the display cases and shelves. Then she called Worm and made arrangements to meet him for dinner.

39

"I've searched the storage room in the basement, Sir."
Lily stood in her black and white uniform with its pointed
collar and lace-trimmed pockets. Of all the employees, she
had been the closest to Rachel. She had been the one Rachel
had confided in whenever she needed motherly advice. And
Lily loved her like a daughter.

"Nothing? No stuffed animals resembling a kangaroo?
Pottery, boxes, or containers?"

Lily shook her head to each question, wisps of short,
gray hair curling around a wise and trusting face. Her
heart-shaped mouth was pursed, tears welling up in her
tired eyes at the mere mention of Rachel's name. "I don't
remember her coming home with anything other than
clothes and accessories."

Robert grabbed her hands and held them. "I'm sorry,
Lily. I know you tried your best. Now I would like you to
expand your search to all the upstairs rooms." Wrapping an
arm around her shoulder, he walked her to the door. He
wasn't sure whom he could trust anymore. How involved
was Eric? Did Nick know anything? And how could he not

see Edie for the type of woman she was? How could he sit across from her at breakfast, live under the same roof, and not want to shake her til she gave him the answers he needed?

"It is important, Lily," Robert continued, "that no one, not my sons, my daughter-in-law, or any other employees know what you are looking for."

"I understand, Mr. Tyler. I'll do my best."

He watched her leave, the one person who had grieved the most over Rachel's death. Robert had spent too much time in denial, especially since Rachel's body had never been found. And now he didn't have the heart to tell her he was on his way to the morgue in Michigan City to identify Rachel's body.

Edie rushed into the hotel suite. "Where is it?" She looked from Luke's hands to the coffee table. "You did get it, didn't you?" Her eyes were large green orbs surrounded by thick lashes.

Luke poured two glasses of cognac and motioned for Edie to sit down.

Edie smiled. "Are we toasting our success?" She curled one shapely leg under her as she sat on the couch. The cognac was hot going down but she savored every drop.

"It wasn't there." Luke's eyes watched her reaction.

"What do you mean it wasn't there?" She set the glass on the coffee table and methodically went over a scenario in her mind. "My god, what if it fell off when those two goons were playing hide-the-body?" She set her fiery gaze on

Luke. "I told you those two morons couldn't be trusted."

Luke knew that unless Edie had followed Joey and Mince that night, there wasn't any way she would know where the body was. And he had gotten pretty good at telling when Edie was lying. If Edie didn't take the earring, then Joey and Mince did. Or maybe he wasn't the only one Edie was entertaining. Maybe she was playing them all against each other.

"What about the necklace? Our buyers will buy only the entire set. That detective has one earring, someone has the other, and the necklace is god knows where." Luke tipped back the glass and swallowed the hot liquid in one gulp. "We're not exactly batting a thousand here." He stared at Edie's face, her long nails tapping on the back of the couch. She had an analytical if not sadistic mind. Eric was no match for her. Luke knew women like her marry only for money, rarely for love.

"I tell you, it's not in the house. I thought for sure it would be in that secret compartment." Edie walked over to the window and stared down at Ogden Park eleven floors below. A horse-drawn carriage was taking passengers on a tour of some of the finer points of Cedar Point.

Luke raised his heavy lids, turning the corners of his eyes down even farther. His voice was soothing, but deceiving because there was a threatening glare to his look. "And this is the first you have known of a secret compartment … after five years?"

She turned and leveled an icy stare at him. "Don't start. We both waited for Rachel to get her memory back. I've waited a long time to get my hands on those diamonds."

The door slammed shut and they turned to see Joey and Mince.

"What diamonds?" the two men demanded.

Joey snarled. "You two are full of surprises, aren't you? I knew there was more to this job than just snatching some rich sister-in-law." He sat his butt down on the arm of the couch and let his eyes drift down Edie's frame.

Mince circled the room, like an overgrown fly looking for a place to land. His gaze took in the large suite, tasteful furnishings, expensive Oriental carpeting. "Yeah, Luke. The dame has put you up in some nice digs while Joey and me, we're crammed in a small room with two double beds. What gives? She offering you a hell of a lot more than sex, I take it?"

Luke placed one beefy arm across the back of the couch. He stared at the two men, then at Edie. "I wouldn't mind knowing about the other earring myself."

"What are you looking at me for?" Edie glanced at each of the three men. "Wait a minute. First you tell me you disposed of the body. Now I find out you were holding onto it. What's going on here?" She sank onto the love seat and crossed her legs.

"You tell us," Mince sneered. He walked around the couch and crawled into a side chair. His skin was white, his fingers short and pudgy.

Luke pulled open the drawer in the end table and tossed the floral scarf in Edie's lap. "I didn't find the other earring on the body, but I found this."

Edie held up her scarf at both ends. "You found my scarf there?" She stared over the scarf at three sets of eyes. "Oh no." Her hands dropped to her lap. "I swear, Luke, I have no idea how it got there. I didn't even know where these idiots put her body."

"I believe you," Luke said simply.

"You are kidding." Mince stood and pulled a gun out from under his shirt. "I smell something fishy, Joey."

"Put the gun away," Luke ordered.

Mince wrinkled his pudgy face. "I don't think so. There's more going on here than just a pair of earrings. Talk fast."

Edie looked at Luke. Luke looked at the gun. "Okay." Luke proceeded to tell them about the Williamsburg Collection. By the time he was done, Mince had placed the gun down and slowly sank into the chair.

"Four hundred million?" Joey licked his lips.

"Don't get any ideas." Edie draped the scarf over her lap, lit another cigarette, and dabbed a piece of tobacco off her tongue. "You're not about ready to suck more money out of us."

Propping a foot up on the coffee table, Luke regarded the situation. His gaze shifted to Edie, whose determined look was a dangerous blend of greed and power. Joey and Mince, on the other hand, just reeked greed.

Luke glanced quickly at Edie and then told the two men, "I'm sure if we're successful there would be a nice bonus for you two."

"How nice?" Mince pressed.

Edie took a long drag off her cigarette, staring at Luke through the smoke. "You guys can iron that out later. We have more pressing matters." Setting the scarf aside, she said, "Let's think this through. There are only two people who could have the other earring."

"The cops are one," Luke said.

The word cops brought a chill to the room.

"Sweet jezzus," Mince whispered. "I ain't goin' to jail. I can tell you that right now."

"Where the hell did you hide the body?" Edie demanded.

"It's in one of the new townhouse freezers at the Dunes Resort," Luke replied.

"Oh, lord." Edie planted an elbow on the armrest and pressed a hand over her eyes. "That's a sure way to lead the police right to me." Shaking her head of auburn waves, she lit another cigarette, fingers trembling. Inhaling long and deep, she cleared her head and let the wheels churn. Taking another long puff, she let the smoke out slowly. Finally, Edie said, "No, I don't think it's the cops. Newspapers would have plastered it all over the front pages. I think it's Dagger. It was his client who supposedly witnessed the murder. He would have been the one to comb the area, pick a lock or two, and find the body. "We have to find Dagger's weakness."

Luke agreed. "What about his fiancée? Isn't she the daughter of that rich guy?"

Edie shook her head. "Dagger broke it off with Sheila. I don't know him that well, but from what I could tell, he would probably throw her to the dogs before trading her for the earring." She took a swig of cognac and smiled slowly. "One thing I do know—he is very protective of Sara." Edie explained, "If you hurt any of Dagger's friends you are his enemy for life. You can anger him by beating up his friends or even stealing his parrot. But Sara, she's our key. I think he'd trade Sara for the earring."

"Sara." Joey's mouth turned up in a sadistic grin. "Oh, yeah."

40

"A part of me didn't believe you, Dagger." Robert's hand shook as he dabbed at his eyes. Rachel had looked as if she were sleeping, accept for the blue tinge to her skin and the bloodstain on her dress. "It feels like it was a lifetime ago that she died. So much time has passed."

Robert followed Dagger down the hall to a waiting room. The grieving husband had just finished identifying his young wife's body. Robert silently gazed out of the picture window. Next door was the county court house and beyond that, a large building circled by a high fence. It was a youth correctional facility.

Robert lowered his body onto the hard bench and slumped against the backrest. "If I had only taken her call more seriously."

Dagger took a seat next to him, leaned forward, elbows on his knees, hands clasped. "You have to quit beating yourself up."

Padre appeared in the doorway with a cup of coffee, which he handed to Robert. "Thought you could use this."

Robert thanked him and set the coffee on the end table.

Padre rolled a chair over to the bench and took a seat across from them. He pulled a notepad from his pocket and leaned forward. Dagger knew Padre's routine by heart. He liked to lean close, speak in a soft tone, as if he were in a confessional. The tone was always congenial, understanding.

Padre asked, "Did you pay the crew five years ago to say that Rachel sailed with them that night when she actually didn't?"

Robert sighed, closed his eyes briefly. "No. Where on earth would you hear such a thing?" He looked from Padre to Dagger. "I thought all the questions had been answered?"

"You hired me to do a job, Mr. Tyler," Dagger said. "And I've come up with some issues that contradict what was reported to the police five years ago."

Robert's shoulders sagged, his face looked haggard. The county morgue was no place to interview a victim's relatives. But they couldn't do it at Robert's home or the precinct without police or the press being curious. As it was, they didn't have much time before the medical examiner's report became public knowledge.

"As far as I know Rachel boarded the yacht that night. If the crew were paid by someone to say she was never there, the money didn't come from me."

Dagger thought back to Pete's reaction to the woman on the yacht. For someone who supposedly was paid to lie about Rachel being on the yacht as Nick professed, Pete had some pretty vivid and fond memories. Dagger asked Tyler, "Were you aware that Edie knew Rachel before you two were married?"

Robert shook his head. "That can't be true."

"We have pictures of them together. But Edie had blonde hair back then," Padre said. "I have a tail on Edie now. I wouldn't bet my pension, though, that we would find a blonde wig or two in her room. If she's as smart as I think she is, she got rid of all the evidence five years ago."

"Damn, what a stupid old fool I've been." With a disbelieving shake of his head, Robert said, "That makes no sense. I could provide Rachel with everything. She had no reason to steal anything. And why would they keep it from the family that they knew each other?" His haggard eyes looked to them for answers, they had none.

After a few moments, Padre turned to Dagger and said, "By the way, I ran those plates through the computer. The pickup was reported stolen two days ago. It's a lousy way to lose your Mustang."

"Mustang, hell. They almost killed Sara."

Robert turned an ashen face toward Dagger. "Don't tell me she was almost killed because of this case."

Padre nodded. "Afraid so."

Robert's gaze drifted from Padre's face down to the open collar of his shirt where portions of a bandage was showing. "I really feel bad that you were almost killed, too, Sergeant.

"There's an upside to it." Padre grinned, "It means we're getting close."

Robert picked up his coffee cup and retreated to the window. Padre and Dagger exchanged unspoken signals. A lifting of his eyebrows meant Padre had no reason not to believe Robert.

Dagger asked Robert, "And what about Rachel's will? Maybe there's something in it that mentions the kangaroo."

Robert shook his head. "We had our wills made up together. There were no surprises. She would have been well taken care of had I died first." He left his cup on a cart next to the doorway. Shoving his hands in his pockets he slowly paced, shoulders slumped. "You know, gentlemen, I didn't build a billion dollar business on stupidity. I know Rachel could have had any young man she wanted. I know money is a magnet for beautiful women like Rachel and Edie. I'm not that blind." He studied the thread-worn carpet as he paced, wondering how many other grieving relatives had walked this same path. The worry lines in his forehead deepened. "I know there were rumors that Rachel and Eric had a quick fling but Eric and Rachel both denied it and I believe them."

"Did Rachel leave any jewelry to your daughter-in-law?" Padre asked.

Robert chuckled. For the first time since he had seen Rachel's body, he actually displayed an emotion other than anguish. "Funny thing was, Rachel didn't like the real stuff. She insisted on only costume jewelry. She knew too many friends who had their real jewels stolen either from their house or right off their bodies. Check our wedding pictures. Other than pearl earrings, all she's wearing is a plain gold band and a gold cross necklace her mother gave her."

Dagger looked quizzically at Padre and after a few minutes, they wandered down the hall, leaving Robert in the waiting room with his anguish and memories.

"You get the same impression I did?" Padre asked.

"Maybe. I'm thinking Rachel may have been completely unaware she was being used to move the jewels from Australia. Who better than a model with suitcases full of costume jewelry? But once she got home and realized what she had, she could have camouflaged the earrings, hid the necklace, maybe threatened to go to the police."

They looked back at Robert, one of the richest and most powerful men in the state. He could buy just about anything he wanted and usually did, from his thousand-dollar suits to fancy cars and high-priced resorts. But all that power and all that money didn't protect him from the one thing everyone experiences eventually, no matter how rich or poor … grief.

41

Dagger was up early the next morning. Whenever he couldn't sleep, whenever his head throbbed, whenever the angry side of him wanted to rear its ugly head, he practiced Tai Chi. If he had practiced it daily, the way he was supposed to, he wouldn't be clenching his teeth at night.

What had happened to Skizzy brought out feelings that had seemed foreign to him. Every time he closed his eyes, he saw a disturbed, phobic man, sinking even lower into his schizophrenia, not that Skizzy ever appeared to be improving.

Facing the expansive living room windows, Dagger inhaled deeply, inspired by the daybreak peering through the trees. His arms moved slowly up, bringing the good Chi toward him. Exhaling, he slowly moved his arms down, while placing his weight on his heels and pivoting to his left. His movements were deliberate in a practiced rhythm. He wore white drawstring pants and a loose-fitting white shirt. His mode of dress coupled with the bandana around his forehead made him look like a martial arts instructor. Matter of fact, used properly, Tai Chi was an excellent method of self-defense.

Just as on the other mornings he practiced Tai Chi, he felt eyes on him. Even in the winter when it was so dark at five in the morning that he could barely see one hand in front of the other, he could still feel eyes peering at the back of his head.

"It's called Tai Chi," Dagger said softly, not wanting to break his concentration. From his peripheral vision he saw Sara rise from the top stoop outside her bedroom and descend the stairs. "It's the ultimate exercise for body, mind and spirit. Reduces stress, strengthens the immune system, and is actually a self-defense technique."

He broke his pattern briefly and turned to face her. When does she ever sleep? Sometimes he would go to bed before her yet she was up before him. Maybe it was youth that kept her looking rested, vibrant, no matter how little sleep she had. Maybe she napped when he wasn't home.

"Come." He guided her in front of him, both facing the windows. "Dip your knees slightly, like when you sit on the edge of the bar stool." He placed his hands on top of hers. "Hold your hands apart as if you are holding an imaginary ball. Don't let the fingertips touch."

"What does this do?"

"Shhhhh. Don't talk. Just feel the Chi. Turn slowly from the waist, first to the left." Their bodies moved in unison. As they turned, their left hands slowly rotated to the top and their right hands to the bottom of the imaginary ball. As they turned back toward the center, their hands moved back to the starting position. "Exhale when we are facing straight ahead." His voice was soft, soothing. "Slowly inhale again, moving the right hand on top as we turn to the right."

They continued the pattern for several minutes. "Do you feel it?" The heat pulsated, radiating between their hands.

"Yes," Sara gasped. "How does it do that?"

"Energy." As Dagger inhaled he realized he was smelling Sara's hair, her skin. Not only was their heat between their hands, but they were generating a good deal of it between their bodies. He could hear Simon's voice in his head, 'Sooner or later, you be looking at her in a whole different light'.

Dagger dropped his hands. "You keep practicing. I'm going to go take a shower."

"Sweetheart, you aren't going to believe this." Sheila's voice gushed through the speaker phone.

"WICKED WITCH, AWK." Einstein recognized Sheila's voice.

"What did you do this time?" Dagger closed both doors to the aviary, while Einstein cranked his neck trying to find out where Sheila's voice was coming from. Dagger checked the clock on the wall. "It's nine in the morning, Sheila. Usually you aren't up until the crack of eleven." He sat down and propped his feet on the desk. He picked up outdated notes and dropped them into a trash can.

"You'll be proud of me. I actually checked this out on my own. That ingrate Worm. I'm going to fire his ass."

Dagger clasped his hands behind his neck and stared up at the skylights. Even Sheila's voice was beginning to grate on his nerves.

Sheila continued, her voice more excited. "I had a friend do a title search on Sara's property. Guess what? There's no record of ownership. We can buy it free and clear."

Dagger looked up at the catwalk to see Sara standing there, her face sullen, eyes accusing. She turned and walked back to her room.

"I doubt you checked thoroughly, Sheila. You can't just check any records. I think you have to go to the Bureau of Indian Affairs or the Interior Department." His mind raced, thinking of how to divert her attention. He flipped through his notes looking for Worm's phone number. "I have another call, Sheila. As usual, you haven't done your homework." He ended the call, pulled his legs off the desk and dialed Worm's number.

"Now is a good time to call Sheila and give her your notice if you haven't already done so." Dagger thought Sheila could be kept busy pacing her father's office whining about Worm quitting and then having to find a replacement for him.

Next, Dagger called Skizzy who was feeling better and bragging about how he had been able to hold his own against the two thugs that beat him up. He agreed to prepare a forged title and bury it in the bureaucratic system somewhere along with a will signed by Sara's grandmother.

He turned from his desk and saw Sara standing by the bar. "She's going to try to do it, isn't she?" She tilted her head, a defiant look in her eyes spelling trouble. Sara was ready to do battle.

"I took care of it, Sara."

She didn't seem convinced and wouldn't be until she

had the actual papers in her hand.

"I'm sorry I didn't take you seriously before. Forgive me?" Dagger fingered the sterling silver wolf hanging from the chain around his neck.

"She has money and connections."

"I know. It will be okay, Sara. I promise."

She nodded and slipped around the corner into the kitchen.

Dagger no sooner poured himself a cup of black coffee, then Simon showed up.

"You're going to have to talk to him," Simon said. "Skizzy has got damn plywood nailed to the windows."

"If it makes him feel safe."

"Safe, hell, he may as well put a Count Dracula coffin in the back room the place is so dark." Simon's eyes brightened as he saw Sara enter the room in a yellow floral sundress. "My, aren't you a breath of sunshine."

Since Dagger had ended his phone call with Sheila, Sara felt it was safe to let Einstein out of the aviary. He immediately flew over to the doorway and whistled.

"WHAT A BODY. AWWWKK."

Dagger yelled, "Hey, watch your beak."

Sara laughed and told Einstein. "Aren't you the fresh one." She offered Einstein some broccoli and then returned to the kitchen.

Cocking his head toward Einstein, Simon said, "Does the bird have good taste or is he hearing you talk in your sleep?"

Dagger snapped the morning paper open and took a quick glance toward the doorway to the kitchen. "Don't start. Einstein just has good taste."

"Uh huh. Then why take a lookie-see to where that sweet young thing is?"

"Because I never know what foul thing is going to come spilling out of your mouth." Dagger buried his face in the papers but thought back to Sara's nude body twirling in the moonlight.

"AWK, WHAT A BODY, WHAT A BODY." Einstein clamped onto the grated door and hung upside down.

The leather cushions hissed as Simon settled onto the couch. He chuckled and said, "You're going to have to teach Einstein a new word or in a few months when you and that sweet thing are knockin' boots he's going to be screaming, 'Oh Dagger, please!'"

Dagger snapped his paper again and glared at Simon.

"Don't give me that look," Simon scolded. "I've been there. You're trying to convince yourself she's just a child. Pretty soon, you be dreamin' about her. Dreams so vivid they keep you up nights."

"You know, Simon." Dagger stood up. "I don't want you to spend too much time here."

Simon chuckled again. "What's the matter? Am I getting a little too close to the truth?" Simon stood and arched his back, dipping left then right. "You need a more comfortable couch," he mumbled.

"Are you leaving, Simon?" Sara asked.

"I was just trying to tell Simon that it isn't safe for him or anyone to spend that much time around me. I don't want anyone else to end up like Skizzy."

"My appearance as a worn-out, flabby postal carrier is

just my cover up. Nobody messes with Simon the Terrible."
Simon laughed heartily.

"COMPANY, COMPANY, AWWK." Einstein flew
over to the monitor and pushed the Entry Key to open the
outside gate.

Dagger grabbed the macaw and cradled him in his arms.
"So that's how those guys got in the other night."

"I can't believe it," Sara laughed. She checked the face
on the monitor. "It's Worm," she announced. "He's going to
fill us in on his investigation." She ran to the kitchen to wait
for their visitor.

"Someone else who needs to keep his distance
from me."

Simon said, "You need to keep an eye on that little lady."

"Trust me. Sara is capable of taking care of herself."

Simon leaned in close and whispered, "That won't stop
them from trying."

42

"Wow." Worm removed his glasses to look closer at the picture of Rachel taken at the medical examiner's office. "What a shame. She was so beautiful,"

"The killers were careful. Crime Lab wasn't able to lift any prints from either the freezer or the townhouse where we believe the murder took place." Dagger passed additional pictures to Worm. "Padre has agreed to talk to you about the investigation." Dagger did a slow inspection of Worm's clothes. "Is Sheila picking out your clothes these days?" Worm was wearing a pale yellow shirt and white linen sportcoat.

Worm's face reddened. "Looks terrible, doesn't it?"

"It looks … summery," Sara offered. "Don't listen to Dagger. Everything in his closet is black and gray."

Dagger looked down at his own black Dockers™. "I only say that because that's the first thing Sheila did was drag me through the malls. When I would refuse to try on clothes, she would buy them and present them like some offering. I always returned them."

"Well, she won't have me to kick around any more. I

called her and quit, like you suggested."

"How did she take it?" Dagger took a peek in the aviary. Einstein was napping so Dagger pulled both doors closed.

"First she was pissed royally. Then she went on and on about how I would never get another job in this town if she had anything to do with it."

Sara asked, "Can she do that?"

"She can try, but Worm will have his exclusive and every paper in the country will be clamoring for his services." Dagger handed Worm some photographs.

"More pictures of Rachel?"

"No." Dagger sat on the armrest, one foot braced on the coffee table. "Those are composite pictures of Edie Tyler with blonde hair. It only proves she was the friend in Rachel's vacation pictures." Dagger checked his watch. "You have an appointment with Padre at two o'clock; and J.C. Kinnecutt, the curator for the Argyle Museum is in town. I'm going to see if he can meet with you at four o'clock."

"Really?" Worm bubbled. "I can't thank you enough." He smoothed a hand over the top of his bristly hair but the hairs popped right back up. "You actually have the curator here in the states?"

"Yes, but don't be surprised if he's reluctant to talk. He seemed to be embarrassed by the whole ordeal and is pretty worried about keeping his job." Dagger pointed to a stack of papers. "You'll find a color picture of the Williamsburg Collection somewhere in that pile."

Worm dragged papers from his briefcase. "I got a lot of information on moissanite from the Internet. It was discovered in a meteorite in the 1800s by Henri Moissan."

"How fascinating," Sara said. She stood behind the couch looking over Worm's shoulder.

"And," Worm continued, "its properties are the closest thing to diamonds yet it's about ten percent the cost of diamonds. They started producing laboratory stones in 1995 but they haven't started to pop up in the market until recently."

Dagger leaned back, his eyes gazing up at the catwalk. "So the public and the jewelry stores didn't know until recently that moissanites were available?"

"But they do make them in a lab," Sara said.

Worm peered over his shoulder at her. "Yes. They are available in yellow, blue, black, gray, and dark green. But the colorless stones are the most popular."

Sara's brows knitted. "They don't make pink ones?"

Sheila threw open the door to her father's office and was pummeled by plumes of foul-smelling cigar smoke. She waved her hands frantically in an attempt to find a patch of unpolluted air to inhale.

"Daddy, you never answered my phone call about Worm. What do I do for an assistant now?"

"Close the door!" Leyton paced the length of his wall of bookcases, leaving a trail of smoke behind him. "I have more pressing matters right now."

"But, Daddy."

"Sit."

Sheila checked her watch. Whenever her father was on

the warpath she was usually his sounding board. He didn't need a hatchet man. That was normally his expertise and he wielded the hatchet with glee.

"Look at these," he mumbled from behind his clenched cigar. He handed Sheila several letters.

She perused them quickly as he rambled about suing the bastard if he ever found out who did it.

"Daddy, these are thank-you letters. What's the problem?"

He stripped off his suit jacket, revealing sweat stains under his armpits. His beefy arms were sunburned from last weekend's golf outing. His face was as red as his arms and it wasn't all from the sun .

"Oh, really? Two hundred thousand dollars to the Native American College Fund, another two hundred thousand to the United Negro College Fund, and," he picked up one of the letters and heaved it across the room, "a lousy hundred thousand bucks to the Legal Fund for Native American Fishing Rights."

"Well, considering how you feel about all those groups, I have to admit I'm surprised."

Leyton plucked the cigar from his mouth. "I didn't write the damn checks. Someone forged my signature."

"What?" Sheila blinked quickly. "And you think I did it?"

"No, of course not. But what am I going to do? There are press releases going out expounding my benevolent virtues. And me," he jabbed a chubby finger at his chest, "the newly elected president of the Great Lakes Fishing Rights Association."

"So someone stole your checkbook?"

He pulled a ledger of checks from his safe. "Look. Every damn check is there. Someone literally forged the check design, the paper, and actually numbered them. I checked with the bank. They gave me the check numbers." He fanned through the blank checks. "They are all here. The sneaky sonofabitch picked some random numbers and forged my signature."

Sheila suddenly started to calculate the dollars. "Daddy, that's half a million dollars!"

"No fuckin' shit."

"Well, stop payment, do something!"

"And how is that going to look in the papers?"

Sheila bolted out of her chair and reached for the phone. "Did you call our family attorney?"

"Put the phone down." He checked his cigar, which had run out of steam. He tossed the slimy stub into the ashtray. "I already checked with Nathan. He closed out the checking account so no other checks can be cashed. And he said the best I can do is resign my newly elected office. But that would be far too embarrassing."

Sheila paced, her three-inch heels grinding into the carpeting as she pivoted, her floral neck scarf trailing behind. This was her specialty—troubleshooting—and the one talent she knew her father respected in her completely. She looked pensive with one arm across her waist, a fist thrust under her chin, one long painted nail anchored between her teeth.

Sheila's eyes brightened as she snapped her fingers. "I've got it. You release a statement that you were the victim of an activist group who forged stolen checks. Don't mention anything about what a racist pig you are." She smiled sweetly playing *Daddy's Girl* to the hilt. "Everyone who knows you knows your feelings. Instead, just disclose that an investigation is ongoing and this was a cruel and practical joke. However," Sheila added as she grabbed a pad of paper and wrote down notes, "it would be far too cruel for even you to demand that the donations be returned. In lieu of this unfortunate event, you are donating," she glanced at her father as he dabbed perspiration from his forehead, "and you are going to have to do this, Daddy," she continued, "you are donating an additional two hundred thousand dollars to the Great Lakes Fishing Rights Association. This way you don't look cold-hearted by stopping payment on the checks and you appease your fellow GLFR members by tossing them more money."

She placed her notes down and waited.

Leyton sank into his chair and expelled a long, heavy sigh. After several moments he nodded in agreement. "You are right, as always. That is really my only out. But if I ever find out who did this, he's going to wish he had never been born."

43

"Daddy is just furious," Sheila cried. She dabbed a tissue at the corner of each eye and sank onto a bar stool. "And then Worm quit and I just can't do all the work on my own. And then, and then .." she stammered, wiping her eyes again, "I find out I can't get this property for you like I promised."

Dagger checked his watch. The last thing he needed on his doorstep was Sheila Monroe, especially when he was expecting Padre.

"I told you it's difficult touching reservation land."

At the sound of Sheila's voice, Einstein flew over to the desk screeching, "WICKED WITCH, WICKED WITCH, AWWK."

Sara rushed in from the kitchen to see what the commotion was about.

"I would like some coffee." Sheila held up a finger only to be met with a blank stare.

"Where do you think you're at, your country club?" Dagger asked.

"Well," Sheila kicked off her three-inch heels, "she is

your secretary. Doesn't she do secretarial things? My father's secretary brings his coffee."

"AWWK, GET OUT." Einstein buried his head under Sara's arm, accepting the security of her gentle stroking and whispers.

"Shhhhh." Sara kissed the top of his head.

"Well, how about a sandwich? I'm starving." Sheila looked at Sara again.

"AWWWKK." Einstein flew up to the catwalk and landed on the railing. Sara ran upstairs to calm him down.

Dagger slipped behind the bar. "All I can offer you is a beer."

"Champagne?" Sheila stood up and leaned over the bar to check the contents on the shelf. She whispered, "Need help?" Her two box-link gold chains slipped out from under her silk blouse.

Dagger couldn't help but notice she had more buttons undone on her blouse than necessary.

Sheila smiled seductively, placing her hand on top of his as he handed her a beer.

"I'm expecting company. Can you make it quick?"

"We have never had a problem making it quick when we needed to. Like two little rabbits." Sheila glanced up toward the catwalk and smiled.

Einstein eyed Sheila, opened his beak, and made several hacking motions, his foot raised like a boxer.

"Come on, Einstein." Sara coaxed him off the rail. "Don't get yourself all riled up over nothing." Sara sat on the catwalk with Einstein in her lap. She tried not to watch as Sheila played with the gold chains around her neck, letting her fingers trace her cleavage. As a way to keep Einstein quiet so she could listen to Sheila and Dagger, Sara offered Einstein a Brazil nut, but he refused it.

"What's this about your father?" Dagger asked.

Sheila told Dagger about the forged checks. He quickly took a long pull on his beer to keep from smiling.

"Well, your father has pissed off a lot of people with his radical viewpoints." Dagger checked his watch.

"I want to hire you."

"Me? For what?"

"To find out who's responsible for this."

"No, thanks. My golden rule: I don't do cheating spouses, missing dogs, deadbeat dads, or check forgers. Besides, your father hates me."

Sheila did that little thing with her finger again, drawing imaginary circles on the top of his hand with the tip of one lacquered nail. Dagger pulled his hand away before the chills started making more than just the tiny hairs on his hand stand up. A reprieve -- the front gate alarm rang.

"COMPANY, COMPANY, AWWK." Einstein flew toward the monitor. Sara tore down the stairs after him.

"Hey," Dagger yelled, diverting Einstein from the monitor to the perch by the desk. "You've been told not to press that buzzer."

"SPREAD 'UM. AWWWKK." Einstein had seen Padre's face on the monitor.

"Dagger, it's not good to yell. You'll upset him," Sara warned.

"For crissake." Sheila slid off the bar stool and slipped on her shoes. "Next thing she'll have him seeing a parrot psychologist."

Dagger let Padre in. Immediately, Einstein pointed one toe at him. Padre made a mock gun with his fingers and pointed it at Einstein.

"Let me out of here. This place is a zoo." Sheila tried to kiss Dagger but he turned to catch the kiss on his cheek. "Think again about my offer, Sweetheart."

"GOOD RIDDANCE, YUK," Einstein screeched.

"Same to you, you overgrown crow." Sheila glanced at Sara but didn't say anything.

She was out the door and in her car before Padre said, "Sweetheart? I thought you broke things off?"

"It hasn't sunk in with her yet."

Sara tapped on the grated door to the aviary. "Past your bedtime, Einstein." Einstein flew up to his favorite tree branch and Sara slid the grated door shut first, then the soundproof Plexiglas door. She checked the humidity controls on the panel near the door for the aviary.

"Sheila has called the precinct at least three times to get an update on her father's forged checks. They keep telling her the chances of catching the guy are zilch." Padre accepted a beer from Dagger and they sat on the couch while Sara retreated to the kitchen. Several moments later they heard the dishwasher humming.

"Sheila tried to hire me to find the guilty party. But I'm not getting involved."

Sara returned with a cup of tea, said her goodnights, and went upstairs to her room.

"Do you have the medical examiner's report?"

"She was definitely shot close range. We'll get Ballistics

on it immediately."

"You are sure these guys are being followed?" Dagger heard the familiar sound of Sara's patio door sliding open.

"We know where they are staying. We'll know if they make a move."

"All we need now is a plan."

The gray wolf darted through the underbrush, around trees, over deteriorating fences, and through creeks as it made its way to the Tyler mansion. The night air was heavy and damp, the remains of an earlier storm clinging to the foliage. The sky was dark and thunder rumbled in the background.

The wolf stopped to listen. Streetlights filtered through the branches; and traffic sounds, although a mile away, sounded to the wolf as if cars were a few feet away.

With a giant push, the wolf leaped for a branch twenty feet from the ground, shifting in mid-flight into the gray hawk. It ruffled its feathers as it shifted its body, letting its talons search for a better grip.

It could see lights in the distance from the Tyler mansion. The hawk lifted off and in less than a minute was on the patio railing outside the third floor library.

Edie paced in front of the patio doors, the phone pressed to her ear, talking to Luke. She slid open the door and welcomed the cool breeze which had followed the earlier storm.

"Are you sure they have a clear plan?" She opened the humidor but changed her mind. A headache was developing, and the last thing she needed was a cigar.

"Yes. We went over it. Why are you so jumpy?"

"I don't know." She rubbed a finger and thumb across her forehead, trying to press away a tension headache. "Can't wait til this is over with. I keep seeing cars following me, wondering if it's the cops, or maybe even your two buddies." Stopping long enough to light a cigarette, she continued pacing. "When are those two idiots taking care of the body? According to the schedule, the resort staff will start to stock those pantries and freezers soon."

"That is their main priority after getting the girl. Now, what about your husband? Is he going to be a problem?"

"No. He hasn't a clue. And I'd never let him in on it anyway. This is my nest egg. He already gambled away as much money as I care to entrust him with."

"And your brother-in-law?"

"I think I've managed to convince him that it wasn't Rachel who Dagger's client saw murdered. And a body will never be found. So ..." Peering out the door, Edie saw two eyes glowing from the railing and jumped back. "My god. What is with these birds?"

"What are you talking about?"

"The bird ... hawk ... whatever was outside your hotel window. It's outside the library window. This is really bizarre. It's like it has been following me." A cold chill ran up Edie's back as she stared at the bird.

"That's ridiculous. You're going to tell me it's the same hawk?"

Edie studied the bird's coloring. "I know it is. It's the eyes. Hawks don't have blue eyes, Luke, do they?"

44

"DON'T TOUCH. AWWK." Einstein gripped the perch, spread his wings, and bobbed his head to look around Sara who was seated at the computer monitor. Morning sunlight filtered through the half-opened blinds embedded in the skylights.

"I can touch, but you can't." Sara turned and handed Einstein a piece of orange. "Now, tell me again about the kangaroo, Einstein." Sara accessed the Internet and went to AOL Net Search. She looked at Einstein, who was busy eating. "Kangaroo, Einstein. What is kangaroo?" She thought back to the night Einstein had blurted out the word. "What was it you said?"

Einstein pulled out the orange long enough to say, "AWWWKK, KANGAROO PAW, KANGAROO PAW."

"Good," Sara smiled, "that's what I wanted to hear." She typed *kangaroo paw* on the search line and waited. A few seconds later 283 matches lit up the screen. "Mangles' Kangaroo Paw?" She read the description of the emblem of the State of Western Australia. Clicking on the first entry, she waited for the screen to fill. The image was familiar.

"Oh my." Turning from the screen, Sara said, "Einstein, I know where the diamonds are!"

Sara drove Dagger's truck toward the Tyler residence. She had been unsuccessful at trying to reach Dagger on his cellular phone. He had planned to meet Padre. There was always the possibility Sara was wrong which is why she wanted to check things out first.

The Cedar Point Police Department was a buzz of activity. Tuesdays seemed to be the chosen day for every lawyer in Cedar Point to pick up an arrest report. Men in power suits nodded at Padre as they walked past. The women in power suits smiled at Dagger. They stood outside a door marked *Homicide.*

"I don't know what it is with you, Dagger," Padre pointed out as another woman in a thigh-high skirt and carrying a briefcase cast one of those, *I'm available* smiles. "Must be that long hair or *I don't have time to shave* look. You've had a stream of ladies here for the taking. Thank god I'm married. I wouldn't want to make the decision on which one."

Dagger stood, arms crossed, leaning against the wall. A smile tugged at the corner of his mouth as the next woman rushed by. "You just give them what they want. Let your gaze tell them they are looking good. Now they can go into court and give the judge hell. By lunch time they won't even remember me."

Padre nodded in agreement and chuckled. "Right, until they go to bed. Look at me." He gestured toward his pinstriped suit. "I've got the power suit thing going, hair trimmed, though slightly receding. But for reasons that escape me, women with all that education and culture go ga-ga over guys with grease under their nails, five-o-clock shadows …" he glanced at Dagger's head, "hair six months past a trim, and in desperate need of a wardrobe."

Dagger grinned. "Yeah, but I clean up nice."

Padre opened the door and led Dagger past three sets of desks butted together in twos. Ceiling fans circulated warm air and an air conditioning unit jammed in one of the windows clattered and droned.

Padre's desk was in a far corner of the room. He sat down and motioned to a chair in front of his desk.

Dagger remained standing. He jammed his hands in his pants pockets and paced, looking up whenever someone entered. "I don't like this," Dagger said. "I've got a bad feeling."

"You always were edgy in a police station."

"Why couldn't you just call me with the information?"

Padre rose. "Come on." He led him down an aisle and into a conference room. When he closed the door, he said, "Feel better?"

Dagger surveyed the twelve-foot-square room with faded green walls. "It's not your office. It's not this room. Hell, it isn't even the building." He paced, clasping his hands in back of his head.

"You look like you're going to jump out of your skin."

"Something doesn't feel right."

Padre pulled a notepad from his pocket. "Maybe you have a premonition of what I'm about to tell you."

Dagger stopped pacing and stared at Padre. He

unclasped his hands and took a seat across the marred table from the sergeant.

Padre studied his notes, pursed his lips in thought. Finally, he said, "I've had my people checking out these three yokels. It seems Joey was a guest of the Boston Police Department during the week Rachel was modeling the Williamsburg Collection. Mince was in California. There are a string of hotel receipts from him. And Luke was in New York, under surveillance by the Justice Department."

Dagger threaded his fingers through his hair. "Damn, maybe Sara is onto something."

"Sara? What did she find out?"

Dagger drove Padre to Sara's house. The answering machine had been left on but that didn't mean Sara wasn't home. She could be outside in the garden or in the throes of cleaning Einstein's aviary and not want to be interrupted.

"Sara?" Dagger called out as he entered the kitchen, Padre close behind.

"Maybe she left a note." Padre checked the kitchen counter, then walked to the phone on the desk. He could barely see the desktop. "Damn, when are you going to get organized?"

Dagger checked the aviary. The doors were closed, Einstein was alone and napping. Next, he ran up the stairs to Sara's room where he located his laptop. This was where Sara had disappeared during Worm's visit. Something Worm had said about moissanite had triggered her curiosity. Dagger brought the laptop downstairs, set it on the coffee table and sat in front of it.

Turning it on, he accessed AOL. "Let's see what she was working on."

"How can you tell?" Padre loosened his tie and took a seat next to Dagger.

"She will usually save something in *My Favorite Places* so she can return to it when she wants." Dagger clicked on *My Favorite Places*. "The last one listed is usually the last one accessed."

He ran the cursor down the list, clicked on the item, and read the contents. "Interesting. Why was she looking up the Mayfair Gallery in London? I'm going to check her Email, see what messages she has sent."

Padre peered at the screen and read along with Dagger. "Sonofabitch," the two men said in unison. The phone rang but Dagger let the answering machine pick it up.

"Mr. Dagger, if you're home, I'd advise you to pick up."

Dagger looked up. He and Padre exchanged glances.

"I've got someone here who wants to speak to you," the voice continued.

After a few moments, a voice said, "Dagger?" It was Sara.

"SARA?" Dagger yelled, as he ran for the phone. "Where are you?"

"Not too fast." The man had taken the phone from Sara.

"Sara, are you all right?" Dagger pressed the record button on the phone so the conversation could be recorded.

"You have something of ours and we've got this gorgeous piece of meat."

"If you hurt her I'll ..."

"That's all up to you. She has a knife to her throat right now, so her life is in your hands."

Dagger knew Sara wouldn't shape-shift, couldn't take the chance of being seen even though it might be her only way to save her life.

"What do you want?" Dagger demanded.

"The diamonds. All of them. Give me your cellular number."

As he gave the caller the cellular number, Dagger pulled his Phoenix Raven from the bottom drawer and checked the clip. "I don't have the necklace."

"Then I would suggest you and old man Tyler get your heads together and figure it out. I'll call you back in thirty minutes. If you don't have the necklace, she dies." He hung up.

"Dammit." Dagger punched the speaker button off. He rifled through papers on his desk until he found a phone number. He grabbed the box containing the diamond earrings, shoved the piece of paper at Padre, and said, "Come on. You call while I drive."

45

Sara struggled against the ropes that bound her hands and the tape across her mouth. She didn't like the way Joey glared at her. His eyes rarely looked at her face, only her body, as if she were some tasty meal and he hadn't eaten in a week. He had weasel features, thin and pointed. He never left her alone, always leering, always playing with the knife.

Her trip earlier to Tyler's to check on what she had discovered on the Internet, had been interrupted when the truck engine died. Sara had let her foot off the clutch a little too long. Then she couldn't get the truck started again. When a man stopped to offer his help, she noticed it was one of the men who had broken into her home and beaten up Dagger. And his friend, the man with the marred face, had opened the driver's side door and forced her to scoot to the middle.

After shoving her down on the seat, Joey had taped her hands and mouth. He had kept her head down so she couldn't see where they were headed. All she could do was concentrate on the sounds outside the truck, anything that could give her a clue where they were going. When the truck finally came to a halt, they lead her down a dirt driveway to a cabin. She could hear the rush of water, maybe from a near-by creek. But no traffic, no human sounds. They were deep in the woods somewhere.

And as they walked, her eyes kept roaming, searching for some trail marker and identifier. And she had found it. A small sign nailed to a tree said *Possum Creek*. They were in a wooded area near a field where Dagger used to take Einstein. But Einstein had kept going too deep into the woods and refused to obey Dagger's commands. All she needed now was one chance to talk to Dagger to possibly give him a clue as to her location.

Mince had just left with Dagger's truck. He was to abandon it somewhere in town. Joey pulled the tape off Sara's mouth. She ran her tongue over her parched lips.

"Like how you do that," Joey sneered. He strolled around the cabin, pulled open the shutters, and let the sunlight stream in. "You can try to scream all you want but we're pretty isolated here."

The cabin was dusty and smelled of stale air and kerosene. A small wood-burning stove was nestled in a corner and a twin-sized bed with a stained bedspread occupied the wall near the window.

Turning away from the window, Joey asked, "I've really been curious, Sweetie. How did you survive that plunge into the quarry the other night?"

Sara blinked and thought back to that harrowing night. "The car mangled the fence. I was able to reach for the fence and hang on until Dagger pulled me up."

Joey circled Sara slowly. She felt trapped, vulnerable, and his eyes had the hunger of a predator. Her wrists were starting to ache and she had to go to the bathroom.

Before leaving, Mince had warned Joey to not do any-thing to Sara until Luke gave him the okay. That had sent chills down her spine. All it meant was whether or not Dagger gave them what they wanted, Joey was still going to kill her.

"Mr. Tyler!" Dagger tore past Lily, who had opened the front door to him and Padre. They ran through the foyer with Lily close behind.

"He's in the dining room," Lily called out, her hands pressed together.

As they entered, the Tyler clan was seated around the table. Edie looked calm, her steepled fingers lightly tapping against her chin. The patio doors were open and a warm breeze filtered through the room. The air was tense, and both Dagger and Padre detected it immediately. They turned to see Luke standing next to the bookcase, a cellular phone in his hand.

"Well, if it isn't the dick-and-dick twins. Did you bring the earrings?"

Dagger and Padre pulled their guns at the same time. Luke just waved his cellular at them. He pointed at Lily and ordered her to join the others at the table.

"If I don't call my partners back, I don't have to tell you what will happen to that sweet, innocent child." He dragged a tapestry upholstered chair from the corner by the door and took a seat.

Undaunted, Dagger walked up to Luke and shoved his

Raven .25 in his face. "You'll get the earrings when Sara is safe."

"That wasn't our deal."

"You're lucky I haven't put a bullet between your eyes."

"Tsk, tsk. So much pent-up frustration, Mr. Dagger." He motioned toward the two men with a long-barreled pistol. "I'll take your weapons, nice and easy. Set them right there on the floor." Luke pointed to a spot about five feet from him. "Oh, and the earrings, too." Dagger shoved his hands in his shirt pockets and retrieved an earring out of each.

"On the floor." Luke picked up the weapons and earrings. "Please, join the rest." Luke was seated about twenty feet from them where he could see everyone. "Has Detective Martinez clued you in on Joey's rap sheet?"

"I read his rap sheet." Dagger said. He and Padre took a seat at the end of the table away from the Tyler clan.

Luke smiled and crossed his arms, the bulk of his muscles oozing from under his short-sleeved shirt, the phone almost hidden under his thick fingers.

"I bet the rap sheet doesn't have the rape and murder of a fifteen-year-old girl in Boston six years ago. Or the rape and mutilation of a twenty-year-old college girl in Florida last year. Or how about the twenty-two-year-old he sodomized and beat so bad she lost her eyesight. That was six months ago in Indianapolis."

Dagger shifted in his seat, looked to Padre who shook his head. It was obvious Padre had not known this about Joey. Dagger's thoughts turned to Sara. He had done his best to teach her about his world. But he had never exposed her to the dredges of society like Luke and his thug friends before. She was fine when Dagger was around for backup. But he wasn't sure how she would handle Joey and Mince.

Robert spoke up. "He said he wants the diamonds."

"They have Sara," Dagger explained to Robert.

"Sara?" Nick jumped to his feet, almost knocking the chair over. "That pervert he just talked about has Sara?" He made a move for the giant.

Luke pointed his pistol at Nick. "Sit," he ordered.

The room grew quiet. The grandfather's clock in the far corner of the room clanged loudly. Lily twisted her hankie while Robert wrapped a consoling arm around her shoulder.

Eric checked his watch. "He has been terrorizing us for the past thirty minutes. Why the hell does he think we would have diamonds?"

Padre glared at Eric and asked, "Why don't you ask your wife?"

Robert and Eric turned to Edie who feigned shock.

"I have never seen this man in my life." Her eyes challenged Padre.

"What the hell is he talking about?" Eric demanded.

"They're bluffing." Edie remained calm and poised.

"I don't know." Dagger shoved his seat back and propped his legs up on the linen-covered table. He took some deep Chi breaths to calm down and watched the glimmers of doubt growing in Nick's and Robert's eyes. "Maybe Nick would like to tell us about the woman he saw the night Rachel disappeared. The woman who let Nick think all these years that he's the one who pushed Rachel and caused her to hit her head."

"What?" Robert gasped.

Nick stared at the table. He ran a trembling hand through his hair and glanced toward the bottles on the bar.

Robert stared at his son from across the table. "Nick?"

Nick turned on Edie. "You were there that night."

"What?" Robert turned to his daughter-in-law. "What the hell is going on under my nose?"

Edie tapped her nails against the linen, averted her eyes from Padre. "Of course, I was. Eric and I found you the next morning."

"I really don't care to hear a trip down memory lane," Luke snarled. He picked up his cellular and turned to Dagger. "You've got five minutes. You and old man Tyler here better get your heads together."

Dagger asked Lily, "Did you have any luck finding the kangaroo?"

Lily shook her head.

"Kangaroo?" Edie asked. "What kangaroo?"

Robert told them about the phone call he received from Rachel more than a week ago and how she had asked if he still had the kangaroo.

"That really was Rachel who was murdered? She has been alive all this time?" Nick slowly rose from the table, his head shaking in denial.

Luke dialed the phone. "Joey, we have a problem here. They can't seem to find the diamonds." Luke's gaze jerked to Dagger. "Oh, really?" He smiled broadly and held the phone out to Dagger. "Your little lady is claiming to know where the necklace is, and she'll only tell you."

This brought Edie out of her chair, her eyes wide in anticipation.

Dagger crossed the room and took the phone. "Sara?"

"I'm fine, so far, Dagger."

"You said you know where the necklace is?" Dagger listened for a while then strolled over to the patio. Sliding the screen door open, he stepped out. "Okay, I'm on the balcony but there's nothing here."

Suddenly, Luke's massive frame was behind him, breathing down his neck. Dagger heard Joey tell Sara, "Just tell him where it's at and give the phone back to me."

"Describe it." Dagger stepped back into the room, his eyes searching, then settling on a plant with red flowers.

Sara asked, "Einstein is okay, isn't he?"

"Sure, of course, Sara."

"Just don't let him out like you did a few months ago when he got lost."

The rest of the Tyler crowd stood and followed Dagger's gaze.

Dagger walked up to Padre and whispered in his ear.

"Hey." Luke leveled his gun at Dagger's back. "What are you talking about? Give me the phone." He pulled the phone from Dagger and spoke with Joey. "Hang on."

Dagger settled back in his seat, hands clasped behind his head, legs propped on the table. His dark eyes danced as they followed Luke's movements. Luke hadn't noticed that Dagger had pressed the mute key on the telephone. Joey wouldn't be able to hear him. That should buy Sara a little time. The detective said, "The diamonds are in the plant."

Padre walked around the plant with the woolly leaves and red flowers. "So this is a Kangaroo Paw." He looked around for something to cover the floor before spilling the contents.

"Kangaroo?" Robert gasped. "Of course. I had forgotten what Rachel called it."

Unconcerned about dirt being spilled on the floor, Luke gave the plant a shove, sending the plant tumbling, spilling the dirt and smashing the terre cotta pot.

"Let me see." Edie muscled her way between Padre and Luke. She knelt on the floor, staining her white slacks. Her long fingers plunged into the dirt. "I feel something," she cried. She raised a wrapped plastic package, pulled at the sealed edges and gasped when she had the necklace in her hands.

The Tyler men watched Edie's reaction with horror.

Padre announced, "I believe we have found the rest of the Williamsburg Collection." He turned to Dagger. "Why aren't you excited?"

Dagger smiled. "I'm waiting for the missing player."

Padre smiled in agreement. "He's a little late."

Robert asked, "He who?"

J.C. Kinnecutt appeared in the doorway. "Guess I didn't fool you, did I, Dagger?"

46

"Oh my god." Edie glared at J.C. and clutched the necklace to her chest. "You!"

"Hello, Sweetheart. Forget to call?" J.C. held a small Smith & Wesson .9mm in his hand.

"Sweetheart?" Eric stammered.

"Something's come up," Luke said into the phone before hanging up, unaware Joey still couldn't hear him. Luke slid a beefy hand around Edie's slender neck and pulled her against his body, his gun pointed at her head.

Lily let out a scream.

"Let's all remain calm," J.C. said. He asked Dagger, "What gave it away?"

"Celia, the desk clerk at the Carmelite Retreat couldn't quite remember specific details about Rachel's fictitious brother, Sean, until Padre called earlier and asked her if the brother had an Australian accent."

"Ahhh. Just a tiny detail, but significant."

"Well, well, Edie." Luke traced her jaw with the barrel of his gun. "Why don't you tell us who your friend is?"

"I was going to call, J.C.," Edie stammered.

299

"Oh really, now?"

"Oh my god," Eric moaned, covering his face.

"Well, now I know it wasn't my imagination that some-one was following me." A nervous laugh escaped from Edie's throat.

"Amazing way to connect the dots. I just followed your father-in-law from Dagger's house and I followed you. Best way to find out who all the players are." J.C. fanned the gun at his audience, "Please, everyone sit down." To Edie he said, "Drop the necklace nice and easy."

One by one the Tyler brood sank back onto their chairs. Lily clung to Robert's hand. Eric huddled close to Nick.

"She ain't giving you jack shit." Luke pulled her tighter. Edie gasped as she strained her eyes in the direction of Luke's gun.

J.C.'s eyes smiled. He had a trusting face and a sincere cadence to his voice. "I do detest violence. It is so messy. But there are circumstances when the situation warrants it." He fired one shot. Edie and the necklace dropped to the floor. He fired off another and Luke dropped to the floor.

All the men jumped to their feet. Eric cried out, "Edie!" Lily screamed.

"Anyone else?" J.C. asked.

"Sara was right about you," Dagger said

J.C. bent down and scooped up the jewelry.

"And what was that?"

"She Emailed the last museum you worked at and sug-gested they check their most valuable collection to see if it was moissanite. Imagine their surprise when they did your little flame trick and those suckers turned bright yellow.We then discovered that moissanite, the fake diamond you used, was never available in pink. You, however, were a pretty good gemologist in your own right and I figured you found a way to make pink ones. No one had ever heard of a pink moissanite so they would never suspect the set you had in the Argyle Museum was fake." When J.C.'s cheshire grin confirmed the revelation, Dagger added, "Edie must have hired you."

"Actually," J.C. explained, "we sort of found each other. Birds of a feather they say. What a perfect way to get the diamonds out of the country. She arranges for her sister-in-law to be the model, I exchange the wonderful replicas for the real thing, and Edie retrieves the jewels back in the states. We find a buyer, split the profits. What a country."

"But," Padre interjected, "Rachel suspected they were real when Edie became obsessed with getting them from her."

"When Edie quarreled with Rachel, she accidentally pushed her and she hit her head." J.C. looked down at Edie's lifeless body. "I helped Edie deliver Rachel to that retreat. I wanted to make sure she actually did have amnesia. Couldn't trust Edie, really." J.C. turned to Eric. "Don't you find that to be true, Mr. Tyler?"

"Can't trust the cops, either," Padre confessed.

Puzzled, J.C. furrowed his brow and gripped his gun tighter.

Smiling, Padre said, "We never come alone." Three members of Cedar Point's elite Swat Team had just arrived.

* * *

Dagger raced his pitted Ford Torino to the forest preserve. He had played Sara's message over in his head while the events unfolded at the Tyler residence. He had taught her to be prepared for anything and to be observant. Dagger was sure Sara was somewhere in Possum Woods.

The sun was setting as he gunned the Ford through the downtown streets and headed for the outskirts. Possum Woods was on the other side of town, a little-known woods except in the fall after the first frost when all the mushroom pickers were out in droves. The creek wasn't big enough for boats and there were no large picnic areas. No walking or jogging trails. The woods would be isolated enough to do whatever Joey wanted to do without any witnesses.

He gripped the steering wheel tighter as he thought of Joey. If things got bad, he knew Sara's instincts would be to flee, to shape-shift. Dagger felt confident until something popped into his head. Sara's instincts would save her, provided she was conscious.

"I have to go to the bathroom," Sara pleaded.

Joey stopped pacing and stared at her. His eyes drifted down her sundress and traced the body beneath the fabric. Slowly he unbuttoned the bottom two buttons of her dress. The fabric fell away, revealing shapely thighs, tan and firm. His lips parted as he exhaled slowly, his eyes closing briefly with thoughts Sara didn't want to imagine.

Slowly he took his knife from his pocket, walked around

in back of Sara's chair and knelt down. He inhaled the scent of her hair and closed his beady eyes as he drank in the smell of her perfume. His bony fingers slid languidly down her arms and when he reached her fingers, he clasped one between his teeth and sucked hard.

Sara fought back the urge to vomit. Everything about him made her skin crawl. He seemed to rarely blink, his eyes appearing psychotic, dangerous. Finally, she heard the knife cutting and felt her wrists released from their binding.

"You leave the door open though."

"Why?"

"Because I said so." His gaze never left her chest as it rose and fell with each labored breath.

"I can't go if you watch."

"Too bad." He checked the time. "I don't know why Luke isn't calling."

She entered the small closet, which contained only a rusty toilet and tank. It hadn't been used much and was rusty from water stain. She closed the door slightly but Joey pushed it open. He stood straddling the threshold between the two rooms, his knife whittling away at the wooden door jam.

Sara started to cry. Her tears were huge and fell like rivers down her cheeks. "I feel sick," she cried. She held her stomach as she neared him. Joey backed away. Moaning, she held a hand to her mouth, and when he least expected it, kicked hard at his groin.

Joey doubled up in pain and Sara proceeded to give him another sampling of what he had received when they had broken into her house. Another kick sent Joey halfway across the room. Sara spun, kicking out again with her leg, planting a foot into his throat.

As Joey hit the floor, Sara ran to the door, unfastened the bolt, and fled.

Flashes of sunlight skipped in and out from between the trees as Dagger raced the car down a dirt road. Dagger pounded the steering wheel. "Think, dammit." He pulled the car to a stop and killed the engine. Leaning over the steering wheel, he stared into the woods, looking for some sign, some hint of movement.

Sara? He tried to reach her telepathically but there was no response. Then he remembered … the lodge! A small house had been used as a storage lodge. It had been vacated over ten years ago but was never torn down.

He checked his gun and rushed out of the car.

Sara's strong legs carried her swiftly away from the house. There were more woods there in which to hide and in the cloak of the dense forest she would be able to shape-shift and get away from him.

"Sara!" Joey's voice echoed off the trees. He gave a shrill yelp as if he were on some fox hunt. "I love it when you fight."

His voice sounded close. She looked back quickly and saw him running like a deer up the hill. Sara speeded up, branches catching her clothing and whipping across her face. Just as she reached the top of the hill and a clearing, she heard Joey closing in.

"That's it, Sweetie. Tire yourself out so you won't fight too much when it counts." His voice cackled, taunting, teasing.

The rushing of the creek grew louder and Sara ran toward the sound. But she stopped quickly and wrapped an arm around a narrow tree. The creek was fast and about thirty feet below. She didn't think she had climbed that high.

"My god." Her heart pounded in her chest. She could jump and shape-shift as she fell, she thought. But it was too late. Joey tackled her from behind.

"Gotcha!" Joey turned Sara around. She kicked furiously struggling to get up. But Joey threw a punch and connected with her chin. Sara fell against a tree and slid down to the damp ground.

She felt hands tearing at her clothes. Her head felt groggy and she tried to shake herself conscious but it hurt too much. Warm air caressed her exposed breasts. She moaned when she felt her panties ripped off her and Joey pushing her legs apart.

"You are going to pay, Sweetheart."

Joey's voice was husky, depraved, as he pressed his mouth against her throat. When she felt his hands fumbling with his zipper, she cried out and forced her eyes open, shook the grogginess from her head.

She gathered all the energy she could, and just as he was ready to penetrate her, she shape-shifted.

"Whaaa?" Joey rocked back on his heels and watched in horror as Sara shifted into a hawk, slipped out from his hold, and flew up to a high branch. He had been too busy concentrating on Sara to hear Dagger rushing up the hill.

Sara had no sooner shifted than Joey felt Dagger's body slam into him.

Dagger's adrenaline was on high. He pummeled Joey, punching him in the midsection several times. Joey staggered, turned and lunged for Dagger. They rolled partway down the hill, over fallen branches and wet leaves. Joey pulled himself up and kicked at Dagger's head. Like the skinny weasel he was, Joey scampered back up the hill and away from Dagger. It would have been so simple to just shoot the sonofabitch but Dagger thought that would be too easy.

At the top of the hill, Joey struggled for his breath. His eyes searched the trees, saw Sara's clothes on the ground. A strange sneer pulled at his lips as he saw the hawk through the branches.

Reaching the top of the hill, Dagger charged, knocking Joey off balance. Dagger popped the palms of his hands against Joey's ears. Joey screamed as he felt one of his ear drums pop. Dagger kicked, sending Joey flying backwards where he lay motionless for a few moments. But he was like a road kill that refused to die, arms and legs still twitching.

Exhausted, Dagger crawled hand over hand through the mud to where Joey lay. The man was still breathing, eyes fluttering trying to regain his senses. Slowly, Dagger rolled the limp body over. He pressed one knee into Joey's back, grabbed his head, and twisted. Joey died instantly.

Dagger? What are you doing? Sara's voice quivered in his head. The sound of Joey's neck breaking sent a shiver through the hawk. Sara had never seen Dagger look that way … dangerous, feral, frightening. She had seen a similar look many times in the past when the hawk would watch an animal on the hunt. Once the prey was killed, the predator would have a menacing, fierce look as it guarded the remains of its meal.

When Dagger jerked his head up to stare at the hawk, the hawk took a few steps backward. *Go home, Sara.* Strands of hair, littered with fragments of leaves fell across his dirt-smudged face. There was pure vengeance in his eyes, and no matter how many attempts Sara made to communicate with him, he shut her out. He never spoke again.

But the hawk didn't leave. It watched tentatively as Dagger hoisted Joey's body up and sent it plunging over the cliff and into the creek below. Then he gathered Sara's clothes and carried them down the hill.

47

Simon rose from the couch the moment Dagger stumbled through the front door. Dagger had called Simon and asked if he and Eunie could stay with Sara until he got home.

"How's she doing?" Dagger whispered, his gaze drifting toward the upstairs.

"Hard to tell. She's quiet, you know? Didn't say much, least not to me."

A stocky woman with skin the color of chocolate teetered down the stairway. She held onto the railing as though not sure of her footing. Because of her enormous chest resting over her waistline, she couldn't see the stairs. Her head was a wad of tight graying curls.

Eunie's jovial eyes smiled, but the corners of her lips frowned when she saw Dagger. "Honey, I hope you don't feel as bad as you look."

Dagger's shirt was torn and ragged, his slacks covered in mud that was now drying. He had brushed them off the best he could before coming into the house.

"I've had better days." He glanced at the second

floor again.

"She's sleeping, finally." Eunie wrapped a strong arm around his waist.

"I really appreciate you two coming over on such short notice." He staggered to the couch and sat down on the arm. Every muscle in his body was starting to awaken and were none too happy.

"She's such a precious little thing," Eunie whispered. "She just curled up in a ball on her window seat and stared out into that dark yard. I don't know what she thought she was seeing." She turned to Simon. "She kept asking me if I heard the rattles. Don't know nothin' about no rattles."

Dagger forced a smile as he brushed his dirt-caked hair from his face. "Her grandmother is buried out by the stream. Sara hung some feathers and rattles from the cross. She said if her grandmother's spirit travels at night, it will be able to find its way back to the grave by listening for the sounds."

Dagger couldn't even picture Sara right now other than the last image in his mind of her fighting off Joey. His eyes settled on Eunie's and he dreaded asking the question but he had to know. "Did Sara say ... were you able to find out if ...?"

Eunie grabbed his hand and patted it. "She's fine. That bastard didn't get to her."

"Did they get the sonofabitch, Dagger?" Simon wobbled over to where his wife stood. They were matching bookends with identical hair, body shape, even their expressions.

Dagger looked sharply at his friend, his jaw tensed, and just hearing reference to Joey's name brought the same savage look to his eyes that the hawk had seen. "Let's just say he got his just rewards and leave it at that." Dagger held

Simon's gaze and knew his friend understood.

Grabbing Simon's arm, Eunie said, "We best be going."

After saying their goodnights, Dagger locked the door behind them, set the alarm, and turned off the lights.

Once in his bedroom, he peeled out of his clothes and stepped into the shower. The water stung as he braced his hands against the shower wall. As the hot water soothed his sore muscles, he wished it could also wash away the events of the day. All his mind kept returning to was the scene of Sara barely conscious lying under Joey, whose hands were tearing at her clothes. The rest was a blur. The adrenaline took over, rumbling through his body like a freight train, unable to control, unable to stop. It had been a long time since that had happened.

After disposing of Joey's body into the creek, Dagger had wanted to be alone, to regain some part of his sanity he had lost on that cliff. So he called Simon and asked if he and his wife could stay with Sara. Then Dagger spent two hours walking the shoreline. He sat for a while on a secluded part of the beach watching Sara's clothes burn. He couldn't leave them on the hill and he didn't think she would ever want to put them on again. It wasn't so much the way he had killed Joey that bothered him. It was the fact that something inside him enjoyed it.

He toweled off and stared at his reflection in the mirror. The cuts and bruises were starting to swell and there was discoloration forming under his skin on his arms, shoulders, and chest. Somehow he hadn't felt the blows.

His fingers combed through his wet hair and he felt the fatigue in his arms. Slowly and painfully, he tugged on a pair of jeans. But they were too unyielding against his sore muscles so he stripped out of those and put on his white cotton drawstring pants. Barefoot and barechested, he walked to the bar and flipped on a dim, overhead light. He poured himself a glass of bourbon, grimaced against the bitter taste, and added ice.

He climbed the stairs to the second floor and peered into Sara's room. She was asleep, lying on her side, the sheet pulled up to her waist. He fought the urge to climb into bed just to hold her, tell her he'd always keep her safe. It amazed him she was able to sleep after her ordeal.

Quietly, he returned to the living room and lowered himself onto the cool leather couch, setting the glass on the coffee table. He answered the phone on the first ring so it wouldn't wake either Einstein or Sara.

"It's about time," Padre said. "I've been trying your cellular for the past two hours."

"I turned it off."

"I know." After a moment of silence, Padre asked, "How's Sara?"

"Sleeping."

"Good, that's good. Listen, I thought you might want to know how this whole deal worked out."

So Dagger let him ramble while he studied the contents of his glass. J.C. had demanded to see the Australian ambassador, but he was busy instructing the Australian police to check J.C.'s apartment.

Nick had been an unfortunate accessory. They can only assume Edie had led him to believe he killed Rachel. Pete, the crew member, wasn't a suspect but was being given a chance to amend his story and identify Edie as the woman on the boat five years ago.

Dagger took another long swallow then said, "Listen, can I possibly read the shortened version in the papers?"

"That reminds me," Padre rambled on, "that young guy got the exclusive you wanted. My office told all the other papers to stop by tomorrow for a press conference, but Mr. Wormley will have his story in the morning edition."

"Good, that will make Sara happy."

"She knew Nick was connected to this whole scenario somehow, didn't she?"

"She felt he was drowning some bad memories in a bottle." Dagger looked at his empty glass and walked to the bar to refill it.

"How did she know where the necklace was?"

Dagger smiled for the first time since the morning. "That was Einstein. Whenever we mentioned the word *kangaroo*, Einstein always spit out the words *Kangaroo Paw*. Sara looked it up on the Internet. Then she remembered seeing an identical plant on the balcony."

Padre laughed. "You have got two partners any cop would kill for."

"You've got that right." Dagger thought back to that blur of time from when he had pulled Joey away from Sara to when he had tossed his limp body over the cliff.

"Oh, and that guy, Mince? One of our beat cops stopped him earlier for driving your stolen truck. Now he's singing like a canary."

"How is Robert Tyler taking it?"

"As well as can be expected. I think the Tyler men will

do just fine by themselves with Lily to mother them." After a pause, Padre said, "Okay, I'll let you get some sleep."

Dagger hung up the phone and held out his hand. It quivered as if tiny rivers of adrenaline were still pulsing through his body. He pressed the cold glass to his forehead, realizing that the bourbon was adding to his headache. He left the half-empty glass on the bar and saw a movement out of the corner of his eye. Sara was standing at the bottom of the stairs, a floral cotton robe buttoned up to her neck as though any amount of skin would be too enticing.

"I didn't hear you come in," she whispered as she stepped out of the shadows.

Dagger wanted to wrap his arms around her, hold her close. But the same fear he had seen in the hawk's eyes was still there. Sara had watched him kill a man, and not just by accident. It had been ruthless, without hesitation, professional.

Dagger slowly walked back to the couch and sat on the coffee table. Sara followed, taking a seat on the couch facing him. The dim glow from the bar light fell across his face and she couldn't help but notice the cuts and bruises.

She reached out and touched his face. Dagger winced.

"It looks painful."

Dagger just stared into her perfect face marred only by that one small bruise, the result of Joey's punch. He resisted the urge to touch her hair, her face. A part of him was afraid she would recoil, revert back to being fearful of any movement he would make.

"I'm sorry I didn't come home right away. I drove around a bit, went by the lake." His voice trailed off.

"I wanted to come home, make sure you were okay."

Sara nodded. "Simon's wife is nice." Her gaze dropped down to his battered knuckles and she stared at his hands as if they were ruthless weapons. But she touched them just the same.

Dagger sandwiched her hands between his and gathered his thoughts. After a few moments he said, "Listen, Sara. There are a lot of things you don't know about me, about the people I used to work for, the things I have done in my past." She pressed her hand to his mouth to silence him but he moved it away. "I've done a good job of forgetting that part of my life, of controlling the anger. But when someone hurts someone close to me ..."

"It's okay." Her heart pounded in her chest and tears welled. "Grandmother told you, didn't she?"

Dagger stared. "Told me what?"

"That's why you killed him. Grandmother told you there can be no witnesses. The wolf will kill. And Joey was a witness to my shifting. You killed Joey so I wouldn't have to."

Dagger cupped her face in his hands and stared intently. Yes, Ada Kills Bull had told him Sara couldn't control the wolf when it wanted to kill witnesses. Instead, she and her grandmother would flee, get as far away as possible so the wolf wouldn't be tempted. Dagger often wondered if it was the necklace with the wolf's head he wore that protected him. But he reminded himself that he had saved the wolf's life.

On the first case Sara had helped him on, he had found the wolf in the woods, its leg shot off. He had wanted to shoot the wolf to put it out of its misery, but then it shape-shifted to Sara. He had been unaware of her special *talents*. She had pleaded with him to take her to her grandmother, not the hospital. And he will always remember his shock when he watched through a crack in the partially closed door to Ada's bedroom. Sara's leg had grown back! She had regenerative powers.

But the fact that the wolf would hunt down Joey wasn't the reason Dagger killed him. So innocent, so trusting. Dagger knew Sara didn't believe, couldn't believe that he was capable of cold-blooded murder. How could he tell her about his past? That Dagger had his own demons he couldn't control? That Chase Dagger wasn't even his real name?

Her fingers touched his swollen lip and traveled to the cut above his eye. "You and I are a lot alike," she whispered. "We both have parts of our lives we have to keep secret. We have only each other to trust."

And with that she rose. Dagger watched her climb the open staircase, the dim light filtering up from the bar, outlining her body, accentuating the curve of her calves. When she had spoken, it was as if they were her grandmother's words, wise and intuitive. She seemed older somehow. And she understood, at least enough to know some things needed no explanation. She had matured before his eyes, no longer the child.

He walked back to the bar, finished his drink, and cursed Simon for being right.

THE END

shape'-shift

The ability to shift between animal and human forms. Thought to be restricted to shaman who would use the powers of the animal spirits to spy on their enemies. Another belief claims shifting is performed by only the men in a tribe who would shift at night to prey on livestock. It is not sure if shape-shifters are more human or animal.

Native mythology

A Chase Dagger Mystery